LEN DEIGHTON

The Ipcress File

D1639281

HARPER

Harper
An imprint of HarperCollins*Publishers*
77–85 Fulham Palace Road,
Hammersmith, London W6 8JB

www.harpercollins.co.uk

This edition 2011

First published in Great Britain by
Hodder & Stoughton 1962

A catalogue record for this book is
available from the British Library

ISBN 978-0-00789972-2

Set in Sabon
Printed and bound in Great Britain by
Clays Ltd, St Ives plc

Mixed Sources
Product group from well-managed
forests and other controlled sources
www.fsc.org   Cert no. SW-COC-001806
© 1996 Forest Stewardship Council

FSC is a non-profit international organisation established to promote the
responsible management of the world's forests. Products carrying the FSC
label are independently certified to assure consumers that they come
from forests that are managed to meet the social, economic and
ecological needs of present and future generations.

Find out more about HarperCollins and the environment at
www.harpercollins.co.uk/green

Cover designer's note

The great challenge I faced when asked to produce the covers for new editions of Len Deighton's books was the existence of the brilliant designs conceived by Ray Hawkey for the original editions.

However, having arrived at a concept, part of the joy I derived in approaching this challenge was the quest to locate the various props which the author had so beautifully detailed in his texts. Deighton has likened a spy story to a game of chess, which led me to transpose the pieces on a chess board with some of the relevant objects specified in each book. I carried this notion throughout the entire quartet of books.

Since smoking was so much part of our culture during the Cold War era, I also set about gathering tobacco-related paraphernalia.

Each chapter of *The Ipcress File* opens with its Gauloises-smoking protagonist's horoscope, so discovering an Aquarius cigarette lighter was a great coup. Finding a Gauloises cigarette packet, designed by Marcel Jacno in 1936, became a more difficult proposition. However, after much searching, I eventually found one via the Internet!

Serendipity sometimes plays an important part in the design process. In seeking an appropriate ashtray, to carry through the 'smoking' theme, I accidentally came across a unique piece shaped like a hand gun, so I aimed it at a red chess pawn, which represents *Ipcress*'s 'Red' Cold War antagonist.

The image of the gun pays homage to the original Hawkey-designed *Ipcress* jacket. I further retained the wooden type font logotype originated by him.

One of my long-time hobbies has been collecting cigarette cards. I was fortunate to find some appropriate images among my personal trove to illustrate the back cover, and these are accompanied by examples of military insignia gathered during my National Service days served in Cold War Korea!

Len Deighton and I shared a great affection for London's Savoy Hotel. My father had served as a waiter there in the 1930s so I have a number of pieces of memorabilia from the Savoy, including the saucer and the cloakroom ticket depicted on the cover.

I was thrilled to locate the 'Made in GDR' syringe in Latvia, of all places. Closer to home, I have kept all my past British passports, together with most of my boarding passes and baggage labels. The

Chubb key and the CND badge – which today has become a fashion accessory – came from other locations around the UK. The 1960s postage stamp on the spine of the cover commemorates the former Soviet spy, Richard Sorge.

During the 1970s, while designing a supplement series for the London *Sunday Times*, I needed a set of fingerprints to illustrate a specific article, so I persuaded the duty sergeant at my local police station to take mine, which are here given a new public airing!

I photographed the cover set-up using natural daylight, with my Canon OS 5D digital camera.

Arnold Schwartzman OBE RDI

Introduction

The Ipcress File was my first attempt to write a book. I was a commercial artist, or 'illustrator' as we are now called. I had never been a journalist or reporter of any kind so I was unaware of how long writing a book was likely to take. Knowing the size of the task is a deterrent for many professional writers, which is why they defer their ambitions often until it is too late. Being unaware of what's ahead can be an advantage. It shines a green light for everything from enlisting in the Foreign Legion to getting married.

So I stumbled into writing this book with a happy optimism that ignorance provides. Was it a depiction of myself? Well, who else did I have? After completing two and a half years of military service I had been, for three years, a student at St. Martin's School of Art in Charing Cross Road. I am a Londoner. I grew up in Marylebone and once art school started I rented a tiny grubby room around the corner from the art school. This cut my travelling time back to five minutes. I grew to know Soho very well indeed. I knew it by day and by night. I was on *hello, how are you?* terms with the 'ladies', the restaurateurs, the gangsters and the bent coppers. When, after some years as an illustrator, I wrote *The Ipcress File* much of its description of Soho was the observed life of an art student resident there.

After three years postgraduate study at the Royal College of Art I celebrated by impulsively applying for a job as flight attendant with British Overseas Airways. In those days this provided three or four days stop-over at the end of each short leg. I spent enough time in Hong Kong, Cairo, Nairobi, Beirut and Tokyo to make good and lasting friendships there. When I became an author, these background experiences of foreign people and places proved of lasting benefit.

I don't know why or how I came to writing books. I had always been a dedicated reader; obsessional is perhaps the better word. At school, having proved to be a total dud at any form of sport – and most other things – I read every book in sight. There was no system to my reading, nor even a pattern of selection. I remember reading Plato's *The Republic* with the same keen attention and superficial understanding as I read Chandler's *The Big Sleep* and H.G. Wells' *The Outline of History* and both volumes of *The Letters of Gertrude Bell*. I filled notebooks as I encountered ideas and opinions that were new to me, and I vividly remember how excited I was to discover that *The Oxford Universal Dictionary* incorporated thousands of quotations from the greatest of great writers.

So I wasn't taking myself too seriously when, as a holiday diversion, I took a school exercise book and a fountain pen, and started this story. Knowing no other style I did it as though I was writing a letter to an old, intimate and trusted friend. I immediately fell into the first person style without knowing much about the literary alternatives.

My memory has always been unreliable, as my wife Ysabele regularly points out to me, but I am convinced that this first book was influenced by my time as the art director of an ultra-smart London advertising agency. I spent my days surrounded by highly educated, witty young men who had been at Eton together. We relaxed in leather armchairs in their exclusive Pall Mall clubs. We exchanged barbed compliments and jocular abuse. They were kind to me, and generous, and I enjoyed it immensely. Later, when I created WOOC(P), the intelligence service offices depicted here, I took the social atmosphere of that sleek and shiny agency and inserted it into some ramshackle offices that I once rented in Charlotte Street.

Using the first person narrative enabled me to tell the story in the distorted way that subjective memory provides. The hero does not tell the exact truth; none of the characters tell the exact truth. I don't mean that they tell the blatant self-serving lies that politicians do, I mean that their memory tilts towards justification and self-regard. What happens in *The Ipcress File* (and in all my other first-person stories) is found somewhere in the uncertainty of contradiction. In navigation, the triangle where three lines of reference fail to intersect is call a 'cocked hat'. My stories are intended to offer no more precision than that. I want the books to provoke different reactions from different readers (as even history must do to some extent).

Publication of *The Ipcress File* coincided with the arrival of the first of the James Bond films. My book was given very generous reviews and more than one of my friends was moved to confide that the critics were using me as a blunt instrument to batter Ian Fleming about the head. Even before publication day, I was taken by Godfrey Smith (a senior figure at *The Daily Express* newspaper) to lunch at the Savoy Grill. We discussed serial rights. The next day I went in my battered old VW Beetle to Pinewood Film Studios and lunch with the unforgettable and in every way astonishing Harry Saltzman. He had co-produced *Dr. No*, which was getting widespread publicity, and had decided that *The Ipcress File* and its unnamed hero could provide a counterweight to the Bond series. On the way to Pinewood my car phone brought a request for an interview with *Newsweek* and there were similar requests from publications in Paris and New York. It was difficult to believe this was all really happening; illustrators were never treated like this. Never! I was nervously unbelieving, and constantly ready to wake up from this frantic dream. Between meetings and interviews I continued my work as a freelance illustrator. My friends delicately ignored my Jekyll and Hyde life, and so did the clients to whom I delivered my drawings. I didn't feel like a writer, I felt like an impostor. I didn't have those intense literary ambitions that writers are supposed to have while they languish in a cobwebbed garret.

Publication proved that I wasn't the only one surprised by the book's success. Despite the serialization and the entire hullabaloo, Hodder and Stoughton resolutely restricted their print order to 4,000 books. These were sold out in a couple of days. Reprinting took weeks and much of the value of the publicity and serialization was lost.

There was one question that remained un-answered. Why did I say that the hero was a north-erner from Burnley? I truly have no idea. I had seen the destination 'Burnley' on parcels I had handled while on a Christmas vacation job at King's Cross sorting office. I suppose that invention marked one tiny reluctance to depict myself exactly as I was.

Perhaps this spy fellow is not me after all.

Len Deighton, 2009

And now I will unclasp a secret book, And
to your quick-conceiving discontents, I'll read
you matter deep and dangerous.

Henry IV

Though it must be said that every species of
birds has a manner peculiar to itself, yet there
is somewhat in most genera at least that at
first sight discriminates them, and enables a
judicious observer to pronounce upon them
with some certainty.

Gilbert White, 1778

The Ipcress File

Secret File No. 1

PROLOGUE

Copy to:	no. 1. Copies 2
Action:	W.O.O.C.(P).
Origin:	Cabinet.
Authority:	PH 6.
Memoranda:	

Please prepare summary of Dossier M/1993 /GH 222223 for Parliamentary Secretary to Minister of Defence.

They came through on the hot* line at about half past two in the afternoon. The Minister didn't quite understand a couple of points in the summary. Perhaps I could see the Minister.

Perhaps.

The Minister's flat overlooked Trafalgar Square and was furnished like Oliver Messel did it for Oscar Wilde. He sat in the Sheraton, I sat in the Hepplewhite and we peeped at each other through the aspidistra plant.

'Just tell me the whole story in your own words, old chap. Smoke?'

I was wondering whose words I might other-

---

* Permanently open line.

wise have used as he skimmed the aspidistra with his slim gold cigarette case. I beat him to the draw with a crumpled packet of Gauloises; I didn't know where to begin.

'I don't know where to begin,' I said. 'The first document in the dossier . . .'

The Minister waved me down. 'Never mind the dossier, my dear chap, just tell me your personal version. Begin with your first meeting with this fellow . . .' he looked down to his small morocco-bound notebook, 'Jay. Tell me about him.'

'Jay. His code-name is changed to Box Four,' I said.

'That's very confusing,' said the Minister, and wrote it down in his book.

'It's a confusing story,' I told him. 'I'm in a very confusing business.'

The Minister said, 'Quite,' a couple of times, and I let a quarter inch of ash away towards the blue Kashan rug.

'I was in Lederer's about 12.55 on a Tuesday morning the first time I saw Jay,' I continued.

'Lederer's?' said the Minister. 'What's that?'

'It's going to be very difficult for me if I have to answer questions as I go along,' I said. 'If it's all the same to you, Minister, I'd prefer you to make a note of the questions, and ask me after-wards.'

'My dear chap, not another word, I promise.'

And throughout the entire explanation he never again interrupted.

2

1

[Aquarius (Jan 20–Feb 19) A difficult day. You will face varied problems. Meet friends and make visits. It may help you to be better organized.]

I don't care what you say, 18,000 pounds (sterling) is a lot of money. The British Government had instructed me to pay it to the man at the corner table who was now using knife and fork to commit ritual murder on a cream pastry.

Jay the Government called this man. He had small piggy eyes, a large moustache and handmade shoes which I knew were size ten. He walked with a slight limp and habitually stroked his eyebrow with his index finger. I knew him as well as I knew anyone, for I had seen film of him in a small, very private cinema in Charlotte Street, every day for a month.

Exactly one month previous I had never heard of Jay. My three weeks' termination of engagement leave had sped to a close. I had spent it doing

3

little or nothing unless you are prepared to consider sorting through my collection of military history books a job fit for a fully grown male. Not many of my friends were so prepared.

I woke up saying to myself 'today's the day' but I didn't feel much like getting out of bed just the same. I could hear the rain even before I drew the curtains back. December in London – the soot-covered tree outside was whipping itself into a frenzy. I closed the curtains quickly, danced across the icy-cold lino, scooped up the morning's post and sat down heavily to wait while the kettle boiled. I struggled into the dark worsted and my only establishment tie – that's the red and blue silk with the square design – but had to wait forty minutes for a cab. They hate to come south of the Thames you see.

It always had made me feel a little self-conscious saying, 'War Office' to cab drivers; at one time I had asked for the pub in Whitehall, or said 'I'll tell you when to stop,' just to avoid having to say it. When I got out the cab had brought me to the Whitehall Place door and I had to walk round the block to the Horseguards Avenue entrance. A Champ vehicle was parked there, a red-necked driver was saying 'Clout it one' to an oily corporal in dungarees. The same old army, I thought. The long lavatory-like passages were dark and dirty, and small white cards with precise military writing labelled each green-painted door: GS 3, Major this, Colonel that, Gentlemen, and odd anonymous tea rooms from which bubbly old ladies in spectacles appeared when not practising alchemy within. Room 134 was just like any other; the standard four green filing cabinets, two green metal cupboards, two desks fixed together face to face by the window, a half full one pound bag of Tate and Lyle sugar on the window-sill.

Ross, the man I had come to see, looked up from the writing that had held his undivided attention since three seconds after I had entered the room. Ross said, 'Well now,' and coughed nervously. Ross and I had come to an arrangement of some years' standing – we had decided to hate each other. Being English, this vitriolic relationship manifested itself in oriental politeness.

'Take a seat. Well now, smoke?' I had told him 'No thanks' for two years at least twice a week. The cheap inlay cigarette box (from Singapore's change alley market) with the butterflies of wood grain, was wafted across my face.

Ross was a regular officer; that is to say he didn't drink gin after 7.30 P.M. or hit ladies without first removing his hat. He had a long thin nose, a moustache like flock wallpaper, sparse, carefully combed hair, and the complexion of a Hovis loaf.

The black phone rang. 'Yes? Oh, it's you, darling,' Ross pronouncing each word with exactly the same amount of toneless indifference. 'To be frank, I was going to.'

For nearly three years I had worked in Military Intelligence. If you listened to certain people you learned that Ross *was* Military Intelligence. He was a quiet intellect happy to work within the strict departmental limitations imposed upon him. Ross didn't mind; hitting platform five at Waterloo with rose-bud in the buttonhole and umbrella at the high port was Ross's beginning to a day of rubber stamp and carbon paper action. At last I was to be freed. Out of the Army, out of Military Intelligence, away from Ross: working as a civilian with civilians in one of the smallest and most important of the Intelligence Units – WOOC(P).

'Well I'll phone you if I have to stay Thursday night.'

I heard the voice at the other end say, 'Are you all right for socks?'

Three typed sheets of carbon copies so bad I couldn't read them (let alone read them upside down) were kept steady and to hand by the office tea money. Ross finished his call and began to talk to me, and I twitched facial muscles to look like a man paying attention.

He located his black briar pipe after heaping the contents of his rough tweed jacket upon his desk top. He found his tobacco in one of the cupboards. 'Well now,' he said. He struck the match I gave him upon his leather elbow patch.

'So you'll be with the provisional people.' He said it with quiet distaste; the Army didn't like anything provisional, let alone people, and they certainly didn't like the WOOC(P), and I suppose they didn't much like me. Ross obviously thought my posting a very fine tentative solution until I could be got out of his life altogether. I won't tell you all Ross said because most of it was pretty dreary and some of it is still secret and buried somewhere in one of those precisely but innocuously labelled files of his. A lot of the time he was having ignition trouble with his pipe and that meant he was going to start the story all through again.

Most of the people at the War House, especially those on the intelligence fringes as I was, had heard of the WOOC(P) and a man called Dalby. His responsibility was direct to the Cabinet. Envied, criticized and opposed by other intelligence units Dalby was almost as powerful as anyone gets in this business. People posted to him ceased to be in the Army for all practical purposes and they were removed from almost all War Office records. In the few rare cases of men going back to normal duty from WOOC(P) they were enlisted all over afresh and given a new serial number from the batch that is reserved for Civil Servants seconded to military duties. Pay was made by an entirely different scale, and I wondered just how long I would have to make the remnants of this month's pay last before the new scale began.

After a search for his small metal-rimmed army spectacles, Ross went through the discharge rigmarole with loving attention to detail. We began by destroying the secret compensation contract that Ross and I had signed in this very room almost three years ago and ended by his checking that I had no mess charges unpaid. It had been a pleasure to work with me, Provisional was clever to get me, he was sorry to lose me and Mr Dalby was lucky to have me and would I leave this package in Room 225 on the way out – the messenger seemed to have missed him this morning.

Dalby's place is in one of those sleazy long streets in the district that would be Soho, if Soho had the strength to cross Oxford Street. There is a new likely-looking office conversion wherein the unwinking blue neon glows even at summer midday, but this isn't Dalby's place. Dalby's department is next door. His is dirtier than average with a genteel profusion of well-worn brass work, telling of the existence of 'The Ex-Officers' Employment Bureau. Est 1917'; 'Acme Films Cutting Rooms'; 'B. Isaacs. Tailor – Theatricals a Speciality'; 'Dalby Inquiry Bureau – staffed by ex-Scotland Yard detectives'. A piece of headed note-paper bore the same banner and the biro'd message, 'Inquiries third floor, please ring.' Each morning at 9.30 I rang, and avoiding the larger cracks in the lino, began the ascent. Each floor had its own character – ageing paint varying from dark brown to dark green. The third floor was dark white. I passed the scaly old dragon that guarded the entrance to Dalby's cavern.

I'll always associate Charlotte Street with the music of the colliery brass bands that I remember from my childhood. The duty drivers and cipher clerks had a little fraternity that sat around in the dispatch office on the second floor. They had a very loud gramophone and they were all brass band fanatics; that's a pretty esoteric failing in London. Up through the warped and broken floorboards came the gleaming polished music. Fairey Aviation had won the Open Championship again that year and the sound of the test piece reached through to every room in the building. It made Dalby feel he was overlooking Horse Guards Parade; it made me feel I was back in Burnley.

I said 'Hello, Alice,' and she nodded and busied herself with a Nescafé tin and a ruinous cup of warm water. I went through to the back office, saw Chico – he'd got a step beyond Alice, his Nescafé was almost dissolved. Chico always looked glad to see me. It made my day; it was his training, I suppose. He'd been to one of those very good schools where you meet kids with influential uncles. I imagine that's how he got into the Horse Guards and now into WOOC(P) too, it must have been like being at school again. His profusion of long lank yellow hair hung heavily across his head like a Shrove Tuesday mishap. He stood 5ft 11in in his Argyll socks, and had an irritating physical stance, in which his thumbs rested high behind his red braces while he rocked on his hand-lasted Oxfords. He had the advantage of both a good brain and a family rich enough to save him using it.

I walked right through the Dalby Inquiry Bureau and down the back stairs. For this whole house belonged to WOOC(P) even though each business on each floor had its own 'front' for our convenience. By 9.40 A.M. each morning I was in the small ramshackle projection room of Acme Films.

The sickly sweet smell of film cement and warm celluloid was so strong that I think they must have sprayed it around. I threw my English B-picture raincoat across a pile of film tins, clean side up, and sank into one of the tip-up cinema seats. As always it was seat twenty-two, the one with the loose bolt, and always by that time I didn't feel much like moving.

The Rheostat made that horrible squeaking noise. The room lights dimmed tiredly and the little projector clattered into action. A screaming white rectangle flung animated abstract shapes of scratch marks at my eyes, then darkened to a business-like grey flannel suit colour.

In crude stick-on letters the film title said JAY. LEEDS. WARREN THREE. (Warren Three was the authority upon which it was filmed.) The picture began. Jay was walking along a crowded pavement. His moustache was gigantic, but cultivated with a care that he gave to everything he did. He limped, but it certainly didn't impair his progress through the crowd. The camera wobbled and then tracked swiftly away. The van in which the movie camera had been hidden had been forced to move faster than Jay by the speed of the traffic. The screen flashed white and the next short, titled length began. Some of the films showed Jay with a companion, code-named HOUSEMARTIN. He was a six feet tall handsome man in a good-quality camel-hair overcoat. His hair was waved, shiny and a little too perfectly grey at the temples. He wore a handful of gold rings, a gold watch strap and a smile full of jacket crowns. It was an indigestible smile – he was never able to swallow it.

Chico operated the projector with tongue-jutting determination. Once in a while he would slip into the programme one of those crisp Charing Cross Road movies that feature girls in the skin. It was Dalby's idea to keep his 'students' awake during these viewings.

'Know your enemies,' was Dalby's theory. He felt if all his staff knew the low-life of the espionage business visually they would stand a better chance of predicting their thought. 'Because he had a picture of Rommel over his bed Montgomery won Alamein.' I don't necessarily believe this – but this was what Dalby kept saying. (Personally I ascribe a lot of value to those extra 600 tanks.)

Dalby was an elegant languid public school Englishman of a type that can usually reconcile his duty with comfort and luxury. He was a little taller than I am: probably 6ft 1in or 6ft 2in. He had long fine hair, and every now and then would grow a little wispy blond moustache. At present he didn't have it. He had a clear complexion that sunburnt easily and very small puncture-type scar tissue high on the left cheek to prove he had been to a German University in '38. It had been a useful experience, and in 1941 enabled him to gain a DSO and bar. A rare event in any Intelligence group but especially in the one he was with. No citations of course.

He was unpublic school enough to wear a small signet ring on his right hand, and whenever he pulled at his face, which was often, he dragged the edge of the ring against the skin. This produced a little red weal due to excessive acidity in the skin. It was fascinating.

He peeped at me over the toes of his suède shoes which rested in the centre of a deskful of important papers, arranged in precise heaps. Spartan furniture (Ministry of Works, contemporary) punctured the cheap lino and a smell of tobacco ash was in the air.

'You are loving it here of course?' Dalby asked.

'I have a clean mind and a pure heart. I get eight hours' sleep every night. I am a loyal, diligent employee and will attempt every day to be worthy of the trust my paternal employer puts in me.'

'I'll make the jokes,' said Dalby.

'Go ahead,' I said. 'I can use a laugh – my eyes have been operating twenty-four frames per second for the last month.'

Dalby tightened a shoe-lace. 'Think you can handle a tricky little special assignment?'

'If it doesn't demand a classical education I might be able to grope around it.'

12

Dalby said, 'Surprise me, do it without complaint or sarcasm.'

'It wouldn't be the same,' I said.

Dalby swung his feet to the floor and became deliberate and serious. 'I've been across to the Senior Intelligence Conference this morning. Home Office are worried sick about these disappearances of their top biochemists. Committees, sub-committees – you should have seen them over there, talk about Mother's Day at the Turkish Bath.'

'Has there been another then?' I asked.

'This morning,' said Dalby, 'one left home at 7.45 A.M., never reached the lab.'

'Defection?' I asked.

Dalby pulled a face and spoke to Alice over the desk intercom, 'Alice, open a file and give me a code-name for this morning's "wandering willie".' Dalby made his wishes known by peremptory unequivocal orders; all his staff preferred them to the complex polite chat of most Departments as especially did I as a refugee from the War Office. Alice's voice came over the intercom like Donald Duck with a head cold. To whatever she said Dalby replied, 'The hell with what the letter from the Home Office said. Do as I say.'

There was a moment or so of silence then Alice used her displeased voice to say a long file number and the code-name RAVEN. All people under long-term surveillance had bird names.

'That's a good girl,' said Dalby in his most charming voice and even over the squawk-box I

13

could hear the lift in Alice's voice as she said, 'Very good, sir.'

Dalby switched off the box and turned back to me. 'They have put a security blackout on this Raven disappearance but I told them that William Hickey will be carrying a photo of his dog by the midday editions. Look at these.' Dalby laid five passport photos across his oiled teak desk. Raven was a man in his late forties, thick black hair, bushy eyebrows, bony nose – there were a hundred like him in St James's at any minute of the day. Dalby said, 'It makes eight top rank Disappearances in . . .' he looked at his desk diary, '. . . six and a half weeks.'

'Surely Home Office aren't asking us to help them,' I said.

'They certainly are not,' said Dalby. 'But if we found Raven I think the Home Secretary would virtually disband his confused little intelligence department. Then we could add their files to ours. Think of that.'

'Find him?' I said. 'How would we start?'

'How would you start?' asked Dalby.

'Haven't the faintest,' I said. 'Go to laboratory, wife doesn't know what's got into him lately, discover dark almond-eyed woman. Bank manager wonders where he's been getting all that money. Fist fight through darkened lab. Glass tubes that would blow the world to shreds. Mad scientist backs to freedom holding phial – flying tackle by me. Up grams Rule Britannia.'

Dalby gave me a look calculated to have me feeling like an employee, he got to his feet and walked across to the big map of Europe that he had had pinned across the wall for the last week. I walked across to him. 'You think that Jay is master minding it,' I said. Dalby looked at the map and still staring at it said, 'Sure of it, absolutely sure of it.'

The map was covered with clear acetate and five small frontier areas from Finland to the Caspian were marked in black greasy pencil. Two places in Syria carried small red flags.

Dalby said, 'Every important illegal movement across these bits of frontier that I have marked are with Jay's OK.

'*Important* movement. I don't mean he stands around checking that the eggs have little lions on.' Dalby tapped the border. 'Somewhere before they get him as far as this we must . . .' Dalby's voice trailed away lost in thought.

'Hi-jack him?' I prompted softly. Dalby's mind had raced on. 'It's January. If only we could do this in January,' he said. January was the month that the Government estimates were prepared. I began to see what he meant. Dalby suddenly became aware of me again and turned on a big flash of boyish charm.

'You see,' said Dalby. 'It's not just a case of the defection of one biochemist . . .'

'Defection? I thought that Jay's speciality was a high-quality line in snatch jobs.'

15

'Hi-jack! Snatch jobs! all that gangland talk. You read too many newspapers that's your trouble. You mean they walk him through the customs and immigration with two heavy-jowled men behind him with their right hands in their overcoat pockets? No. No. No,' he said the three 'noes' softly, paused and added two more. '. . . this isn't a mere emigration of one little chemist,' (Dalby made him sound like an assistant from Boots) 'who has probably been selling them stuff for years. In fact given the choice I'm not sure I wouldn't let him go. It's those—people at the Home Office. They should know about these things before they occur: not start crying in their beer afterwards.' He picked two cigarettes out of his case, threw one to me and balanced the other between his fingers. 'They are all right running the Special Branch, HM prisons and Cruelty to Animal Inspectors but as soon as they get into *our* business they have trouble touching bottom.'* Dalby continued to do balancing tricks with the cigarette to which he had been talking. Then he looked up and began to talk to me. 'Do you honestly believe that given all the Home Office Security files we couldn't do a thousand times better than they have ever done?'

'I think we could,' I said. He was so pleased with my answer that he stopped toying with the cigarette and lit it in a burst of energy. He inhaled

* The Denning report published September, 1963 revealed that the Home Secretary is in control of British Counter Intelligence.

the smoke then tried to snort it down his nostrils. He choked. His face went red. 'Shall I get you a glass of water?' I asked, and his face went redder. I must have ruined the drama of the moment. Dalby recovered his breath and went on.

'You can see now that this is something more than an ordinary case, it's a test case.'

'I sense impending Jesuitical pleas.'

'Exactly,' said Dalby with a malevolent smile. He loved to be cast as the villain, especially if it could be done with schoolboy-scholarship. 'You remember the Jesuit motto.' He was always surprised to find I had read any sort of book.

'When the end is lawful the means are also lawful,' I answered.

He beamed and pinched the bridge of his nose between finger and thumb. I had made him very happy.

'If it pleases you that much,' I said, 'I'm sorry I can't muster it in dog-Latin.'

'It's all right, all right,' said Dalby. He traversed his cigarette then changed the range and elevation until it had me in its sights. He spoke slowly, carefully articulating each syllable. 'Go and buy this Raven for me.'

'From Jay.'

'From anyone who has him – I'm broadminded.'

'How much can I spend, Daddy?'

He moved his chair an inch nearer the desk with a loud crash. 'Look here, every point of entry has the stopper jammed tightly upon it.' He gave a little bitter laugh. 'It makes you laugh, doesn't it. I remember when we asked HO to close the airports for one hour last July. The list of excuses they gave us. But when someone slips through *their* little butter-fingers and *they* are going to be asked some awkward questions, anything goes. Anyway, Jay is a bright lad; he'll know what's going on; he'll have this Raven on ice for a week and then move him when all goes quiet. If meanwhile we make him anything like a decent offer . . .' Dalby's voice trailed off as he slipped his mind into over-drive, '. . . say 18,000 quid. We pick him up from anywhere Jay says – no questions asked.'

'18,000,' I said.

'You can go up to twenty-three if you are sure they are on the level. But on our terms. Payment after delivery. Into a Swiss bank. Strictly no cash and I don't want Raven dead. Or even damaged.'

'OK,' I said. I suddenly felt very small and young and called upon to do something that I wasn't sure I could manage. If this was the run of the mill job at WOOC(P) they deserved their high pay and expense accounts. 'Shall I start by locating Jay?' It seemed a foolish thing to say but I felt in dire need of an instruction book.

Dalby flapped a palm. I sat down again. 'Done,' he said. He flipped a switch on his squawk-box. Alice's voice, electronically distorted, spoke from the room downstairs. 'Yes, sir,' she said.

'What's Jay doing?'

There was a couple of clicks and Alice's voice

came back to the office again. 'At 12.10 he was in Lederer's coffee-house.'

'Thanks, Alice,' said Dalby.

'Cease surveillance, sir?'

'Not yet, Alice. I'll tell you when.' To me he said, 'There you are then. Off you go.'

I doused my cigarette and stood up. 'Two other last things,' said Dalby. 'I am authorizing you for 1,200 a year expenses. And,' he paused, 'don't contact me if anything goes wrong, because I won't know what the hell you are talking about.'

2

[*Aquarius (Jan 20–Feb 19) New business opportunities begin well in unusual surroundings that
provide chance of a gamble.*]

I walked down Charlotte Street towards Soho. It
was that sort of January morning that had enough
sunshine to point up the dirt without raising the
temperature. I was probably seeking excuses to
delay; I bought two packets of Gauloises, sank a
quick grappa with Mario and Franco at the
Terrazza, bought a *Statesman*, some Normandy
butter and garlic sausage. The girl in the delicatessen was small, dark and rather delicious. We
had been flirting across the mozzarella for years.
Again we exchanged offers with neither side taking
up the option.

In spite of my dawdling I was still in Lederer's
coffee-house by 12.55. Led's is one of those con-
tinental-style coffee-houses where coffee comes in
a glass. The customers, who mostly think of them-

selves as clientele, are those smooth-rugged characters with sun-lamp complexions, half a dozen 10in by 8in glossies, an agent and more time than money on their hands.

Jay was there, skin like polished ivory, small piggy eyes and a luxuriant growth of facial hair. Small talk ricocheted around me as reputations hit the dust.

'She's marvellous in *small* parts,' an expensive gingery-pink rinse was saying, and people were dropping names, using one-word abbreviations of West End shows and trying to leave without paying for their coffee.

The back of Jay's large head touched the red flocked wallpaper between the notice that told customers not to expect dairy cream in their pastries and the one that cautioned them against passing betting slips. Jay had seen me, of course. He'd priced my coat and measured the pink-haired girl in the flick of an eyelid. I waited for Jay to stroke his eyebrow with his right index finger and I knew that he would. He did. I'd never seen him before but I knew him from the flick of the finger to the lopsided way he walked downstairs. I knew that he'd paid sixty guineas for each of his suits except the flannel one, which by some quirk of a tailor's reasoning had cost fifty-eight and a half guineas. I knew all about Jay except how to ask him to sell me a biochemist for £18,000.

I sat down and burnt my raincoat on the bars of the fire. An unassisted thirty-eight with a sneer under contract eased her chair three-sixteenths of an inch to give me more space, and nosed deeper into *Variety*. She hated me because I was trying to pick her up, or not trying perhaps, but anyway, she had her reasons. On the far side of Jay's table I saw the handsome face of Housemartin, his co-star in the Charlotte Street film library. I lit a Gauloise and blew a smoke ring. The thirty-eight sucked her teeth. I noticed Housemartin lean across to Jay and whisper in his ear while they both looked at me. Then Jay nodded.

The waitress – a young fifty-three with imitation pastry cream on her pinafore – came across to my table. My friend with *Variety* stretched out a hand, white and lifeless like some animal that had never been exposed to daylight. It touched the glass of cold coffee and dragged it away from the waitress. I ordered Russian tea and apple strudel.

Had it been Chico sitting there he would have been making time with the Minox camera, and dusting the waitress for Jay's prints, but I knew we had more footage on Jay than MGM have on Ben Hur, so I sat tight and edged into the strudel.

When I had finished my tea and bun I had no further excuse for delay. I searched through my pockets for some visiting cards. There was an engraved one that said 'Bertram Loess – Assessor and Valuer', another printed one that said 'Brian Serck Inter News Press Agency', and a small imitation leather folder that gave me Right of Entry under the Factories Act because I was a weights and measures inspector. None of those suited the present situation so I went across to Jay's table, touched a forelock and said the first thing that came into my head – 'Beamish,' I said, 'Stanley Beamish.' Jay nodded. It was the head of a Buddha coming unsoldered. 'Is there somewhere we can talk?' I said. 'I have a financial proposition to put to you.' But Jay was not going to be hurried; he took out his thin wallet, produced a white rectangle and passed it to me. I read – 'Henry Carpenter – Import Export'. I'd always favoured foreign names on the ground that there is nothing more authentically English than a foreign name. Perhaps I should tell Jay. He picked up his card and delicately with his big scarred finger-tips on the points returned it to his crocodile-skin wallet. He consulted a watch with a dial like the control panel of a Boeing 707, and eased himself back in his chair.

'You shall take me to lunch,' said Jay, as though he were conferring a favour.

'I can't,' I said. 'I have three months' back pay outstanding and my expense account was only confirmed this morning.' Jay was thunderstruck at striking this rich vein of honesty. 'How much,' said Jay. 'How much is your expense account?'

'1,200,' I said.

'A year?' said Jay.

'Yes,' I said.

'Not enough,' said Jay, and he jabbed my chest to emphasize it. 'Ask them for 2,000 at least.'

'Yes,' I said obediently. I didn't think Dalby would stand for it, but there seemed no point in contradicting Jay at this stage of the proceedings.

'I know somewhere very cheap,' said Jay. As I saw it, a finer way out of the situation was for Jay to buy me lunch, but I know that this never even occurred to him. We all paid our bills, and I picked up my groceries, and then the three of us trailed out along Wardour Street, Jay in the lead. The lunch hour in Central London – the traffic was thick and most of the pedestrians the same. We walked past grim-faced soldiers in photo-shop windows. Stainless-steel orange squeezers and moron-manipulated pin-tables metronoming away the sunny afternoon in long thin slices of boredom. Through wonderlands of wireless entrails from the little edible condensers to gutted radar receivers for thirty-nine and six. On, shuffling past plastic chop suey, big-bellied naked girls and 'Luncheon Vouchers Accepted' notices, until we paused before a wide illustrated doorway – 'Vicki from Montmartre' and 'Striptease in the Snow' said the freshly-painted signs. 'Danse de Desir – Non Stop Striptease Revue' and the little yellow bulbs winked lecherously in the dusty sunlight.

We went inside. Jay was smiling and tapping Housemartin on the nose and the usherette on the bottom at the same time. The manager gave me a close scrutiny but decided I wasn't from West End Central. I suppose I didn't look wealthy enough.

I closed my eyes for a moment to accustom myself to the dark. On my left was a room with about sixty seats and a stage as big as a fireplace – it looked a slum in total darkness. I'd hate to see it with a window open.

In the cardboard proscenium a fat girl in black underwear was singing a song with the mad abandon that fitted 2.10 P.M. on a Tuesday afternoon.

'We'll wait here,' said the handsome House-martin, and Jay went up the staircase near the sign that said – 'Barbarossa – club members only' – and an arrow pointing upwards. We waited – you wouldn't have thought that I was trying to do an £18,000 deal. The garlic sausage, the *Statesman*, the Normandy butter, had become a malleable shapeless lump. I didn't think Dalby would wear that on my expenses, so I decided to hang on to it a little longer. Drums rolled, cymbals 'zinged', lights and gelatines clicked and clattered. Girls came on and went off. Girls thin, fat, tall and short. Girls in various stages of dress and undress; pink girls and green girls, little girls and old girls, and still more girls, relentlessly. Housemartin seemed to like it.

Finally he went to the gents, excusing himself with one of the less imaginative vulgarisms. A cig-arette-girl, clad in a handful of sequins, tried to sell me a souvenir programme. I'd seen better print jobs on winkle bags, but then it was only costing twelve and six, and it was made in England. She

offered me a pink felt Pluto, too. I declined gratefully. She sorted through the other things on the
tray. 'I'll have a packet of Gauloises,' I said. She
smiled a crooked little smile – her lipstick was lopsided – she seemed to have very little skill at putting things on. She dropped her head to grope for
the cigarettes. 'Do you know what the packet
looks like?' she said. I helped her look. While her
head was close to mine she said, in her pinched
Northumberland accent, 'Go home. There's
nothing to be gained here.' She found the cigarettes and gave them to me. I gave her a ten-
shilling note. 'Thanks,' she said, offering no
change.

'Not at all,' I said. 'Thank *you*.' I watched her
as she made her journey through the wispy audience of middle-aged tycoons. When she reached
the rear of the auditorium she sold something to
a plump man at the bar. She moved on out of my
range of vision.

I looked around me; no one seemed to be
watching. I walked up the stairs. It was all vel-
veteen and tinsel stars. There was only one door
on this landing – it was locked. I went up another
floor. A notice said, 'Private – Staff Only'; I pushed
through the swing door. There was a long corridor ahead of me. Four doors opened to the right.
None to the left. I opened the first door. It was a
toilet. It was empty. The next door in the line-up
said 'Manager'; I tapped and opened it. There was
a comfortable office: half a dozen bottles of booze,

large armchair, a studio couch. A television set said '. . . begin to feel the tummy muscles stretching and relaxing . . .'

There was no one there. I walked across to the window. In the street below a man with a barrow was arranging the fruit best side forward. I went down the corridor and opened the next door – there was a complex and fleshy array of about twenty semi-nude chorus girls, changing their tiny costumes. A loudspeaker brought the sound of the piano and drums from downstairs. No one screamed, one or two of the girls looked up and then continued with their conversation. I closed the door quietly and went to the last door.

It was a large room devoid of any furniture; the windows were blocked up. From a loudspeaker came the same piano and drums. In the floor of the room were six panels of armour glass. The light came from the room below. I walked to the nearest glass panel and looked down through it. Below me was a small green baize table with sealed packs of cards, and ashtrays, and four gold-painted chairs. I walked to the centre of the room. The glass panels here were bigger. I looked down upon clean bright yellow and red numbers demarking black rectangles on the green felt. Inset into the table a nice new roulette wheel twinkled merrily. There was no sign of anyone unless you included the pale man in dark jacket and pin-stripe trousers who was lying full length along the gaming table. It looked like, and it just had to be; Raven.

3

There was no other door to the room and the windows were blocked. I went back along the corridor and down the stairs. I tried the door again as I had on the way up; I reached the same conclusion. I moved it gently and heard the bolt rattle. I rapped it with my knuckles – it was solid. I went upstairs quickly and back into the observation room. From below the glass would look like mirror, but anyone in this room could see the cards all the players were holding.

I hadn't yet offered a deal to Jay. If that was Raven I was bound to recover him, seize him, or whatever the terminology is. I went quickly back to the manager's office. The woman on the TV was saying '. . . down together . . .' I lifted his heavy typewriter off his desk and carried it along

28

the corridor. Two girls in scanties came pushing out of the dressing-room and, seeing me, the tall one called through the doorway, 'Watch your pockets girls, he's back again,' and her friend said, 'He must be a reporter,' and they both giggled and ran downstairs. I humped the huge typewriter into the observation room in time to see a figure enter the gaming room downstairs. It was Housemartin, and he now had a grease stain on the lapel of his camel-hair coat. He looked as hot and bothered as I felt, and he hadn't had my troubles with the typewriter or the girls.

Housemartin was a big man. Because he wore suits with shoulders six inches outboard of the shoulder bone didn't mean that he wasn't beefy enough already. He picked the limp Raven off the big *crème de menthe* coloured table like a Queen's scout with a rucksack, and marched off through the far door. I was groaning under the weight of the Olivetti and now I let go. It went through the big six-foot panel without a ripple. The surface shattered into a white opacity except for a large round hole through which I saw the typewriter hit the roulette wheel dead centre and continue its downward path to the floor – the hole in the gaming table mouthed its circular surprise. I kicked the splintery edges of the broken glass but still tore the seat of my trousers as I slid through the panel and dropped on to the gaming table below. I picked myself up and rubbed the torn place in my trousers. Suddenly the music from the loudspeaker ceased, and I heard one of the strippers running upstairs shouting.

Over the loudspeakers a voice said, 'Ladies and Gentlemen, the police are checking the premises; please remain in your seats . . .' By that time I was across the gaming room and through the doorway through which Housemartin and Raven had gone. I went down the stone staircase two steps at a time. There were two doorways, one had 'emergency exit' painted on it. I put my weight against the crunchbars and opened it a couple of inches. I was in a semi-basement. There were four uniformed policemen standing ten feet away along the pavement. I closed the door and tried the other door. It opened. Inside were three middle-aged men in business suits. One was flushing the contents of his pockets down the toilet. One was standing in another toilet helping the third through a very small window. The sight through this window of the point of a blue helmet had me moving back up the stairs again. I had passed a door on the way down. I pushed at it now. It was made of metal, and was very heavy. It moved slowly and I found myself in an alley full of bent dustbins, wet cardboard cartons and crates with 'No deposit' stencilled upon them. At the end of the alley was a tall gate with a chain and padlock. Facing me was another metal door. I walked through it into a man in a greasy white jacket shouting 'Make it spaghetti and chips twice.' He looked me over suspiciously and said, 'You want a meal?'

'Yes,' I said quickly

'That's all right then, sit down. I'm not doing no more coffee except with food.' I nodded. 'I take your order in a minute,' he said.

I sat down and felt in my pocket for cigarettes. I had three and a half packets in one pocket and a quarter of a pound of garlic sausage, and a soft metal foil parcel of butter in the other. It was then that I discovered there a brand new hypodermic syringe in a black cardboard box, and I thought, 'What did that cigarette-girl mean by "Go home. There is nothing to be gained here"?'

4

I used the emergency number to go through to our secret exchange: Ghost – which was our section of the special Government telephone exchange: Federal.

Ghost switchboard gave the usual eighty seconds of 'Number unobtainable' signal – to deter callers who dialled it by accident – then I gave the week's code-words 'MICHAEL'S BIRTHDAY', and was connected to the duty officer. He plugged me in to Dalby who might have been anywhere – half-way across the world, perhaps. I conveyed the situation to him without going into details. He felt it was all his fault, and said how pleased he was that I hadn't got mixed up with the 'blue pointed head mob'. 'You will be doing a job with me next week. It might be very tricky.'

'Fine,' I said.

'I'll speak to Alice about it, meanwhile I want you to change your papers.' He rang off. I went home to a garlic sausage sandwich. '1,200,' I thought. 'That's twenty-four pounds a week.'

*   *   *

32

'Changing papers' is a long and dreary process.

It meant photographs, documents, finger-prints and complications. A small roomful of civilian clerks at the War Office are busy the whole year through, doing nothing else. On Thursday I went to the little room at the top of the building to the department run by Mr Nevinson. On the door the small white ticket in its painted frame said, 'Documents. Personnel Reclassifications and Personnel deceased'. Mr Nevinson and his colleagues have the highest security clearance of anyone in government employ and, as they all know very well, they are under continuous security surveillance. Through these hands at some time or other go papers for every important agent in HM Govt employ.

For example; take the time my picture appeared in *The Burnley Daily Gazette* in July 1939, when I won the fifth form mathematics prize; the following year the whole of the sixth appeared in a class photograph. If you try to see those issues now at the library, at the offices of *The Burnley Daily Gazette*, or at Colindale even, you'll discover the thoroughness of Mr Nevinson. When your papers are changed your whole life is turned over like top-soil; new passport of course, but also new birth-certificate, radio and TV licences, marriage-certificates; and all the old ones are thoroughly destroyed. It takes four days. Today Mr Nevinson was starting on me.

'Look at the camera, thank you. Sign here, thank

you; and here, thank you; and again here, thank you; thumbs together, thank you; fingers together, thank you; now altogether, thank you; now you can wash your hands, thank you. We'll be in touch. Soap and towel on the filing cabinet!'

5

[*Aquarius (Jan 20–Feb 19) Don't make hasty
decisions about a prospect you have in mind.
A difference of opinion may provide a chance
for a journey.*]

Monday I got to Charlotte Street usual time. A
little grey rusting Morris 1000 knelt at the kerb,
Alice at the controls. I was pretending I hadn't
seen her when she called out to me. I got into the
car, the motor revved, away we went. We drove
in silence a little way when I said, 'I can't find the
bag of wet cement to put my feet into.' She turned
and cracked her make-up a little. Encouraged, I
asked her where we were going.

'To bait a Raven trap, I believe,' she said.

There seemed no answer to that. After a few
minutes she spoke again. 'Look at this,' she said,
handing me a felt toy exactly like the one I had
declined to buy in the strip club the week before.
'There.' She jabbed a finger while driving, talking

and tuning the car radio. I looked at the pink spotted felt dog; some stuffing was coming out of its head. I prodded it around. 'You're looking for this?' Alice had a Minox in her hand. She gave me a sour look, or perhaps I already had one.

'I was pretty stupid . . .' I said.

'Try not to stay that way,' she almost smiled. If she went on that way she'd soon have a crackle finish.

In Vauxhall Bridge Road we pulled into the kerb behind a black Rover car. Alice gave me a buff envelope about 10in by 6in and 3/4in thick sealed with wax, and opened the door. I followed her. She ushered me into the rear seat of the Rover. The driver had a short haircut, white shirt, black tie and navy blue DB raincoat. Alice smacked the roof of the car with the flat of her hand; show jumper style. The car pulled away through the 'back doubles' of Victoria. I opened the buff envelope. Inside was a new passport, thumbed, bent and back-dated to look old; two keys; a sheet of paper with typing on it; three passport photos, and one of those multi-leaved airline tickets. I was booked BOAC first-class single LON/BEI. The typewritten sheet gave plane times and said, – 'BA712. LAP 11.25. Beirut International Airport 20.00. Photo Identity: RAVEN. Juke box. Upstairs. BEI Airport. Destroy by burning immediately.' It gave no date. Attached to one key was a number: '025.' I looked at the man in the photos, then burned the typewritten sheets and the photos, and lit a cigarette.

We turned left out of Beauchamp Place on to the all too lavishly tended stretch of road that connects Maidenhead with Harrods. The driver's first words were spoken at the Airport. 'The overnight lockers are across the hall,' he said.

I left the car and driver, and fitted my key into 025, one of a wall-full of metal twenty-four-hour lockers. It swung open and I left the key in the lock. Inside was a dark leather brief-case and a blue canvas zip bag with bulging side pockets. I took them across the hall to check in for my flight.

'Is this all your baggage, sir?' She weighed in my wardrobe case, took my ticket, straightened her strap, fluttered her eyelids and gave me a boarding card.

I took my brief-case, walked to the bookstall, bought *New Statesman*, *Daily Worker* and *History Today*, then took off towards my Exit. A bundle of people surged around kissing and greeting and 'how lovelying' their way across from the customs. In a dirty raincoat, hemmed in every-which-way was Ross. I didn't want to see him, and it was mutual, but for a moment the crowd forced us together like unconnected elements among so many molecular constructions. I beamed at him – I knew this would irritate him most.

Through the big shed-like customs hall.

The BOAC girl called the flight in a resonant metallic voice – 'BOAC announce the departure of flight BA712 to . . .' We walked across the apron. The aeroplane had swarms of white garbed engineers and loaders in blue battledress making like busy past the airport policeman. I clanked up the steps.

There was that smell of blue upholstery and fan-heated ovens. A steward took my name, boarding card and dirty trench coat and I moved up front with my fellow first-class passengers, towards a flurried-looking hostess who'd just done a four-minute mile. Something like the Eton wall game was going on in the narrow gangway. I made towards a petite dark girl looking very much alone, but the only people who get to sit next to girls like that are the men who model the airline adverts. I was next to a thick-necked idiot of about twenty-two stone. He sat down with a hat and overcoat on and wouldn't give either to the steward. He had boxes and bags and a packet of sandwiches. I strapped in and he looked at me in amazement. 'Floorn before?' I gave him the side focus and nodded like I was deep in contemplation. The steward helped him strap in, the steward helped him find his brief-case, he helped him understand that although the plane went to Sydney via Colombo he only need go to Rome. The steward showed him how to fit on, and tie up, his life-jacket, how the light switched itself on in water, where to find the whistle and turn on the compressed air. Told him he couldn't buy a drink until we were airborne. Showed him where to find his maps and told him how high we were. (We were still on the ground.) When we got to the end of the runway we hung around while an Alitalia DC8 came in, then with a screaming great roar, the brakes were off and we rolled, gaining speed, down the wide runway. Past airport buildings and parked aircraft, a couple of jolts as the machine gained buoyancy and airspeed. The cars on the London Road became smaller and the sun glinted dully on the many sheets of water around the Airport. Strange castles, baronial mansions, that appear only when you are in an aeroplane. One by one I remembered them and again promised myself a journey in search of them some day.

About Guildford the stewardess offered us the free alcohol that together with six extra inches of seat space makes the cost of a first-class ticket worth while, if you are on expenses. Gravel Gertie, of course, wanted something odd – 'A port and lemon.' The hostess explained they didn't have such a thing. He decided to 'Leave it to you, love, I don't do much travelling.'

Our drinks arrived. He passed me my glass of sherry and insisted upon bumping our glasses together like mating tortoises, and saying, 'Cheerio, Chin-chin.'

I nodded coolly as the spilt sherry pioneered its sticky route down my ankle.

'Over the teeth, over the gums, look out stomach, here she comes,' he chanted, and was such a helpless roistering jelly of merriment at his own wit that only a small fraction of his drink did in fact complete the journey. I wrote ROUNDELAYS into the crossword. 'I'm going to Rome,' said Gertie. 'Have you ever been there?'

I nodded without looking up.

'I missed the 9.45 plane. That's the one I should have been on, but I missed it. This one doesn't always go to Rome, but that 9.45 goes direct to Rome.'

I crossed out ROUNDELAYS and wrote RONDO-LETTO. He kept saying 'I'll go no more a-roaming,' and laughing a little high-pitched laugh, his great floppy face crouching behind his pink-tinted rimless spectacles. I was into the competition page of the *Statesman* when the stewardess offered me a selection of pieces of toast as large as a penny garnished with smoke salmon and caviare. Fatso said, 'What are we 'aving to eat, luv, spaghetti?' A thought that drove him wild with hysterical mirth, in fact he repeated the word to me a couple of times and roared with laughter. A toy dinner came along on a trolley; I declined the fat man's thick sausage sandwiches. I had frozen chicken, frozen *pomme parisienne* and frozen peas. I began to envy Fatso his sausage sandwiches. By the time we were crossing the suburbs of Paris the champagne appeared. I felt mollified. I crossed out RON-DOLETTO and wrote in DITHYRAMBS which made twenty-one down AWE instead of EWE. It was beginning to shape up.

We skimmed our way into the clouds like a nose into beer froth. 'We are approaching Rome – Fiumicino Airport. Transit time is forty-five

minutes. Please do not leave small valuable arti-
cles in the aircraft. Passengers may remain aboard
but smoking is not permitted during refuelling.
Please remain seated after landing. Light refresh-
ments will be available in the airport restaurant.
Thank you.'

I accidentally knocked Fatso's glasses out of his
hand on to the floor, one pane suffered a crack
but held together. While we apologized together
we came in over the eternal city. The old Roman
aqueducts were clearly visible, so was Fatso's
wallet, so I lifted it, offered him my seat – 'Your
first view of Rome.'

'When in Rome . . .' he was saying as I took
off to the forward toilet, I heard his high-pitched
laugh. 'Occupied.' Damn. I stepped into the bright
chromium galley. No one there. I leaned into the
baggage recess. I flipped through Fatso's wallet. A
wad of fivers, some pressed leaves, two blank
postcards with views of Marble Arch, a five-shilling
book of stamps, some dirty Italian money and a
Diner's Club card in the name of HARRISON B J D
and some photos. I had to be very quick. I saw
the stewardess walking slowly down the aisle
checking passengers' seat belts, and the lights were
up. 'NO SMOKING, FASTEN SEAT BELTS.' She was going
to give me the rush. I pulled the photos out – three
passport pictures of a dark-haired, smooth stockbroker type, full, profile and three-quarter. The
photo was different but the man was my pin-up,
too – the mysterious Raven. The other three photos

41

were also passport style – full face, profile and three-quarter positions of a dark-haired, round-faced character; deep sunk eyes with bags under horn-rimmed glasses, chin jutting and cleft. On the back of the photos was written '5ft 11in; muscular inclined to overweight. No visible scar tissue; hair dark brown, eyes blue'. I looked at the familiar face again. I knew the eyes were blue, even though the photograph was in black and white. I'd seen the face before; most mornings I shaved it. I realized who Fatso was. He was the fat man sitting at the bar in the strip-club when the cigarette girl told me to 'Go home.'

I stuffed them back, palmed the wallet, said 'OK' to the protesting hostess. I got back to my seat as the flaps went down, the plane shuddered like Gordon Pirie running into a roomful of cotton wool. Fatso was back in his own seat; my cardigan had fallen to the floor over my brief-case. I sat down quickly, strapped in. I could see the Railway Junction now and as we levelled off for the approach the G glued me to the seat springs. I could see the south side of the perimeter as we came in, and beyond the bright yellow Shell Aviation bowsers I noticed a twin-engined shoulder wing Grumman S2F-3. It was painted white and the word 'NAVY' was written in square black letters aft of the American insignia.

The tyres touched tarmac. I leaped forward to pick up my mohair cardigan. As I did so I flipped Fatso's wallet well under his seat. Now I saw the clean knife cut along the back of my new brief-case – still unopened. Not one of those long, amateur sorts of cuts, but a small, professional, 'poultry-cleaning' one. Just enough to investigate the contents. I leaned back. Fatso offered me a peppermint. 'Do as the Romans do,' he went on, eyes smiling through the cracked lens.

Fiumicino Airport, Rome, is one of those straight-sided 'Contemporary Economy' affairs. I went into the main entrance; to the left was the restaurant but up the stairs to the right a post office and money exchange. I was killing a minute with the paperbacks when I heard a soft voice say, 'Hello, Harry.'

Now my name isn't Harry, but in this business it's hard to remember whether it ever had been. I turned to face the speaker – my driver from London. He had a hard bony skull, with hair painted across it in Brylcreem. His eyes were black and counter-sunk deep into his face like gun positions. His chin was blue and hardened by wind, rain and monsoon and forty years of shaving hard against the bone. He wore black tie and white shirt and navy blue raincoat with shoulder straps. If he was a crew member he had removed his shoulder badges and taken care to leave his uniform cap elsewhere. If he wasn't, it was little wonder that he chose to wear the undress uniform of all the world's airline crews.

His eyes moved in constant watchfulness over my shoulder. He ran the palm of his right hand hard across the side of his head to press down his already flattened hair. 'Seat nineteen . . .'

'Is trouble,' I completed it in the phraseology of the department. He looked a little sheepish. 'Now you tell me,' I said peevishly. 'He's already shivved my hand baggage.'

'As long as there is still a tin inside,' he said.

'There's a tin inside,' I told him.

He rubbed the side of his jaw pensively, and finally said, 'Be last out at Beirut. Leave that,' we both eyed the case, 'for me to take through customs.' He said good-bye then turned to go, but came back to cheer me up. 'We're doing seat nineteen's hold baggage now,' he said.

As I thanked him I heard the Italian voice on the loudspeaker saying, 'British Overseas Airways Corporation denunca che departe dela Comet volo BA712 a Beirut, Bahrain, Bombay, Colombo, Singapore, Jakarta, Darwin and Sydney a tutto passagere . . .'

The Colosseum – Rome's rotten tooth – sank behind us, white, ghostly and sensational. I slept till Athens. Fatso hadn't re-embarked. I felt tired and out-gambited. I slept again.

I woke for coffee as we crossed the brown coast of Lebanon. Thin streaks of white crests buffered in from the blue Med. I noticed that there were many tall white buildings built since my first visit here in the days of Medway II.* The circuit over

---

* See Appendix: Medway II, p. 327.

44

the coast-side airport is generally a bumpy passage, for immediately after the airport the ground rises in blunt green mountains. Everything is hot, foreboding and very old.

Polite soldier-like officials in khaki uniforms did a line of backwards Arabic in immaculate penmanship across my passport and stamped it. I had cleared customs and immigration.

I dumped my wardrobe case into a Mercedes taxi – after letting two cabs go by – then gave the driver some Lebanese pounds and told him to wait. He was a villainous-looking Moslem in brown woollen hat, bright red cardigan and tennis shoes. I hurried upstairs. Having coffee near the juke-box was the 'driver'. He gave me my brief-case, a heavy brown packet, a heavy brown look, a heavy brown coffee. I dealt with each in silence. He gave me the address of my hotel in town.

The Mercedes touched seventy-five as we passed the dense wood of tall umbrella pines along the wide modern road to the town. Further away on the mountain slopes the cedar trees stood, national symbol and steady export for over 5,000 years. 'Hew me cedar trees out of Lebanon,' Solomon had commanded and from them built his temple. But my driver didn't care.

6

*[Aquarius (Jan 20–Feb 19) Someone else's fore-
thought may enable you to surprise a rival.]*

Peering between the slats of the wide venetian
blind, the yellow and orange stucco buildings conspired to hide the sea. In the warmth of midday
I see a black moustachioed villain hitting the horn
of a pink Caddie; the cause of his annoyance a
child leading a camel with a predilection for acacia
trees. Across the road two fat men sit on rusty
folding chairs drinking arak and laughing; a foot
or so above their heads a coloured litho Nasser is
not amused. In economy-sized cafés behind doors
artfully contrived to preserve a décor of absolute
darkness they are serving economy-sized coffees
of similar darkness with exotic pastries of honey-
smothered nuts and seeds. Clients – young Turks,
Greeks dressed like left bank intellectuals – find
their seats by the light of a juke-box inside which
Yves Montand and Sarah Vaughan are crowded.

Outside in the blinding sunlight, antiquated trams spew out agile targets for the Mercedes taxis. Dark-skinned young men with long black hair parade along the water's edge in bikinis almost big enough to conceal a comb. Below me in the street two young men on rusty cycles balancing a long tray of unleavened bread between them, are nearly brought down by a frenetic dog which yelps its fear and anger. In the souks men from the desert pass among money-changers – the carpet men and the sellers of saddles for horse, camel and bicycle. In Room 624 bars of sunlight lay heavily across the carpet. The hotel intercom hummed with old tapes of Sinatra, but he was losing a battle with the noise of the air-conditioning. Room 624, which the department had booked for me, came complete with private bath, private refrigerator, scales, magnifying mirrors, softened water, phones by bed, phones by bath. I poured another large cup of black coffee and decided to investigate my baggage. The blue wardrobe bag unzipped to reveal – a light-weight blue worsted suit, a seersucker jacket, a used overall with zip front and more pockets than I knew how to use. In the bag's side pockets were some new white and plain-coloured cotton shirts, a couple of plain ties, one wool, one silk, a belt, a slim leather and Italian, and a pair of red braces; didn't miss a trick that Alice. I was going to like working for WOOC(P). In the brief-case was a heavy tin. I looked at the label. It read 'WD 310/213. Bomb. Sticky'. The heavy packet

that the man in the blue raincoat had given me
was an envelope inside which was a waterproof-
lined brown bag. It was the sort of thing you
would find in the pocket of your seat when looking
for matches on an aeroplane. It is also the sort of
thing that aircrews, loaders, and engineers from
Rangoon to Rio use for transporting their little
'finds'. Cakes, chicken, ball-point pens, packs of
cards, butter – the jetsam of the airlines. Inside
this one was a hammerless Smith and Wesson,
safety catch built into the grip, six chambers
crowded with bullets. I tried to remember the rules
about unfamiliar* pistols. In an accompanying box
were twenty-five rounds, two spare chambers
(greased to hold the shells in tight), and a cutaway
holster. It covered little more than the barrel,
having a small spring clip for rigidity. I strapped
the belt across my shoulder. It fitted very well. I
played with this in front of the mirror, making
like *Wagon Train*, then drank the rest of my cold
coffee. Orders would come soon enough: Orders
for a last attempt to grab Raven the biochemist
before he disappeared beyond our reach.

The road inland from Beirut winds up into the
mountains; gritty little villages hold on tight to the
olive trees. The red earth gives way to rock, and
far below to the north lies St George's Bay, where
the dragon got his, way back, that was. Up here

* See Appendix, p. 327.

48

where the snow hangs around six months of the year the ground is dotted with little Alpine flowers and yellow broom, in some places wild liquorice grows. Once the heights are crossed the road drops suddenly and there is a route across the valley before the crossing of the next range – the Anti Lebanon, behind which lies 500 miles of nothing but sand till Persia. Much nearer than that, though, just along the road in fact, is Syria.

At many places the roadway cuts corners, and a shelf hangs almost over the road. A full grown man can, if he keeps very still, perch between two pieces of rock at one place I know. If while in this position he looks east he can see the road for over a hundred yards; if he looks towards Beirut he can see even farther – about three hundred yards, and what's more, he can, through night glasses, watch the road crossing the mountain. If he has friends up the road in either direction and a small trans-receiver he can talk to them. Although he shouldn't do so indiscriminately in case the police radio accidentally monitors the call. Along about 3.30 A.M. a man in this position will have counted the stars, almost fallen off the rock easing his back-ache and be seeing double through the night glasses. The metal of the trans-receiver will be sending pains of cold through hand and ear, and he will have begun to compile a list of friends prepared to help him in the matter of finding some other type of employment, and I won't blame him. It was 3.32 A.M. when I saw the headlights coming down the

49

mountain road. Through the night glasses I could see it was wide and rolled like an American car. I switched in my set and saw the movement up the road as the radio man gave it to Dalby. 'One motor, over a thousand yards. No traffic. Out.' Dalby grunted.

I read off the ranges army style until finally the large grey Pontiac slid under me, headlights probing the soft sides of the road. The beams were way above Dalby's head. I could imagine him, crouching there, perfectly still. In these sorts of situation Dalby sat back and let his subconscious take over; he didn't have to think – he was a natural hooligan. The car had slowed as Dalby knew it must, and as it neared him he stood up and posed, like the statue of the discus thrower, aimed – then lobbed his parcel of trouble. It was a sticky bomb about as big as two cans of soup end to end; on impact its very small explosive charge spread a sort of napalm through tank visors. Burnt cars and contents don't worry policemen the way blown-up shot-up ones do. The charge exploded. Dalby dropped almost flat, some flaming pieces of horror narrowly missed him, but mostly they hit radiator and tyre. The car hadn't slackened speed, and now Dalby was on his feet and running behind it. We'd parked the old car from Beirut obliquely across the path; the man driving our target must have been dead from the first impact, for he made no attempt to collide side to side in sheer, but just ploughed into the old Simca carrying it about eight feet. By now Dalby was alongside. He had the door open and I heard pistol shots as he groped into the rear seat. My trans-receiver made a click as someone switched in and said in a panicky voice, which forgot procedure, 'What you doing, what you doing?' For a fraction of a second I thought he was asking Dalby; then I saw it.

Below me on the road was another car. Maybe he had been following all the time with lights off, or perhaps he'd come down the other valley road from Baalbek and Homs. I looked down on this stretch of road which was as light as day now; the figures frozen like a photo in the intense light of the white hot flames. I could see Dalby's radio man from the Embassy standing there in an anorak like a scoutmaster on holiday, his white horse-like face staring thunderstruck at me. Dalby's feet were visible under the open door and I noticed that Simon was standing behind him instead of going around the other side of the car to help. In this second of time I so badly wanted it to be the duty of someone else to do it. Someone else for blaming when this little Nash turned round and roared away. But I had let it approach unseen, I had volunteered for the look-out so as not to do what Dalby was doing – lying on his belly over a red hot petrol tank among people with no reason to be friendly. So I did what I had to do. I did it quickly and I didn't watch. I needn't have used two sticky bombs; it had a flimsy roof.

Simon had got Dalby's car out on to the roadway by the time I had scrambled down. In the back the radio man was sitting guarding our one captive – the smooth stockbroker whose picture both Fatso and I had carried. The man I had seen lying unconscious upon the gaming table. Dalby had gone to look at the Nash while I vomited as inconspicuously as possible. The heavy smell hung across the roadway and was worse than a brewed-up tank ever made. This smell was a special smell, an evil smell, and my lungs were heavy with it. The two burnt out cars still flickered and spat flames as something dripped on to the red glowing metal. We each of us had removed our overalls and thrown them into the flames. It was Simon's job to make sure they burnt enough to be unrecognizable. I remember wondering if the zips would melt, but I said nothing.

The sky had begun to lighten in the east, and the silence had turned brittle in the way it does when night gives way to dawn. The hills had grown lighter, too, and I thought I could discern a goat here and there. Soon the villages would be awake in the land that St Paul walked, and men would be milking by day where we had been killing by night.

Dalby came back out of earshot and said, 'Nobody likes it.'

I said, 'At first.'

'Not ever, if they work with me.'

Dalby got into the rear seat next to Raven, and

the radio man sat watching them with his pistol cocked.

I heard Dalby say, 'I'm very sorry, sir,' in a firm flat voice, and then he produced one of those tiny toothpaste tubes with the needle that were in wartime first-aid kits. Drawing back the man's sleeve Dalby stabbed it into him. He made no attempt to say or do anything. He sat there in a state of shock. Dalby put the used morphia syrette tube into a matchbox, and the car pulled away, past the whitened twisted wrecks of the three cars; the melted rubber was dribbling and flaring in the road. We turned off the Beirut road at Shtora and headed north up the valley through Baalbek. The pagan and Roman ruins were strategically placed to guard the valley. The six gigantic pillars of the Great Temple were visible through the poplar trees in the streaky dawn light, as they had stood each dawn since the standards of Imperial Rome stood alongside them. I felt Dalby lean forward across my seat-back; he was passing me a rose-tinted pair of spectacles. 'They came from the Nash.' I saw that one pane was cracked. I turned them over in my hand. If there's anything more pathetic than a dead man's dog, it's a dead man's spectacles. Every bend and shine belonged to its wearer and to no one else, nor would ever.

Dalby said, 'ONI.* Both of them. US Embassy car; probably there to do what we did. Serve the

* ONI – Office of Naval Intelligence US Navy.

nosy—right. They should tell us what they are doing.' He caught my glance at Raven. 'Oh, don't worry about him, he's way out.'

I remembered the US Navy's white S2F-3 'Tracker' at Rome, and another at Beirut that was the same one.

7

I saw Dalby butting his head back, his long fair hair flashing in the hot sunshine. He shouted something I couldn't hear, and disappeared behind one of the gigantic smooth-sided Corinthian columns. In scale with him the ruins of Baalbek's temple were vast against the clear desert sky. I jumped down the broken steps and a couple of lizards twinkled out of sight. Dalby had caught the sun this morning and I could feel the tightening of my skin across my nose and forehead. A little scatter of sand blew across my feet as a draught of wind flicked a finger along the valley floor. As Dalby came nearer I saw that he'd found a piece of tile that had cleverly eluded two millennia of tourists. On the far side of the site beyond the little round temple of Venus a group of American girls in red blazers were standing in a semicircle listening to an old white-bearded Arab. I could tell that he'd got to the bit about the sex orgies and the Rites of the God Moloch even though the wind carried his voice away. Dalby had caught up to me now.

'OK for lunch?' he asked, and in his proprietorial manner led the way towards it without waiting for a reply.

We had all slept late that morning in the rather grand villa out there on the Baalbek road. Simon was a Lt-Col in the RAMC and some sort of specialist. He had never been involved in a stunt like last night's before. I felt a little guilty at my unspoken criticism. He was back there now, keeping an eye on the man who had held centre stage last night. The villa was discreetly situated and under the quiet control of an elderly Armenian couple who accepted our arrival last night without surprise. The house stood in the middle of a vast acreage of terraced garden. Azaleas, cyclamen and olive trees all but hid the building which was 'U' shaped in plan. Behind the house across the open end, an irregular-shaped pool was cut into the natural rock. Under the clear blue water at one end a Roman statue was transfixed in athletic pose, and there were no changing-rooms, beach-chairs, parasols or diving-boards to mar the pool's natural appearance. The walls of the house facing inwards were glass from floor to ceiling, with bright plain curtains which moved on electrically propelled runners. At night when the lights were on throughout the house and the curtains fully open, and when the coloured lights illuminated the Roman statue, the paved central loggia made a perfect helicopter landing space, while the double-glazed windows kept the worst of the sound out.

Here at the temple the air was clear and clean and soft and because morning gives a dimension of magic to any place it was soft and sharp at the same time. The fluted columns had been burnished by the centuries of wind but under the hand the surface was as rough as pumice and as pitted as a honeycomb. A dirty child with torn trousers and a pair of American canvas shoes drove three goats clanking along the road to the north. 'Cigarette,' he called to Dalby, and Dalby gave him two.

Dalby was especially relaxed and expansive; it seemed a good chance to find out more about the opposition that we had just outwitted. I asked him about Jay – 'But what's his cover story – what's his angle, his business?'

'He runs, or more accurately he pays someone to run a research unit in Aargau.' He stopped, and I nodded. 'You know where it is?'

'Yes,' I said.

'Where?' asked Dalby.

'Forgive me if my lack of ignorance is an embarrassment to you. The Canton of Aargau is in the north of Switzerland, the river Aar joins the Rhine there.'

'Oh, yes, forgive me, the finance king is bound to know Switzerland.'

'That's right,' I said. 'Now let's take it from there – what sort of research unit?'

'Well they have sociologists and psychiatrists

and statistics people and they have money from various industrial foundations to investigate what they call "synthesized environment".'

I said, 'You've lost me now – without trying.'

'Not surprisingly, for they hardly know what they are doing themselves, but the idea is this. Take German industry for an example. German industry has been short of labour for ages and they have imported workmen from almost every European country – with excellent results. That is to say – put an unskilled labourer from one of the Greek islands, who has never seen a machine before, in the German factory, he learns how to operate it just as quickly as a worker from Düsseldorf.' Dalby looked up. 'You are receiving me?'

'Loud and clear,' I said. 'So what's the problem – peachy for the West Germans.'

'In that sort of situation – no problems, but if a West German builds a factory in Greece and employs local labour they can't even teach them to switch on the lights in some cases.

'Therefore, these boffins in Aargau feel that to be in an environment where everyone knows what they are doing, and attach no difficulty to doing it, means that the new arrival will adopt the same attitude. If on the other hand the individual finds himself among people lacking confidence, he will raise barriers to ever mastering his job – and so will the others. This is what "synthesized environment" means. It could be very important to industry, especially to industries being formed in countries with a rural population.'

'It could be important from our point of view, too.'

'We have a file on it,' said Dalby dryly.

That's about all that Dalby volunteered on the subject of Jay, but I had lots of other chatty topics of discussion ready as we walked back to the villa. I asked him about his new IBM machine, about the Chester Committee Report on the Intelligence Services, and how it was likely to affect us, and about my arrears of pay (now approaching four months) and whether I couldn't have the whole of my expenses available to me in cash against petty cash vouchers instead of submitting accounts and settling down to a long wait as I did now.

It was Dalby's day for proving that he could be one of the boys. He wore his short-sleeved shirt outside his denim trousers and an old pair of suède shoes, against which he kicked every small movable object we encountered. I asked him about Mr Adem, our host, and about him he was more forthcoming than he had ever been about pay and expenses.

Dalby had got him from Ross, who had got him from the US Anti-Narcotics Bureau (Mediterranean Div). He had run Indian hemp* across the Syrian border as a section of a chain to New York. The Americans had done a deal with

* See Appendix: Indian Hemp, p. 328.

him in 1951 and, although the pay wasn't up to drug traffic rates, he had been happy to avoid a spell up the river. In the NATO Intelligence Service regroupings of '53 Adem had come into British service. He was about in his mid-sixties; gentle and humorous with a face like an apple that's been stored through the winter. He was a fine judge of horses, wines and heroin, and had an encyclopaedic knowledge of an area stretching from Northern Turkey to Jerusalem. If you trod on a beetle for miles around you'd find he had it under contract. His role was a giver of information and understanding this, he had, or showed, no curiosity about the affairs of his employers. His salary was virtually unlimited, with one proviso – no cash. As Dalby put it, 'We pay any reasonable bill he runs up, but he never handles a pound himself.'

'It's going to be difficult for him to retire,' I said.

'It will be damn well impossible if I have anything to do with it,' said Dalby. 'He's hooked, we need him.'

'You mean he never tries to re-channel some of his debts into cash?' I asked, just to be provocative.

Dalby's face cracked open in one of those big boyish laughs he gave out when he felt proud of his even teeth. 'He does!

'When we first gave him the Sud Aviation Jet helicopter,' Dalby went on, 'I told him to jazz it around somewhat. "Live it up and be proud of it," I said. "Give a few of the big Government boys a ride around." I wanted him to be seen up and down the shore line, occasionally riding out to sea. With a Lebanese big-wig aboard, inquiries were not going to be encouraged.'

We'd reached the sloping driveway, and beyond the lemon trees I could just see the light green Cadillac in which Adem had met us a few kilometres along the road in the small hours.

'So?' I said. 'It worked?'

'Worked?' Dalby tilted his head, pulled his earlobe and smiled in admiration as he thought about it. 'He brought twenty kilos of heroin across from Syria within seven days of getting his licence. Twenty kilos,' Dalby said, his thin lips forming the words yet again in tacit joy at the sheer ambition of the old man.

'At five shillings a dose that's a lot of green,' I agreed.

'It was a big improvement on Indian hemp. The sort of ruffians he knows can get 100,000 doses from a kilo, and five shillings is the Beirut price, in London it's going to be more like ten. A couple of runs like that and he could buy Cyprus as a weekend place. It gave me a problem, but I told him I'd break his head if he did it again, and in the long run it was beneficial. When the news of the shipment leaked out – it's bound to in a place like this – well, people never trust a completely honest individual.'

The smell of Dgaj Muhshy (chicken stuffed with

nutmeg, thyme, pine nuts, lamb and rice, and cooked with celery) taunted the nostrils. The old man was dressed in a shirt of bright yellow locally-made silk and was poking away among his vegetable garden as we got to the front door.

'Hello,' muttered Dalby. 'The old swine is probably growing his own.'

The soft wind blew across the high-ceilinged dining-room. The décor, except for two beautiful gold thread brocades of very old Persian design, reflected Adem's peasant origin more than his present-day affluence. The scrubbed woodwork, the small-patterned cloths, an enormous dresser, crowded with plates, saucers, jugs and cups. The rugs on the wall of simple dark-toned peasant weaves. All this provided a background against which a food opera was played out. First sambousiks (small pastries containing curried meat served freshly baked) were served. I looked at old Adem as he stood at the end of the table; under his bulbous nose hung an enormous grey moustache which, because of his thinning hair, gave one the curious feeling that his face was upside down. His skin was hard and tanned in such a way that when his face was relaxed and serious, the wrinkles around the mouth and eyes were white; but he was seldom serious.

He divided up the huge joint of lamb with a well-worn horn-sided folding knife that came from his pocket and was used in every operation from vegetable gardening to changing a tyre. I had watched him do both with the same smooth enjoyable efficiency. His mouth contorted with the effort of his hands, and each slice was delivered with a great flashing smile of his brown uneven teeth.

'It's good?' he asked me.

I told him to be careful or he'd have a guest for life. It was the right thing to say. He was a born host and, as Dalby said, I am a born guest.

That afternoon as the sun reached its apogee Adem and I sat talking and drinking under the trees. Adem did the talking, I did the drinking. He told me of his uncle who had killed a lion single-handed with only a spear in 1928. 'A challenge. He went to this lion in challenge. In his right hand he had a spear.' Adem raised his right hand, fingers clenched. 'This arm,' he raised his left arm, 'is tied with clothes and bandage for guarding.' Adem demonstrated guarding. 'After this lion die he is called "Hamid the lion-killer"; he never work again.'

'Never works again?'

'Never. A man who kills a lion, everyone gives him money and food, everything; never work again.'

'I can see the attraction,' I said. 'Are there lions about here now?'

'Not here. To the north perhaps; many times I go. Many animal; many gazelle, many leopard, ibex . . . bears. But they become less each year. Many people hunt.'

'Like your Uncle Hamid.'

63

Adem looked serious, then he laughed a big laugh. 'Not like him. People with guns. I do not like this.'

'You go north hunting?' Now I was doing it.

'Not the hunt. I go to look. I stay very still, very, very still, near water, and I watch them come.'

'You never photograph them?'

'No, I watch. It is just for me, not for pictures. Just for me and the animal.'

I imagined Adem holed up overnight in the bleak brown area to the north watching and sniffing the night air and never taking a film or a bullet. I told him of Xenophon's men who chased the ostrich and wild ass. He liked that part of the story but found the effort of imagining a greater period of time than two generations very difficult. As far as Adem was concerned, Xenophon was a contemporary of A. W. Kinglake. Adem told me of the attempts to conserve the wild life farther north, and of the money they needed. When I told Dalby he said that the old man would do anything to get his hands on cash, but I'm simple enough to believe the old man.

Soon only the higher parts of the landscape were catching the horizontal sunlight and a lone blackcap had sung his song from all the little lemon trees. From inside the house the crick-crack of freshly ignited fruit-tree wood proclaimed the approach of dinner-time.

Totem poles of lamb, aubergine, onion and green pepper were being skewered, seasoned and readied on the big open hearth. As Adem finished speaking a radio somewhere within the house pierced the grey velvet twilight with a needle of sound.

The polished opening notes of the second movement of the *Jupiter*. It seemed that every living thing across the vast desert spaces heard the disturbing, chilling sound. For those few minutes of time as the wire edge modulated to a minor key and as the rhythm and syncopation caught, slipped and re-engaged like a trio on a trapeze, there was only me and Adem and Mozart alive in that cruel, dead, lonely place.

We were three days with the old man of the mountains, then John reappeared from Beirut with a vast radio set. It took him nearly three hours, but finally he made contact with a Battle-class RN destroyer that was NATOing down the Lebanese coastline.

Simon, the army quack, whose name was Painter, as far as anyone's name is anything in this business, seldom came out of the upstairs room. But when they had fixed a rendezous time with the destroyer, Painter decided that the captive could eat dinner with us. Raven. He was well code-named this captive Raven. He was thinner and weaker than he'd looked even two days previously when Dalby had dragged him out of the Pontiac, but he was good-humoured in a different sort of way. His white shirt had grown a little dirty, and in his baggy pin-stripe trousers and a new dark linen jacket he looked like the manager of a Bingo saloon. His eyeballs, deep and darkly sunken, moved quickly and nervously, and I noticed that he repeatedly glanced towards Painter. As they reached the bottom of the stairs our guest paused. He seemed to sense our curiosity and interest in the role he played. Our chatter ceased, and the only sound came from an upstairs radio tuned to the 'Voice of the Arab'; its strange polyphonic discord set the eerie background to the curious scene. His voice was the clear, carefully articulated tones of English management.

'Good evening, gentlemen,' he said flatly. 'Good evening and er, thank you.' He came through like a whisky ad. Dalby strode across to him in a paternal way, and led him to the table like guest night at Boodles. 'Most kind, Dalby, most kind,' he said.

All through the meal little was said that didn't touch on the weather or the garden or horses, mostly horses, and old Adem finished quickly and went up to catch the forecast. The destroyer was making good time down the coast in the gathering twilight; visual contact wouldn't be the simplest thing, although with fuel for over three hundred miles the helicopter had a safe enough margin of search.

They sat inside the big plexiglass dome of the SE-3130 Alouette 2 like goldfish expecting food. Simon Painter sat on one side of the azoic Raven on the folding seats in the rear. Dalby sat in the front left side observer's seat as he received the final few words of Adem's short lecture on the use of the Decca navigation equipment. Adem's face was more serious now as he fingered the joystick-like cyclic pitch control, and worried about how to bring this Alouette down on the temporary landing platform that wouldn't be much bigger than the forward gun turret upon which it was being erected at that minute. On the bodywork I could read the notices: 'Danger Rotors' and a serial number, and inside the cabin a small plastic panel and engraved upon it the procedure in case of fire. The words shuddered as the motor started. Like a back-fire in Trafalgar Square it was followed by the sound of a thousand wings beating the air, clattering across the valley and echoing back to us again. The 400-horse-power Turbomeca power unit was alive, and above my head the thirty-foot rotor-blades shaved the face of the night. The controls reflected little pimples of yellow light into Adem's spectacles, and our distinguished visitor waved a limp hand airily towards us in kingly fashion. 'Farewell troublesome Raven,' I thought.

Adem's left hand pulled the collective lever, twisting the throttle gently as he did so. The limp blades were flung horizontal by the centrifugal surge of the motor, and the rev counter moved slowly around the dial. The big rotors twisted in response to Adem's movement of the 'collective', and hammered the heavy evening air down upon our ears. Like a clumsy Billy Bunter the machine heaved itself hand over hand into the sky. A touch of rudder had the tail rotor slip it sideways, and, silhouetted against the five-o'clock-shadowed chin of twilight, they hedge-hopped in 100 mph gallops towards the sea. Adem the horseman took the cedar tree jumps in fine form.

Walking back towards the house, I decided to try DITHYRAMBE with a final E. This would make ten down EAT, not SAT or OAT. I really was getting it now.

8

*[Aquarius (Jan 20–Feb 19) Keep an open mind.
You will get to know an old friend better. Avoid
business gatherings and concentrate on financial
affairs. Above all don't make impulsive decisions.]*

April is a hell of a month to be in London, and
on the Tuesday I had to go to Sheffield to see some
of our people there. It was a long meeting and
little was settled about the co-relation of filing systems, but they would let us use their staff on our
phone and cable lines. Thursday I was busy
working back over a back-log of new information
on the Jay operation, when Dalby came in. I hadn't
seen him since his helicopter trip. He was tanned
and handsome looking, and was wearing the dark
grey suit, white shirt and St Paul's tie that was
part of his equipment for dealing with Defence
Ministers' private secretaries. He asked me how
things were. It was strictly rhetorical stuff, but I
told him that I was still two months behind with

pay and three with allowances, that I still hadn't settled the business of dating my new substantive rank and a claim for £35 in overseas special pay is overdue by ten and a half months.

'OK,' said Dalby. 'In lieu of all you claim I'll take you for lunch.'

Dalby didn't fool around with expenses; we went into Wiltons and settled for the best of everything. The iced Israeli melon was sweet, tender and cold like the blonde waitress. Corrugated iron manufacturers and chinless advertising men shared the joys of our expense-account society with zombie-like debs with Eton-tied uncles. It was a nice change from the sandwich bar in Charlotte Street, where I played a sort of rugby scrum each lunchtime with only two PhD's, three physicists and a medical research specialist for company, standing up to toasted bacon sandwich and a cup of stuff that resembles coffee in no aspect but price.

Over the lobster Dalby asked me how things were going in the work on Jay. I told him that it was going just great and I hope someone will tell me what I'm doing some day. I wouldn't have remembered Thursday at all, apart from the fine lobster salad and carefully-made mayonnaise, if it hadn't been for what Dalby then said. He poured me a little more champagne and crunching it back into the ice bucket, said, 'You're working with the same information that I am. Unless I'm wrong we are moving in from opposite ends to the same conclusion.' Then he changed the subject.

However, my complaint about working in the dark must have had some effect, for on Friday they started to tell me things.

That Friday morning my post brought me an electricity bill for over £12, and a snotty printed form that said it is understood that the above-named article of War Department property has been retained by you contrary to section something or other of the Army Act. It should be returned to officer i.c. special issue room – War Office, London. The word 'returned' was crossed through and 'delivered personally' written instead; across the top there was scrawled 'officer's sidearm Colt .45 pistol'. The message ended, 'You will be informed in due course whether further action will be taken.' I carefully posted that into the garbage bin under the sink and poured a strong clear bowl of Blue Mountain coffee. I stood there on that cold April morning, hot coffee-bowl cupped between my hands, and gazed blankly out across the chimneys, crippled and hump-backed, the shiny sloping roofs, backyards of burgeoning trees and flowering sheets and shirts. I weighed the desirability of pulling the still-warm bedding over my still-unawakened body. Reluctantly I turned on the shower.

About eleven A.M. Alice entered my office with a rose-decorated cracked cup of Nescafé, a basilisk look and a new green-laced file. She gave me all three, picked up the fountain pen I had borrowed the week before, and marched out. I put aside the paper-clip chain I was working on, and started flipping through the file. It had the usual employment bureau rubber stamp and 14143/6/C written in large flomaster lettering. Typewritten on light-green paper, it was yet another file on the man we called Jay. I had never seen a green file before but it had a much higher security clearance than the ordinary white ones. I read of his university progress and his training in Jungian psychology (discontinued after two years) and his unsuccessful excursion into the timber business. It had the usual outline of Jay's career up to June 1942, then instead of the gap in the story I read of Jay, then Christian Stakowski, being recruited into Polish Army Intelligence based in London. He made two very hazardous trips into southern Poland, the second time his air pick-up failing to contact. His next emergence from the unknown was when he appeared in Cairo reporting back to the Polish Army, who gave him the VM,* in December '42. He was sent back to England and did the eight-month course at the place they had in Horsham. By this time the chain of cells he worked with in Poland had been decimated and a photostat in the file shows that Polish Army counter-intelligence had the possibility that he had done a deal with the Germans added to his papers. Another letter dated May '43 points this possibility up by showing that the arrests along his chain were all by the same department of German Investigation.

* VIRTUTI MILITARI, The Polish VC.

The Polish Underground had many different political origins – Jay, finding himself a member of the National Armed Forces (a Right-wing extremist group), probably did a deal with the German Abwehr. In so doing he was regarded as a hero by the Communist-dominated AL (or people's army) for reducing fascist power. A massive treble-cross!

There is a gap then, and next in September '45, Stakowski, now with the papers of a Polish sergeant WOWC is filtered back into Poland among soldiers released from German POW camps. In Warsaw he obtains a lowly secretarial job with the new Communist Government, and reports back to an Intelligence outfit financed by the Board of Trade of all people! His reports concern industrial espionage especially the movement of German reparation production into Russia. In 1947 his reporting languishes and a note says that he was probably working for the US Central Intelligence Agency, who recruited a lot of agents in Europe at that time on the '8 year system', an offer whereby agents after eight years in the field would be paid a small pension, shipped to the US and settle down to listen to the grass grow. It was received enthusiastically in the US-oriented Europe of '47, although there is no record from 1955 onwards of any pay-offs. In 1950, WOWC, with little or no promotion in his Government job, tenth secretary in a timber bureau, on the pretext of being under suspicion flees to England on a passport that his job enabled him to wangle. In England he sinks as happily into the Right-wing Polish community as he had into the Communist Government.

The file ends with about twenty intercepted US Embassy phone calls to him concerned mostly with the activities of London merchant banks. The Embassy are especially interested in the finances of the Common Market. I sipped my coffee and came to the most interesting part of all. The last item is on notepaper with a discreet coat of arms. It is headed Combined Services Information Clearing House C-SICH, through which all information available in Great Britain is shared to appropriate branches. The many large commercial concerns, which have industrial espionage teams spying on competitors, must submit monthly reports to C-SICH. It is one of these that is quoted as saying that WOWC or Jay is positively not in receipt of regular sums of money from the Russian Government. His income is 'very large but from diverse sources and irregular amounts'. Alice thoughtread me ending the file, came in, took the closed file out of my hands, checked the binding for tears and riffled quickly through the page corners, her eagle eye checking the page numbers for omission. Satisfied, she straightened up my blotter and brushed an eyebrow with her moistened little finger, and collected my empty rose coffee-cup. In hasty little pinched steps she walked across the narrow room.

I cleared my throat. 'Alice,' I said. She turned

and watched me blankly. She paused a moment, then raised an eyebrow. She had her tight-fitting tweed two-piece on today, and her hair had been slightly intimidated in a high-class coiffeur joint.

'Your seams are crooked.'

If I thought I'd make her angry or happy I couldn't have been more wrong. She nodded her head deferentially like a Chinese mandarin and went on her way.

9

Dalby had buzzed me for a meeting at three o'clock. It was in the board-room downstairs. The large red-brown shiny oval table reflected the grey windows with the rain dribbling downward. The electric light shone from a gaunt chandelier-type thing of thin poor-quality glass. Dalby stood with his Bedford-cord behind in front of a puny, one-bar electric fire that looked and felt diminutive in the large Victorian fire-place in which the brass shovel and poker were kept polished. Above his head a vast portrait of a man in frock-coat and beard had almost entirely relapsed into the brown gloom of the coach varnish. Uncomfortable upright chairs unused by dint of their discomfort stood at attention like family retainers along the dead-flower-print wallpaper. High up on the wall above the picture rail a large clock tick-tocked away the sparse daylight hours. A minute or so before three, Painter, the doctor, came in. Dalby continued screening his face with the *Guardian*, so we nodded to each other. Chico was sitting down already. I had no particular reason to speak to Chico. He was in one of those moods where he kept saying things like, 'What about old Davenport then – do you know old "Coca-Cola" Davenport?' Then if not stopped immediately he'd tell me how he got his nickname. 'You must know "Bumble-bee" Tracy then . . .' No, no more, Chico for the present.

I sat down in one of the large chairs and began, while looking official, thinking of dates at random and trying to remember what happened. '1200 – fifteen years before Mongols' I wrote, 'end of Romanesque arch. Four years before fourth Crusade. Battle of Hattin means Europe is defeated in East.' I was really getting into it now. 'Magna Carta . . .'

'D'you mind?' It was Dalby. Everyone was seated and ready to go. Dalby hated me concentrating. 'Going into one of your trances,' he called it. Dalby began now. I looked around. Painter, about forty, a thin rat-faced character, was on my right. He was wearing a good-quality blue blazer, white shirt, soft collar, and a plain dark crimson tie. From his cuffs his links shone dull genuine gold, and a handkerchief peeped coyly. His hands were long and supple and had the dry whiteness that doctors' hands get from being washed too much.

Opposite me across the table was an army type. Gentle in disposition, his gold spectacle frames glinted among hair whitened by Indian sun. He wore a cheap, dark ready-made suit with a regimental tie. I guessed him to be a Captain or a Major of fifty-three, past any chance of further promotion. His eyes were grey and moved slowly, taking in his surroundings with care and awe. His large hairy hands held on to his brief-case before him on the table, as though even here there was a danger of it being stolen before he could reveal his strange mysteries. Captain Carswell, for so I discovered was his name, had come from H.38 to us with some interesting statistics, Dalby was saying.

The clock tick-tocked on, adding a second or so to its seventy years of tick.

'If you are in H.38 you must know "Rice-Mould" Billingsby,' Chico was saying to Carswell, who looked at him, almost surprised to find an imbecile in the room.

'Yes,' he said slowly. His voice had a clear firm ring of outdoor authority. 'There is a Major-General Billingsby in the department.'

'Yes, uncle of a fren,' said Chico brightly, rather like he might have said, 'Checkmate' at the Moscow World Chess Championships.

Then Carswell began his story with a lot of officialese like he was compiling a report, but soon got into the swing of it. After the Burgess and Maclean affair his department had been given the job of doing a statistical analysis in conjunction with the registry of missing persons at the Yard. Carswell had asked permission to process the figures first then to look for patterns afterwards, instead of looking for anything in particular. He then started to do breakdowns just anyway it occurred to him. He gave a lot of credit to the sergeant clerk he worked with, but I think it was Carswell who found in the job a sort of musical freedom working in purely abstract terms. Anyway, whoever is to be credited, some very interesting patterns grew out of it. Finding some strange characteristics, they left the 'missing persons figures' in favour of any combinations among the top-grade security clearances. With no particular purpose they fired cards through sorting machines to look for any common feature.

He explained, 'Although there were few resemblances in any one group from an occupational or geographical point of view, there were resemblances across those groups. For instance . . .'

It was a long explanation that Carswell gave us and he loved every tedious minute of it. It was a long time later that I understood how important was the work he was doing.

He produced his delicately drawn graphs and talked of S.1's (Security Grade Ones) – important chemists, physicists, electronics engineers, political advisers, etc, people essential to the running of the country. Carswell had noticed that groups of these S.1's were found together in certain parts of England which were neither holiday centres nor conference places.

The kidnapping of an S.1 (if he was valuable)

was easy to understand. Raven was an important S.1 and Jay had kidnapped him and come within an ace of delivering him over the border before we had grabbed him back, with our pocket-sized commando attack. But, so far, there had been no more kidnappings, and these meetings in Britain were different; something none of us understood.

10

[Aquarius (Jan 20–Feb 19) Once again you will need tact and discretion, but persistence and hard work will bear fruit in the long run. An old friend will smooth out a difficulty.]

Dalby seconded Carswell to work with me. I got him a little private office just big enough for him and the sergeant – Murray – to work in, a promotion to temporary Major and a suit that fitted him. I took him round to my tailor and we decided that a dull grey-green soft tweed, with dark brown waistcoat, gave him the country squire look right for an unemployed officer. Sgt Murray went for a check jacket with grey flannels. They worked each day diligently from 9 A.M. to 6 P.M., then returned to their wives in Fulham and Bromley. I had my own work to do but I dropped into Carswell now and again. By now he was concentrating on the S.1's (S.2's being too numerous and g-k's (cabinet ministers, etc) being too few to get conclusive results from. Carswell was a statistician but even to him it was evident that unless other common factors could be found the concentrations were meaningless. Carswell and Murray turned up common factors like owning two cars, long holidays, visits to America, holidays in North Africa, etc, but then, of course, these things were bound to form patterns in a group where age-groups, income and education were markedly similar. Other behaviour patterns were less easy to explain. Among the groups concentrating at one place (which Carswell called the 'concens'), among the 'concens' there was an above-average number who had been members of a political or quasi-political group, all but one having Right-wing aims. I asked Carswell to write a description of a concen and a description of an S.1 from the figures he had.

Quite a few had had a serious illness within the last five years, many being fevers, none of the concens were left-handed, they had a great number of bachelors, and a slightly greater number of decorations for valour. Public schools and divorced parents were absolutely at average level. I wrote all this down on a sheet of 10in by 8in writing paper and pinned it above my table. I was still looking at it when Dalby came in. He was affecting a silver-topped umbrella of late. He followed his usual debating tactics, waving a sheet of paper covered with my writing.

'Look here – I'll be damned if I'm passing this. Damned if I will.' Dalby moved one half-eaten egg and anchovy sandwich, toasted. A speciality of Wally's delicatessen downstairs in Charlotte Street. He then moved the SARS to SORC volume of the *Britannica* and *Barnes' History of the Regiments*, a Leica 3 with the 13.5 cm and a bottle of Carbon Tetrachloride, and was able to sit down on the desk. He waved the sheet of paper under my nose, still cursing away. He read, 'Eight poplin shirts, white, for Sgt Murray; two dozen Irish linen handkerchiefs for Major Carswell; four pairs of hand-stitched hide shoes, including cost of last.'

'Cost of last,' said Dalby again. 'What's that mean?'

'Last,' I said. 'Last – what the cobbler threw at his wife, you know.'

Dalby continued reading from my expense account for the month. 'Then this item: "To entertainment, drinks and dinner: Mirabelle Restaurant twenty-three pounds." What is this, you, Chico, Carswell and Murray at the –' he paused, and mouthed the words incredulously and slowly, '– Mirabelle Restaurant!! You're supposed to spend £103 per month. This lot comes to £191 18s 6d. How's that?'

It seemed he expected an answer. 'I'm keeping a few items over till next month,' I said.

That went down like a lead balloon. Dalby had stopped joking now, he began looking really annoyed, he scratched the side of his face nervously and kept waving my expense sheet so that it made crackling noises in the air.

'Ross said you were an impertinent —. You'll impertinent your way right out of here before long. You'll see.' His rage had gone suddenly, but it seemed a shame to leave it like that.

'In all those expensive clothes,' I asked plaintively, 'do you expect us to eat in a Wimpy Bar?' Dalby rolled with the punch, he didn't even know what a Wimpy Bar was; he just couldn't bear the thought of a sergeant brushing waiters with him at the Mirabelle. That's why I continually did it, and why I itemized it in the most unequivocal way I knew. Dalby at this stage executed a famous military manoeuvre known as the 'War Office two-step', generally used for withdrawing intact when out-ranked. He started explaining that there was no need for Carswell and Murray to buy things off my expense sheet. Carswell can have his own. I didn't particularly want Murray to have an expense sheet but I was interested to see whether I could angle Dalby into having to give him one.

'Accounts will never in a million years let you give a sergeant with less than two years' provisional service a sheet of money.'

I followed up, 'You know that's the sort of thing they are dead fussy about; – no, you *might* get away with giving him free use of Carswell's petty cash, but what they says goes when it comes to money sheets.'

Dalby sat there with a sardonic look clamped across his head like a pair of earphones. 'When you have quite finished, for reasons known only to yourself, getting Sergeant Murray an expense sheet, let me say that I have considered the matter carefully and both of them can have one.' Dalby leaned back and put his suède ankle boots on the back of the only comfortable chair in the office. He picked up the two books that lay on the top of the old brief-case that I intended to lose and replace from expenses at the earliest possible moment. He read the spines aloud, '*Experimental Induction of Psychoneuroses in Personality and Behaviour Disorders*, Vol 1, by Liddell, and Shorvon's *Abreactions*. I saw them on your desk this morning but I don't think it will get us closer to Jay.

'Now I know you are a little miffed at working with what you consider inadequate information, but we'll settle all that.' He paused for a long time, as though thinking carefully before committing himself by what he was about to say, as indeed I'm sure he was doing. 'I'm letting you take over this whole department,' he said at last. 'Now don't get all excited, it's only going to be for about three months, in fact less if I'm lucky. You are a bit stupid, and you haven't had the advantage of a classical education.'

Dalby was having a little genteel fun with me. 'But I am sure you will be able to overcome your disadvantages.'

'Why think so? You never overcame your advantages.'

It followed the usual pattern of our preliminaries. We got down to business. The handing-over

85

ceremony consisted of Dalby and Alice showing me how to work the IBM. I had a feeling that a certain amount of the documentation had been removed, but perhaps that's just me being paranoiac. He was moving out the next day and he wasn't telling me what he was doing. I asked him in particular about Jay. Dalby said, 'It's all in the documents. Read it up.'

'I'd rather hear it from you, get the hang of the way you're thinking.' Of course, I really wanted to avoid reading all that damn bumf.

Anyway, Dalby gave me an outline. 'When Jay settled in London in '50 he was working on small-time espionage for the Americans. We didn't want him, in fact, doing just economic and industrial work, it wasn't really our decision. He had an office in Praed Street and seemed to be doing OK apart from his homework for the Yanks. The first time we got interested in him was the Burgess and Maclean business. We had a memo in saying we mustn't pull him for it. We didn't have any idea of doing so, but it started us off thinking.'

I interrupted, 'Who sent the memo?'

'It wasn't written or recorded. I wasn't in charge then. If you ever find out let me know. It's one of my big unsolved mysteries. But he has friends upstairs.'

There was only one level that Dalby called upstairs.

'The Government?' I said.

'The Cabinet,' said Dalby. 'Mind you, don't

quote me, we have no evidence at all, not one thing that connects him with any illegal dealings since '50. We checked Jay's movements during the Burgess and Maclean business. They definitely correlate. When Maclean was Head of Chancery at the British Embassy Cairo, Jay was in Cairo twice. Although we have no trace of him visiting or phoning Tatsfield where Maclean lived, they did cross paths.

'On the 25th May '51, Maclean drove with Burgess in a hired car to Southampton. At twelve the *Falaise* cross-Channel packet left on a round trip to St Malo and the Channel Islands with Burgess and Maclean and Jay aboard. Of the three people, only Jay returned to England.

'When, a lot later, two bank drafts arrived each for £1,000 and both for Mrs —* (Maclean's mother-in-law) and drawn on Swiss Bank Corporation and Union Bank of Switzerland respectively, another bank draft followed, this time for £25,000. It was drawn on the Swiss Bank Corporation and paid into the London and S. Hellenic Bank to the account of Mr Aristo. I need hardly tell you that Mr Aristo is Jay, or there's nothing illegal in receiving twenty-five thousand quid. I think Jay is in the import and export business as his cards say, but he finally found that the second most valuable commodity today is information.'

'And?'

* Name withdrawn from MS.

'The most valuable?'

'People with information,' I suggested.

'Yes, that's what I think, but you'll not get me to say so at this stage in the game.'

'Was that fellow Raven we grabbed at Baalbek part of this scene?'

'He was the chemical warfare biochemist from the Research place at Porton. But the number of people they take are very small. Naturally the Press Department (Security) keep any names out of the papers. We're not having another Burgess and Maclean shindy, questions in the House and all that.'

'You think the work Carswell is doing has Jay involved?'

'No, I think that although the money Jay gets for a B & M operation is vast, he is smart enough to realize that to continue that is to live on borrowed time. I think he grabs an S.1 now and again when he needs some mad money but certainly not on the sort of scale that Carswell is talking of. He'd have to run coaches and advertise in the *Observer*. I'd leave Carswell right out of your calculations until he starts getting something a little more concrete. You'll look an absolute clown talking to the Permanent Under-secretary about . . .' He turned to the list I'd pinned up '. . . right-handed "concens" with fever.' He eased his weight off my desk and bent his knees, quickly sweeping his hand under my desk top. He switched off the miniature tape recorder I had had going. He walked to the door, then came back. 'Just one more small thing, you secret service man, you, try and have a haircut while I'm away and I'll use my influence about your back pay!'

I heard him clumping down the back stairs shouting to Chico to prepare the film he wanted to see before leaving. I collected up my history books, cameras and my sugar, and moved into Dalby's office.

It was easily the lightest room in the building, and if you didn't move more than a couple of feet from the window you could see to read a newspaper.

There were plenty of newspapers. It all had that brown veneered respectable look; on the wall were a couple of well-framed military prints of soldiers in red coats and shakos, sitting on horses. Under the windows was Dalby's latest toy – a low, grey IBM machine. Dalby was a young ambitious man, active and aggressive and one of the best bosses I ever had, but no one could suggest that he had ever had an original idea in his whole life and he'd never missed them. He recognized one when he saw one – he fought for it, utilized it, and what's more, gave its originator all the credit.

This IBM machine was the key to WOOC(P)'s reputation, for it enabled us to have files of information around which no one could correlate except with the machine set the correct way. For instance, a list of three hundred names meant nothing, a list of three hundred house numbers meant nothing, a list of three hundred street names, cities, and a pile of photos meant nothing. On the machine and suddenly – each photo had an address. On the machine again and thirty cards were rejected, and only Dalby knew whether those thirty were left-handed pistol shots, Young Conservatives, or bricklayers fluent in Mandarin. Dalby liked it, it was quick, more efficient than humans, and it made Dalby one of the most powerful men in England.

Sunday I went along to the office about ten-thirty. I didn't normally go in on Sunday but there was a book in the information room I wanted. I got there about ten-thirty and wandered into Dalby's office. The Sunday papers were there in place on top of Saturday's. The cover was off the IBM machine, and I could hear Alice fiddling about making coffee. I sat down behind Dalby's magnificent oiled teak desk. Its smooth light-brown top had the sensual colour of the beach at Nice, when it is covered with girls, you understand. Inlaid with old English craftsmanship into the Danish teak desk top were four metal switches and coloured lights, BLUE, GREEN, RED and WHITE. The BLUE switch put any calls being made in the building to tap into the phone here. GREEN made a tape of what was being said. WHITE switched any calls made in Dalby's absence into the tape so that he could play it back next morning. RED was to call every phone in this building simultaneously – no one can remember it being used except once when Dalby shouted for some ink over it.

I looked up. Alice was standing in the doorway, holding two willow-pattern cups. She wore a floral print dress of the sort favoured by Mrs Khrushchev, heavy nylons and strap shoes. Her hair was almost feminine today but that did nothing to offset the sourness of her white regular features.

'Coffee,' she said. I didn't contradict her, but Alice's fusion of milk, warm water and the coffee powder was like something flushed from a radiator.

'That's nice of you, Alice,' I said. 'You really don't have to work Sundays, too, do you?'

Her face screwed into a smile like an old gardening glove. 'It's quieter on Sundays, sir – I seem to get more done.' She set the cups down and looked around the room. It was untidy again and she tutted and straightened up a pile of newspapers, took my raincoat off the chair and hung it behind the door. 'You're managing to work the machine now?' she asked.

'After a fashion,' I told her. 'There are still a few things I don't understand. The selector for the photos for instance.' I passed her a package of photos with the strip of perforated paper along one side. Alice took the bundle without looking at it, her eyes were level with mine. She said, 'You are an awful lot too honest for this work. You'd better learn who to confide your weaknesses to before it's too late.'

I said nothing, so she said, 'I'll go and get my glasses and see if I can make the photo-selector work.'

Old Alice was getting quite mellow. I wondered if I could ask her to sew up the trousers I had torn at the Barbarossa Club.

Carswell had spent about a week on S.1's who had suffered from housebreaking or burglary with an eye to espionage by this means. He was getting very interested in the patterns and needed Murray to help him tie it down. Murray was a bit reluctant to leave his 'concens', but they were now finding smaller concens throughout the whole period. What had looked most mysterious in terms of one high point per year could now be seen as a wavy line of varying height. It was just a matter of how far above average was abnormal. As Carswell had most reluctantly agreed, there are also geographical areas which at any one time are abnormally *low* in S.1's. He had drawn this up, marking the areas in varying shades of green cross-hatched mapping pen lines according to percentage below average. The areas were called evacuations, and the individual S.1's temporarily out of the areas called 'evacs'. I am not a statistician but it all struck me as being pretty damn foolish. Carswell wasn't the type for a legpull, but he was the only person in the building from whom I could take the idea of 'evacs' without getting the needle. We had done pretty well by the old man. I just wasn't sure whether he wasn't trying to dig himself a niche in the time-honoured army way. I was getting pretty fed up with his housebreaking stats, too, and began to feel that those two were taking me for a ride.

I think Carswell could see I was getting fed up with it. On Tuesday I had Carswell in for a drink in the office. He seemed a bit depressed. He had three beers in quick succession and then began to tell me of his childhood in India. His father had insisted upon Carswell going into the regiment. The polo, the pig-sticking, the punitive actions against the tribesmen who enjoyed the fighting as much as the young English aristocrats did, the sun, horses galloping in the open hill country, drinks and mess dinners, the other young subalterns wrecking the mess in horseplay. All these things were things of his father's life, and when his father died he immediately asked for a posting to another unit. He chose a unit as diametrically opposed to his father's as he could think of; Indian Army Statistical Office, Calcutta. He had no interest or aptitude for the work. He did it as quiet rebellion against his life until then.

'For perhaps two years the work was pure drudgery; especially since, for a brain as inactive as mine was, the elementary calculations were slow and tedious. But after a little while I got used to the tedium, understanding that these parts of my work were as essential to the arabesques of the final pattern as the rest bars are to a symphony.'

He was telling me not to be bull-headed in a nice sort of way. Carswell must have been the only officer in the entire British army who had deliberately thrown away a commission in a crack cavalry regiment in exchange for a dreary office job that had left him nudging sixty, a substantive captain, with little or no prospect of a move past substantive major, if that.

I think we had both been overdoing it from a work point of view. We decided to go home. Through the window I could see the delicatessen crowded with people in wet raincoats. I phoned down for Murray, and asked him if he would like to come up for a drink. My red emergency phone rang before I'd put the internal one down. The operator with the Scotch accent said, 'CRO calling you, sir. Class four, priority. Please scramble.'

I pushed the scrambler button and switched in the green switch of the recording apparatus. I heard the operator tell them they were through to me.

A high-pitched falsetto voice that I had spoken with before said, 'Hello, Criminal Records Office, Scotland Yard. Military Liaison Officer Captain Keightley speaking.'

I said, 'Yes, Keightley?' I knew my evening by the coal fire with a history book had gone bang.

11

[Aquarius (Jan 20–Feb 19) Don't be surprised if trips to other people's houses bring whispers of insincerity for you will also discover a new friendship.]

'We've had a call from Shoreditch Police Station, sir. Frightfully funny business really.' All Keightley's 'r's were pronounced like a 'w'. 'They have a fellow there. Traffic accident. His car scraped a traffic signal I believe.'

'Yes,' I said. 'So?'

'Well sir, the constable asked him for his licence and so on . . .'

'Keightley, get to the point please.'

'Well, sir, this johnny in the car. We've no record here at the CRO, not a white card that is, but there is a green card for him. You know it's for suspected persons without a criminal record.'

'Yes, I know that. Tell me, how did you locate his card? Did he give his name?'

'No, sir. That's just it. You see, this johnny is dressed up in a Metropolitan Police, Chief Inspector's uniform. Luckily the constable had worked in CRO for a year, recognized him and remembered the face. He thought we had a white card but we only have a green one. It's endorsed to your department, with one of those star marks for top priority. So I phoned you. What we want to know, sir, is, shall we tell Shoreditch that there is a green card? There may be an Interpol card of course. Do you want him? That's what I want to know, sir.'

'Listen, Keightley. Tell Shoreditch I want this man held. In fact I want him stripped. I want them to be most careful. Watch for cyanide pills. This could be very important. Tell the chief there that I'm holding him personally responsible for the prisoner's safety. I want him under lock and key from the minute you finish talking to them, and he's to be kept under constant observation. Oh, yes, and make sure the constable that brought him in is available – they should make that copper a sergeant on the spot. Pulling in an inspector, indeed: some nerve; and tell them I'm leaving right away. I'll be there before 7.30.'

'Yes, sir, right away, sir.'

'Oh, and Keightley.'

'Sir?'

'You did right to tell me immediately, whatever the outcome.'

'Thank you, sir.'

I buzzed my controller on the big exchange and they had a black Jaguar at the ready. I locked the IBM and the recorder, I pressed the white button that set the phone to automatic recording. Murray still hadn't finished his drink and asked me if he could come for the ride. I don't have fixed rules about that sort of thing so I said OK. Carswell decided to call it a day. We walked across to Tottenham Court Road and within an instant of reaching the corner the car swept us in. The driver was one of the civilians the police let us have just after the war so he needed no guidance to Shoreditch Police Station. We moved across into the New Oxford Street traffic and up Theobalds Road. I let the driver use the bell and he pulled over to the offside of Clerkenwell Road and shot the speedometer up to seventy.

We were half-way across City Road when a yellow newspaper van coming north from Moorgate realized that we weren't stopping either. The van wheels locked as the driver hit the brake pedal. Our driver pushed the accelerator even harder, which gave the van an inch or so of clearance as it slid across behind us with white hot brakes and the driver's face to match. The last thing I wanted at this stage was that sort of complication.

'Careful,' I said, in what I considered masterful restraint.

'That's all right, sir,' said the driver, mistaking vexation for nervousness. 'They've got rubber mudguards on those paper vans.'

I realized why the police had let us have him.

It had really begun to rain in earnest now and the streets were a kaleidoscope of reflected tail-lights and neon. As we drew up in front of the Police Station three policemen were standing in the doorway. I'm glad they weren't fooling about as far as security was concerned. The driver left the car and came into the station with us. He probably thought he'd see someone he knew. Murray and I were greeted by the sergeant that Keightley had spoken to.

'All absolutely under control, sir,' he said proudly. 'No sooner said than done. Your other two people are parking their car. They needn't have troubled . . .'

'Other two people?' I said. A cold colicky pain kneaded my stomach. I knew that I needn't have troubled either. When we got to him he was naked, horizontal and very dead. I turned the body over. He was a strong, good-looking man of about thirty-five. He looked older close to than when I'd seen him before. We could cross Housemartin off our files. Just as Jay's people were crossing him off theirs right now. It was 7.33. His uniform gave clues – a packet of cigarettes, some money – £3 15s 0d, a handkerchief. I sent immediately for the police constable who had pulled him in. I asked him everything that had happened.

PC Viney came in with a half-written report and a small stub of pencil. He was almost bald, a thick-set man, perhaps an ex-army athlete, a little towards the plump side, he even now would make a formidable opponent. His thin hair, white at the temples, framed his very small ears set well back; a large nose was red from the night air; and his lower jaw was carried well forward in the way that guardsmen and policemen cope with chin straps that don't fit under the jaw. Under his open tunic he wore a badly knitted red pullover with blue braces over the top. His attitude was relaxed and shrewd, as could be expected from someone who had pulled in a man dressed as an inspector.

The sergeant behind me was leaning in the cell door saying, 'In thirty-five years of service . . .' loud enough for me to hear, and worrying himself sick about his pension.

I turned back to the constable. He told me that he had suspected Housemartin's demeanour right from first sight, but would never have come to close enough quarters to recognize him if he hadn't hit the traffic light. Did he think that the man had come from any of the nearby houses? He thought he might have been pulling out into traffic.

'Now don't worry about law court stuff, constable,' I told him. 'I'd sooner you told me something that's a flimsy guess than hesitate because we can't prove it. Now just let's suppose that this man did pull away from the kerb and that he had come from one of the houses in that street. Think carefully of that row of houses. Do you know it well?'

'Yes, sir, fairly well. They all have their

peculiarities. Quite a few of the houses have front rooms where the curtains are never pulled back or changed, but that's the English front room, isn't it, sir?'

'The sort of house I'd be interested in is one where new tenants have moved in during the last six months. A house where new people have been seen going in and out. People not of the neighbourhood, that is. Is there a house that is particularly secluded? It would have a garage and the driver might be able to enter the house direct from the garage.'

Viney said, 'All the houses there stand back from the street, but one in particular is secluded because the owner has bought the undeveloped site on each side of the house. Of course, the houses either side of it are also secluded, but only on one side. Number 40 is one side, that's all flats – young married couples mostly. Mrs Grant owns that. On the other side 44 is a very low building; the husband there is a waiter in the West End. I see him about two to two-thirty on the night beat. I know that Mr Edwards at the Car Mart made an offer for one of the sites. We kept pinching him for obstruction. He left his cars in the road. After we'd had him every day nearly for about a week, he came up to see the sergeant. I think really he told us about buying the site to show he was trying. But anyway, they wouldn't sell. When I think of it, that's the only house that I can't remember any of the occupiers from. They had a lot of building done. Conversion into flats I imagine. About February. But there are no "to let" signs up. Not that you need 'em, word of mouth is enough.'

'You've hit it, constable. I'll buy your big secluded house with alterations.'

Keightley had phoned up the station and got them all in a rare state when he heard what had happened. Murray had heard Keightley's high-pitched little voice saying, 'Murder? Murder? Murder in a police station?' Coming as Keightley's voice did from CRO it worried them far more than anything I might say.

I had them do all the unit checks for finger-prints and Identikit descriptions of the two men – but knowing Jay's set-up it was unlikely they would have a record of any sort, or leave prints. The con-stable recognizing Housemartin from a photo he'd seen once at CRO* was the sort of fluke that hap-pens only very rarely. I turned to PC Viney who had brought me a cup of tea from the canteen. He stood, his uniform jacket undone, waiting and appraising my next action. I said to him, 'Show me on the map, would you? And then I will want to use a phone in private – a scrambled line if possible.'

The information room at Scotland Yard came through in seconds. 'Shoreditch Police Station. I want to speak with an officer of 3H Security Clearance or above; my authority is WOOC(P).'

___
* Criminal Records Office.

'Hold the line, sir.'

The unshaded light made bright reflections in the shiny-cream paintwork. Faintly through the closed door I could hear the canteen radio singing 'There's a Small Hotel'. My tea sat on the worn desk and I fiddled nervously with an old shell case made into a pen-and-ink stand. Finally the phone made clicking sounds and the information room came back on the line.

'Chief Inspector Banbury, CID here.'

Luckily I knew 'Cuff-links' Banbury from the old days. It saved a lot of preliminary checking with code words. Or rather it would have done, except that 'Cuff-links' insisted on going through it all. I wanted thirty officers, at least five of them armed, and four vehicles without police identification.

'All the plain-finish vehicles are in the Richmond garage,' Cuff-links said.

'Then borrow private cars from your coppers. Try West End Central, they've got big cars there.' My sarcasm was lost on Cuff-links; he just carried on being smooth and efficient. 'I want one car to have radio link. I shall be briefing them en route. Include a couple of hook ladders and a jemmy. Tell your press office that I want "complete blackout", and put someone on the radio link that won't shoot his mouth. That's all, chief. Phone me back when they are on the road – say thirty minutes.'

'No, about an hour.'

'No good, chief, this is a 3H Security. If you can't do better than that I'll get authority to use my soldiers.'

'Well, I'll try for forty minutes.'

'Thanks, chief. See you.' It was 7.58.

I went upstairs. Murray was leaning over a big scrubbed table with the elderly constable, a sergeant and an inspector with a neatly trimmed moustache. I asked the sergeant who the inspector was. It didn't make any of them madly happy, but 'twice bitten could get to be a habit'. Murray had worked out a sensible way of hitting 42 Acacia Drive. He had dug out a photo of the street and had drawn a diagram showing heights of garden walls and deploying twenty-five men. Murray had also implied by unknown subtle means that his rank was considerably higher than sergeant. The inspector was deferring to his suggestions and the police sergeant was saying, 'Yes sir, good sir, very good, sir.' I told the policemen that they could come along if they wished, but explained that since I had put 'complete blackout' on the operation, any leakage would be actionable under the Official Secrets Act.

Murray used a propelling pencil with changeable coloured leads to mark in the extra five men; then we stood around drinking another cup of sweet tea. By now the canteen was organized for the top brass. I had a swallow-pattern cup with a saucer to match and a spoon. Murray decided that this was a good time to ask about his living-out

103

allowance. It was nearly three months behind. I said I'd do what I could.

At 8.21, after a knock at the door, a constable said a military police vehicle had just driven into the courtyard, the driver asking for 'Mr' Murray. Murray said he thought a Champ vehicle with radio equipment 'might be useful'. He'd asked for it to drive in instead of parking conspicuously. Murray and I went downstairs to see if the radio could get the Scotland Yard wavelength. He told me that by having a Provost vehicle we automatically got a revolver and ammunition and what he described as 'other useful things'. Murray was proving so unlike what I imagined that I decided to recheck his security clearance the next day.

12

Acacia Drive was a wide wet street in one of those districts where the suburbs creep stealthily in towards Central London. The soot-caked hedges loomed almost as high as the puny trees encased in their iron cages. Here and there a dirty net curtain let a glimmer from a 40-watt bulb escape to join the feeble street lighting.

We waited while the last two men got into position. A door opened somewhere down the street, firing a yellow shaft of light into the gloom. A man in a cloth cap pulled a silver fabric cover from a shrouded car. It proved to be not the one he was looking for. He lifted the silver skirt of the next car. The third one had the right number plate. He drove it off down the street which now became a dark and silent car mortuary once more.

No. 42 had two gates joined by a semicircular driveway of crunchy gravel. On the top floor one very small window showed a light. The Champ vehicle was nearer to the house than any of the private cars the police had used. In the back seat the military policeman was listening to the radio sets of the plainclothes men positioning themselves in the back garden. He gave us the high sign with thumb touching forefinger. Murray and I decided to force a window at the side of the house. The MP was to talk out a description of signals we gave him by torch. Murray had the jemmy and I had a sheet of brown paper covered with police canteen golden syrup.

The gravel crunched underfoot and an aeroplane winking coloured lights vibrated against the cloud. It had almost stopped raining, but the house shone wetly. The grounds were extensive and once across the path we plunged into the kitchen garden that lay alongside the house. The soles of my feet began to squelch as the soaked long grass sprinkled my legs, trousers and socks. We paused alongside the greenhouse through which the moon played shadow games, making mythical monsters of pots and beans and flowers. Every few seconds the house changed character, at one time menacing and sinister, and again the innocent abode of law-abiding citizens about to be attacked by my private army. The luminous watch said 9.11. Over the far side of the grounds I saw a movement by one of the policemen. The wind had dropped and now the aircraft had passed over it seemed very quiet and still. In the distance I heard a train. I stood there unhappily, my feet were wet and made little sucking sounds. I felt Murray touch my elbow with the cold metal jemmy. Looking round I found him pretending it was an accident. I took the hint. The side window was higher than it had looked from the road. Reaching up with the sticky brown paper I smoothed it across the glass and a little syrup ran down my wrist. Murray stuck the jemmy into the woodwork, but it was locked right enough. The window to the left was barred, so he hit the brown-paper-covered pane with the iron. A muffled syrupy crunch and then the broken glass fell inwards hinged on the brown paper. Murray was groping for the fastenings as we did a Charleston in slow motion on the flower-bed. The window swung open and Murray dived head first through. I saw the soles of his hand-made shoes (eighteen guineas) with a small sticky rectangular price tab still affixed under the instep. I passed the army pistol into his hand and followed.

The moonlight poked a finger into a small lounge; the furniture old and comfortable; the fireplace held an electric fire with plastic logs; and scattered across the sofa was some clothing. Suddenly a clock chimed loudly. Murray was out in the hallway. Down the staircase someone had dropped sheets of blue lined writing paper. I knew that the house was empty, but we continued to creep around until 9.28.

Except for a couple to look after the house, the policemen had all been packed off in the cars. The gambling party, we told them, had been cancelled at the last minute. Murray and I went down the road for a cup of 'coffee' in one of the Espresso palaces – rubber plants and buns to match. A sour-faced young waitress flung a smelly dishcloth around the table, said 'Two cappercheeny,' then went back to the three young men in black imitation-leather jackets and jeans, with genuine rivets, for a conversation about motor cycles.

13

[*Aquarius (Jan 20–Feb 19) Pay special attention to insurance arrangements. Romance may be expected to delay social commitments.*]

I talked to Murray about everything except the job. Murray was a tall and large-muscled man who, had he been a few years younger, would have made a John Osborne hero. His face was large, square and bony, and it would be equally easy to imagine him as an RSM or the leader of a wildcat strike.

He was efficient and responsive to orders in a way that more than faintly criticized his superiors by its very efficacy. It reminded me of those NCOs who drilled officer cadets. His hair was tightly arranged across his lumpy skull. His eyes, thin slits, as though he constantly peered into brightness, would wrinkle and smile without provocation. Unlike Chico, Murray's smile wasn't motivated by a desire to join other men – it separated him quite deliberately from them. We talked about Bertold Brecht and the 1937 Firearms Act, and it amused Murray that I was probing around amongst his acquisition of knowledge. He'd not liked the peacetime army and it was understandable, there was no place in it for a man with a paperback edition of Kierkegaard in his pocket. The sergeants tried to talk like officers and the officers like gentlemen, he said. The mess was full of men who'd sit in a cinema all the weekend and come back with stories about house-parties on the river.

'Georgian houses,' Murray said, and he had a great love for beautiful buildings. 'The only Georgian houses they'd ever been to were George the Fifth ones along the by-pass.'

By the time we had got back to 42 the finger-print men and photographers had done their stuff and Chico and Ross had arrived. Ross resented my sudden rise to power and had got his department into the act probably via Keightley. Chico was wearing his short tweed overcoat with the gigantic pattern and looking like a bookies' clerk. I noticed his chin had got those pimples again that I called 'caviare rash'. He and Ross were poking about in the greenhouse when we arrived. I heard Ross say, 'Mine aren't coming on at all, I think it was the early frost.' Chico countered this with a quote from his gardener, then we all started on 42.

You couldn't find a house more normal than

that one, as far as the rooms on the ground floor and first floor were concerned. Old wounded furniture, balding carpets and sullen wallpaper. The ultra-modern kitchen was well stocked with food, both fresh and tinned, and a machine that minced up waste and sluiced it away. The bathroom upstairs was unusually well-fitted for England – shower, scales, pink mirror and extensive indirect lighting. One room on the ground floor was equipped as an office and had in one corner a wooden phone-booth with glass panels and a little gadget that fitted into the phone dial which, when locked, prevented it being used.

A few books remained on the shelves, a *Roget*, a business directory, a thick blue-bound volume, the French edition of *Plans of the Great Cities of the World showing Principal Roads and Exits*, the *AA Road Book, ABC Railway Guide, and a Chambers's Dictionary.*

The filing cases were so new that the paint squeaked. A couple of hundred blank file cards lay inside. I walked into the rose-wallpapered hall and upstairs. The staircase between the first and second floor had been removed. A cheap, unpainted wooden ladder poked its top into a dimly lit rectangle in the ceiling. Murray and Chico deferred to me in the matter of ascending. Ross was downstairs still checking the phone books for underlinings, finger-marks and page removals. I climbed the splintery ladder. As my head rose past the second-floor level I saw what the police cameraman had been talking about. The light from several unshaded 25-watt bulbs fell across the uneven wooden floor. Here and there plaster walls had been badly damaged and revealed brickwork inadequately distempered over. I hoisted my fourteen stone through the hatchway and augmented the dull glow with my torch. I looked into each of the little wooden rooms. Some of them had windows facing down into the cobbled centre courtyard – the central feature of the house built as a hollow square. The outward-facing windows were completely bricked up. Chico came up to me, bright-eyed; he'd found a pair of plimsolls, blue and white, size ten, in one room, and had a theory about the whole thing.

'A small private zoo, sir. My cousin's aunt, the Duchess of Winchester, let him build one, sir. Frightfully interesting. This would be for food, sir, this room. Those scrubbed buckets, sir, everything terribly clean. I helped him many weekends, sir. Then one time we had a stunning house-party there. I wish you had been there, I'm sure you would have been interested, sir.' Chico's adam's apple had become more and more prominent as his voice pitch rose.

I was trying to do the most difficult job I'd ever heard about. To help me I had a rose-cultivator downstairs, and a refugee from the Royal Enclosure. A fine team to pit against half the world in arms.

'It's *just* like my friend's zoo, sir.'

112

There was certainly a lot to support Chico's observation. The gaunt cell-like room in which we were standing had a little coke-burning stove with the stove pipe leading out through the wall. Piled in a corner were some old army-style cooking pans. The floorboards were scrubbed white. I looked through the little unwashed window into the shiny little courtyard, at the rough plastered walls, pitted and broken and at the metal guarded wall-light.

'It's exactly like my *friend*'s, sir.' Anybody with Chico for a friend didn't need an enemy. I nodded.

The rain dabbed spasmodically at the glass pane, and another plane ground its way across a damp skyful of cloud. I tried to see it but the window-frame confined my view to a downward slant. I walked along the corridor, through the heavy wooden door and into the strangest room of all.

It was one of the largest rooms – about 20ft by 25ft. In the centre of the floor stood a heavy metal water tank 8ft by 8ft and 5ft high. There was four feet of water in it. Waterproof cloth had been roughly tacked to the floor. 'There's something in there,' Chico shouted. He was poking around in the water tank with a stick he had found in the garden. It took the police nearly an hour to get all the pieces of the tape recorder, and a harness from the floor of the tank.

The movie camera men from Charlotte Street and two CID men from the forensic lab were in the hallway downstairs, and I decided to leave the place to them for a few hours.

The birds had awakened and a thin streak of wet dawn could be seen as I poured myself a cup of Blue Mountain coffee with cream, and went to bed with a backlog of memoranda from Alice, and still found time to send a fiver to Adem for his fauna preservation. The way I looked at it, I was fauna too.

I was still tired when I showered the next morning. I picked a suitable dark grey striped wool and nylon, with a white shirt, and handkerchief, plain brown tie, and brown shoes to add a touch of rebellion. I must get those brown trousers mended.

I read my copy of *The Stage* in the cab. We put in a regular classified advert to let Dalby know what was going on. It said:

'Touring SOLO talent. Girl dancers (military number) very tall man for panto parts for certain Midland towns. Send photo details. Central London novelty act now complete. Scripts badly needed. Phone Miss Varley. Dalby casting.'

Alice was handling contact with Dalby in the field, but even without the master code-book it seemed pretty clear that she was having a go at me. My cab turned into Scotland Yard. The Commissioner has a very large corner room. His leather chairs were old and shiny but the finish was bright and tasteful. An expensively framed Stubbs print of a man and horse dominated one wall; below it the open fire crackled and flared with damp coal. Through the multi-paned window I could see the traffic creeping over Westminster Bridge. A stubby black tug dragged a train of dirt-filled barges against the oily water flow, and below me on the embankment a short man in a torn wet raincoat was trying to get a bent bicycle into the back of a taxicab. The Commissioner was going on about the house business. He had that Commanding Officer manner from which it was hard to tell exactly which element caused him distress, or indeed, if any aspect did. He started for the third time going through the injustice – the word sounded ironic coming from him – of Charlotte Street being given unlimited funds. I'd told him twice that my office could fit under his kneehole desk, and my view commanded a fly-blown delicatessen. This time I let him run through the whole thing without interruption for the duration of two cigarettes. He was slowing down now he had got to the use we made of the Criminal Records Office and the Forensic Science Laboratory without cost, and the right of search, and how little I knew about it. If the old man knew half the things Dalby got up to he would flip his lid. I made a firm and immediate decision to curtail Chico's participation as far as our illegal activities were concerned; he was easily the most loquacious and not the most tactful. The Commissioner broke through my reverie.

'That fellow with you, dark chap, good talker.'

I went cold.

'Murray?' I said, hoping. 'Sergeant Murray – statistics expert. *He* was at the house last night.'

'No! No! No! *Young* feller-me-lad, er, now, er . . .'

I said, in a dull voice, 'Chillcott-Oakes, Phillip Chillcott-Oakes.'

'Yes, a charming chap, *ab*solute charmer – that's him.' He smiled for the first time and leaned across to me in a conspiratorial gesture. 'At school with my youngest!' he said.

The pub across the road had just opened. I downed a couple of Dubonnet and bitter lemons. What chance did I stand between the Communists on the one side and the Establishment on the other – they were both out-thinking me at every move.

14

[Aquarius (Jan 20–Feb 19) Let your head rule your heart. Steer well clear of controversy both at home and at work.]

Tuesday was a big echoing summer's day. I could hear the neighbour's black Airedale dog, and they could hear my FM. I sorted the letters from the mat; *Times* magazine subscription dept said I was missing the chance of a lifetime. My mother's eldest sister wished I was in Geneva; so did I, except that my aunt was there. A War Office letter confirmed my discharge from the Army and told me that I was not subject to reserve training commitments, but was subject to the Official Secrets Act in respect of information and documents. The dairy said to order cream early for the holiday and had I tried Chokko, the new chocolate drink that everyone was raving about.

At the office I started going through the documents in my locked 'In tray'. Some stuff about chemical warfare documents on microfilm. The US Defense Dept seemed pretty sure that a BOAC engineer was handling them. I marked it for Special Branch LAP. The Public Information Officer at Scotland Yard was being very nice about the house business but said the press was getting a line on it. Alice said he'd been on the phone twice, what should she say. 'Tell him to tell the newspapers that a high court judge, a Cabinet Minister and two press barons were watching a blue film, but that if they play their cards right we won't give the story to ITN.'

'Yes, sir,' said Alice.

The FSO sent a report on the house. I read quickly through: 'Road dust, stains on floorboard; could be blood, very old; possibly from wartime bombing.'

Finger-prints – there were a lot, mostly mine, and unidentified; they were going through the single print collection and 'scenes of crime' (where other unidentified prints were filed under the place in which they were found).

I had to see Ross at three. Now that I had taken over from Dalby it was one of my weekly ordeals. I sent out for sandwiches – cream cheese with pineapple, and ham with mango chutney. The delicatessen sent them with rye bread. I spent ten minutes throwing caraway seeds into the ashtray until Chico appeared, then I downed the last round, seeds and all. He put a reel of 16mm film on the desk and hung around to make conversation. I gave him the rich-man-with-ulcers-type grunt and nod, and he finally went away.

I sat for a long time staring into my Nescafé, but no particular line of action occurred. The opposition may have fumbled the pass but I hadn't detected a gap in the defence, unless any of the documents in front of me now meant anything. It didn't seem much to me. There was nothing to make me sure it was a matter for us to deal with even, let alone to connect it with Jay. It's only writers who expect every lead the hero meddles in to turn out to be threads of the same case. Here in the office were about 600 file numbers; if all the villains were brought to justice simultaneously it would make Auschwitz look like the last scene of *Hamlet*.

Should I continue to fool with the leads in the house business? What leads? I decided to sound out Ross. I'd see whether his department were going on with it. I took a cab down to a sleazy drinking club off Jermyn Street. It was a couple of rooms on the first floor. Red plush everywhere, and not a chink of daylight. Beyond the highly polished baby grand piano, and a vast basket of too perfect flowers, sat a balding man with spectacles and a regimental tie. It was Ross. He was at least half an hour early. I sat down next to him. Our weekly meetings usually took about ten minutes and consisted of agreeing to the Army Intelligence Memoranda sheet for the Cabinet, and an inter-change of certain financing arrangements for which our two departments overlapped. The waiter brought me a Tio Pepe and Ross ordered another pink gin. He looked like he'd had a few already. His big domed frontal area was wrinkled and pale. Why did he like this place?

He asked me for a cigarette. This wasn't like Ross, but I flicked him a couple of inches of Gauloise. I ignited it. The match lit the interior like a magnesium flare. Sammy Davis sang, 'Love in Bloom' and a gentle firm Parker-like sax *vibrato* made the plastic flowers quiver. The barman – a tall ex-pug with a tan out of a bottle, and a tie-knot the size of a large garden pea, was rubbing an old duster around spotless unused ashtrays and taking sly sips at a half-pint of Guinness. Ross began to talk.

'To be frank, the memorandum isn't quite ready yet; my girl is typing it this afternoon.'

I was determined not to say 'That's OK.' The odd couple of times I had been late with my data Ross had 'hurumped' for half an hour. Ross looked at me for a minute and tugged his battered black pipe out of his pocket. He still had my Gauloise only half-finished. Ross was in a nervous state today. I wanted to know if he intended to have his people continue to work on the 'haunted house' as someone had christened it. I also knew that with Ross the direct approach was fatal.

'You've never been down to my little place, have you?' It was pretty rhetorical. The idea of Ross and I having an overlapping social life was hilarious. 'It's quite pretty now; at the bottom of the garden there are three lovely old chestnut trees. Laid out between them Anna Olivier, Caroline Testout and Mrs John Laing. When the yellow catkins are on the trees in June, with Gustave Nabonnand and Dorothy Perkins, why you could be in the heart of the countryside. Except for the house next door of course. Those chestnuts when I bought the place in 1935, no, tell a lie, end of '34, the builders would have cleared the site bald. It was country then, not a house for miles – behind us, I mean; next door was there. Didn't have a bus service, nothing. Mind you, didn't affect me much. I was in Aden by the summer of '35. My wife, you're not married, but my wife, a wonderful woman, at that time the garden – well, it was nothing. Hard work, that's all. I was only a lieutenant then.'

'Ross,' I said, 'Mrs Laing and Dorothy Perkins *are* roses, aren't they?'

'Of course they are,' said Ross. 'What did you think they are?'

I tilted my forehead at the inquiring look of the barman, and a Tio Pepe and pink gin arrived very promptly. He paused long enough to give our ashtray a rebore. Ross had paused in his house agent but he soon went into it again.

'I was at the SCRUBS in '39,* gave me a chance to get the garden going. That's when I put the

* See Appendix, p. 329.

acacias in. It's a picture now. A three-bedroom one only seven doors away, not a patch on ours, not a patch, went for six-and-a-half thousand. I said to the wife at the time, "Then ours must be worth eight." And we'd get it too. It's fantastic the prices detached ones go for.' Ross swallowed a gulp of pink gin and said, 'But the truth is –'

I wondered what the truth was and how long it would take to get round to it.

'The truth is with the boy at school, and at a critical time – couldn't possibly cut back on the boy now, he'll be at university in eighteen months; well, truth is it's been a frightful expense. You've always been a bit of a, well I might almost say a protégé of mine. Last year when you first started hinting about a transfer, well, I can't tell you the hoo-ha there was in the C5 subcommittee. You remember O'Brien, why, he even said it to you. But I just thought you were the sort worth sticking by. And well, I was right, and you've turned up trumps.'

This cant from Ross was more than I could stand – all this 'sticking by you'. What did he want – money, a transfer, Dalby's job? It was way out of character except in that it was badly done. Everything Ross handled had that in common. Did he want a fiver? Five hundred? Did he have the imagination to ask for much more? I wasn't enjoying seeing Ross crawl but he'd given me so many toffee-nosed dressing downs that I didn't feel inclined to soften the way for his application. But now he was changing his line.

'With Dalby away and you running the show, well, it's been mentioned, the Minister's private secretary was most pleased with the Swiss Bank stuff. You have someone inside?' He paused. It was a question, but not one I felt like answering. 'Will he go on with giving us names and code-numbers?' He paused again, and I remembered all the difficulties he'd made for me when I did the deal with the bank. 'Oh, I see I really shouldn't ask. But the important thing is you are getting known. To be frank, it means that you won't be stuck in a cul-de-sac the way I have since Joe One.'*

I muttered something about it being an important cul-de-sac.

'Yes, you think so, but not everyone does, you see. Frankly I'm walled in, financially. Now take the case of the *Al Gumhuria* file.'

I knew the *Al Gumhuria* work; it was one of Ross's favourites. *Al Gumhuria* was Nasser's house organ, the official news outlet. Ross had got through to someone working on it. Later on, when *Al Akhbar (The News)*, Cairo's best-known newspaper, and *Al Ahram (The Pyramids)* were nation-alized, his contact had even more sway.

From his agent there Ross had built up a complete picture of the Russian military aid throughout the Near East.

Ross's people still had a few strings to pull

* The first Russian Hydrogen bomb. Summer 1949. See Appendix, p. 329.

even in Nasser's government, and his boy there never looked back. But as his standard of living rose, so, he thought, should the payments for his extra-curricular activity. I could see Ross felt badly about losing one of the best contacts he'd ever made, just for the sake of a few thousand quid, and I'd heard from devious sources that his agent was beginning to dry up. Probably doing a deal with the Americans for ten times what Ross was paying. If his contact moved on, you could bet the Onassis yacht to a warm snowball that Ross would finally lose the whole network.

'You could do great things there, great things, but I just haven't got the money, or department to do it. I can see the sort of report you'd do. It would go to minister level without a doubt. Minister level.'

He sat and thought about minister level like he'd been asked to write the eleventh commandment.

I nudged his reverie. 'But I don't even have a file number on it. You've got it.'

'Precisely, old boy. Now we're getting down to tin tacks. Now if I were a stranger, you'd have the funds to buy a dossier, wouldn't you?' He rushed on without pausing. 'You have more leeway in these things than I have, or we have, I should say. Well, for a fair sum it's all yours.' He sat back but he didn't relax.

At first I thought I had trouble understanding him, so I played it back at half speed.

'You mean,' I said, 'that my department should buy this file from your department?'

He tapped his pipe against the table leg.

'It sounds strange, I know, but this is a pretty irregular business, old man. It's not like a nine to five job. Not that I'd offer it to anyone else, like the . . .'

'Russians?' I said.

His face had become more and more static over the last few minutes, but now it froze stiff like a Notre-Dame gargoyle, his mouth set to gush rain-water. 'I was going to say "Navy", but since you've chosen to be so bloody impertinent . . . Your friend Dalby wouldn't have been so "boy-scoutish" about an offer like this; perhaps I'll have a word with him.'

He'd chosen his words well; he made me feel like a cad for mentioning the Russians; brought Dalby into the conversation, gently reminding me that I was only acting in his stead anyway, and finally calling me 'boy-scoutish' which he knew would hit me where it hurt. Me, the slick modern intelligence agent. Six months with the CIA and two button-down shirts to prove it.

'Look Ross,' I said. 'Let's clear it up. You need some money urgently for some reason I can only guess at. You're prepared to sell information. But you won't sell it to anyone who really wants it, like the Russians or the Chinese, 'cos that would be unsporting, like pinching knives and forks from the mess. So you look around for someone on your side but without your genteel education, without your feeling for social niceties about who it's nice to sell information to. You look for someone like me, an outsider whom you've never liked anyway, and give my heart-strings a tug and then my purse-strings. You don't care what I do with the dossier. For all you care I could get a knighthood on the strength of it, or chuck it over the back wall of the Russian Embassy. You've got the nerve to sell something that doesn't belong to you to someone you don't like. Well, you're right. That is the sort of business we're in, and it's the sort of business that a lot of people that got those reports for you wish they were still in. But they're not, they're good and dead in some dirty back alley somewhere, and they aren't going to be around for your share-out. We've got 600 open files in my office, that's no secret, and my only interest at the moment is making it five hundred and ninety-nine even if I don't get the Minister's certificate of Good Housekeeping doing it.' I gulped down my Tio Pepe and almost choked on it – it would have spoiled the effect. I chucked a pound note into the spilt drink and left without looking back. Lee Konitz moved into 'Autumn in New York', and as I went downstairs I heard Ross blowing into his briar pipe.

15

[*Aquarius (Jan 20–Feb 19) Entertainment of various kinds will help to enliven routines of family and business.*]

Outside in Bury Street, the dirty old London air smelt clean. People like Ross just *always* gave me a bad time. If I was pally with them I hated myself; when I rowed with them I felt guilty for enjoying it.

In Trafalgar Square the sun was nourishing a mixed collection of tourists, with bags of pigeon food and cameras. I avoided a couple of down-at-heel street photographers and caught a bus outside the National Gallery to Goodge Street.

When I got into the office Alice was guarding the portals. 'Keightley has been ringing,' she said. If she'd just do something about her hair and put on some make-up Alice could be quite attractive. She followed me into Dalby's room. 'And I said you'd be at the War Office cinema at five. There's something special on there.'

I said OK, and that Ross's memoranda sheet would be over later, and would she deal with it. She said that her clearance wasn't high enough but when I didn't reply, she said she'd check it and add our stuff. Alice couldn't hold a conversation with me without constantly arranging the pens, pencils, trays and notebooks on my desk. She lined them up, sighted down them and took away each pencil and sharpened it.

'One of these days I'll come in and find my desk set white-washed.'

Alice looked up with one of those pained expressions with which she always greeted sarcasm. It beat me why she didn't ever tell me that it was the lowest form of wit. I could see the words forming a couple of times.

'Look, Alice, surely with your vast knowledge of the screened personnel available to us you must be able to locate a sexy little dark number to do these things of everyday for me. Unless you're getting a crush on me. Alice, is that it?'

She gave me the 'turn-to-stone' look.

'No kidding, Alice, rank has its privileges. I don't ask for much out of this life but I need someone to précis the intelligence memoranda, watch my calorie count, and sew up tears in my trousers.'

Just to show I wasn't kidding I typed out a requisition of the sort for 'Goods to the value of £700 or over,' and wrote, 'Additional Personnel. One female assistant to temp. OC as discussed. Earliest.'

I gave it to Alice, who read it without her expression changing. She picked up a couple of files from my 'Out' tray and marched to the door. She turned to face me and said, 'Don't use military nomenclature on civilian stationery, and don't leave your trays unlocked.'

'Your seams are crooked, Alice,' I said. She went out.

As you go into the basement at the War Office the décor of drab light-green and cream paint is enlivened by the big square sectioned air-conditioning plant, painted a wild bolshie red. I turned the corner at the bottom of the stairs to find a dour Scots sergeant of military police standing outside the cinema. Talking in the corner were Carswell, Murray and Ross. With them was a heavily built civilian with long black hair combed straight back. He wore a Guards Armoured Div tie, and a white handkerchief folded as a rectangle in his top pocket. His complexion was ruddy, almost unnaturally so, and given the slightest opportunity, he threw back his head to reveal his very even, perfect, white teeth. Nearer to the handkerchief-sized screen was Chico, his bright eyes anxiously darting about to detect a joke coming so he could laugh, and thereby prove he had a sense of humour. He was conversing with a slim elderly major who had half a dozen strands of hair artistically arranged across his head. If they had to have a major here to project the film it might be worth watching.

Ross seemed to be running the show, and when I arrived nodded as though I hadn't seen him for weeks. He addressed the nine of us (two of Ross's people had just arrived):

'There's no more information on this one, chaps, but any recognition, of location even, would be much appreciated.' He leaned through the door. 'That's the lot, sergeant. No one else now.'

'Sir!' I heard the sergeant growl.

'Oh,' said Ross, turning back to his audience, 'and I'm sorry, chaps, no smoking as of last week.'

The lights dimmed down and we had a few hundred feet of unedited 16mm silent cine-film.

Some of the shots were out of focus and some were under-exposed. They mostly showed men indoors. The ages ran from about thirty to fifty. The men were well-dressed and in the main clean shaven. It was hard to be quite sure if they were filmed with or without the subjects knowing. The lights came on. We all looked at each other blankly. I called to Ross, 'Where did it come from? I mean, what's it about?'

'To be frank,' said Ross – I waited for the lie – 'we are not quite sure for the time being. It's possible there is more to come.' The thickset character nodded satisfaction. Anyone who found that explanation satisfactory was easy to please. I felt sure he belonged to Ross and I hoped Carswell and Murray hadn't been indiscreet. I didn't want to join in with Ross's idiot game of cloak and dagger stuff between departments, but in view of

130

Ross's most recent move the less he was told the better.

'Any other questions?' Ross said, just like he'd answered the first one. There was another silence and I stifled the impulse to clap. The jolly fat doorman said, 'Good day, sir,' as I left the Horse-guards Avenue entrance, and walked down Whitehall to Keightley at Scotland Yard.

Inside the entrance an elderly policeman was speaking into a phone. 'Room 284?' he said. 'Hello Room 284? I'm trying to locate the tea trolley.'

I saw Keightley in the hallway. He always looked out of place among all those policemen. His slick hair and deeply lined pale, freckled face, and white moustache gave a first impression of greater age than was really the case. He had a pair of heavy black spectacles of the sort with straight side bars. These latter facilitated his pulling his glasses half off his face just before telling or showing you some-thing, then snapping them back on his nose to lend emphasis to what he was saying. His timing and execution were perfect. I'd never seen him miss his face yet. He came down to collect me. In his hand he had a film tin about eight inches across.

'I think you'll agree,' he had his glasses well off his face now, and was peering over them, 'your journey was well worth while.' They snapped into place, little images of the doorway reflected in the lenses. He rattled the tin heavily and led the way to his office. It was cramped for space, as are so many of the offices at the Yard. I closed the door behind me. Keightley began to remove the heap of papers, files and maps from the knee-hole desk that used up most of the floor space.

An old crone appeared from nowhere with a cup of muddy coffee on a wet tin tray. I wanted to tell her that there was a call out for her, but I resisted the impulse. Keightley got an old black crusty pipe going and finally, after we'd been through the niceties of British meetings, he leaned back and began to let me have it.

'The haunted house,' he began, and smiled, while rubbing the stem of his pipe along his moustache. 'These people,' Keightley always referred to the Metropolitan Police as 'these people', 'did a very thorough job for you. "Finger-prints". Normally we only do a check going back five years, except for murder or treason cases; for them and you we did the whole eighteen-year collection.' He paused. 'Then they did all the special collections; the "scenes of crime" collections; the Indian seamen collection . . .' Keightley poked a match into the bowl of his pipe and sucked his cheeks inwards . . . 'Of men jumping ship, and the sacrilege collection.' He paused again. 'Nothing anywhere. Forensic Science,' he tapped his second finger. 'We did the usual tests. The old bloodstains were Group "O", but then forty-two per cent of the country is Group "O".'

'Keightley,' I interrupted. 'Your time is valuable, so is mine, I know all this. Just tell me what you sent the message about.'

'Procedure: house exterior,' he tapped his next finger. I knew it was no good. I'd have to go through the whole thing. Getting Keightley to tell one punch line immediately was like trying to get an aspirin without first removing the cotton wool. He gave me all the stuff – digging down to eighteen inches in the kitchen garden. Using a mine detector over floors and lath and plaster walls and in the garden. He listed the books they'd found and the oxygen cylinders, the tinned food and the complicated safety harness bolted to the tank. 'It wasn't till then, sir, that we found the film tin. I don't think it was hidden at all. In fact, at first we thought it must be something the FS* boys had brought with them.'

By now I guessed that it was the tin Keightley was talking about. I held out my hand hoping that he'd pass it to me. But no such luck. Keightley had a captive audience and wasn't letting go.

'We checked all the equipment, then I decided that if they were carrying things out to cars in the drive and in a big hurry – and doubtless they were in a big hurry.' I nodded. Keightley was on his feet, acting the whole thing out for me. 'Coming out with huge armfuls of stuff.'

'What sort of stuff?' I asked. I was interested in Keightley's fantasy life; anything would be a relief in a day like this was turning out to be.

'Ah,' Keightley laid his head on one side and

* Forensic Science.

133

looked at me. 'Ah,' he said again. He looked like the wine waiter at the Tour d'Argent being asked for a bottle of Tizer. 'That's what *you'll* have to tell *me*, sir, what *sort* of stuff.'

'Then let's for a minute say "Ships in bottles",' I said.

'Warships, sir?'

'Yes, nuclear submarines, sea-borne missile platforms, floating Coca-Cola depot boats, *Life* magazine colour-section printing-machine barges, thinking men's filter replacement transports, psychological-obsolescence tankers, and deep-frozen do-nut supply ships.'

'Yes, sir,' Keightley pretended that his pipe had gone out and clamped a match-box over the bowl to make a great show of fanning it back to red sparking life. His cheeks popped in and out. He looked up, smiled weakly and said, 'You'd probably like to hear it, sir.' He opened the film tin and removed a reel of ¼ in recording tape.

'Remember though, sir, I'm not saying they did originate from the occupiers.'

'They?' I stared insolently. 'You mean this tape *and* the film you sent Ross at the War House?'

It wrecked Keightley. Mind you, I don't blame him. He was just trying to keep everyone happy; but not blaming him and not preventing a future incident of the same kind is a different thing again. Keightley's loosely captive eyeballs circuited their red bloodshot linings. We sat silently for perhaps thirty seconds, then I said, 'Listen, Keightley, Ross's department is all military. Anything that passes your eyeballs or eardrums and has even a sniff of civilian in it comes to Dalby, or as the situation is at present, to me, or failing that, Alice. If I ever have cause to think that you are funnelling information of any sort at all, Keightley, any sort at all, into unauthorized channels, you'll find yourself lance-corporal in charge of restricted documents in the officers' mess, Aden. Unless I can think of something worse. I won't ever repeat this threat, Keightley, but don't imagine it's not going to be forever hanging over your bonce like Damocles' chopper. Now let's see what you found at the bottom of the garden. And don't start tapping your bloody finger-tips again.'

He played the tape through on the big grey Ferrograph. The sound was of an abstract quality. It was like a Rowton House production of the 'Messiah' heard through a wall and played at half speed.

'Animal, vegetable or mineral?' I asked.

'Human voices, these people say.'

I listened to the undulating and horrisonous mewl, to the bleating, braying, yelping howl, and found it as difficult to listen to as it was to label. I nodded. 'It doesn't do a thing for me,' I told him, 'but I'll take it away and think about it. It might grow on me.'

Keightley gave me the reel and the tin, and a quiet good-bye.

16

The next day I didn't go into the office in the morning. I drifted up to the Charing Cross Road on a number 1 bus, then cut off across Soho. I wanted to get a few groceries, some coffee, aubergines, andouillettes, some black bread, that sort of thing. The girl in the delicatessen had trimmed her eyebrows – I didn't like them so much like that. She looked constantly surprised. With the clientele in that shop perhaps she was. I decided to have a cup of coffee in Led's. The coffee may not be so good there – but the cheesecake was fine and I like the customers.

It seemed gloomy inside after the hot sunshine. I kicked the threadbare section of carpeting and eased myself into one of their rickety wooden chairs. Two Cona coffee-pots were bubbling away noisily.

My coffee came. I relaxed with the *Daily Express*. A hearsay report from a reliable source said that a girl featured weekly in a badly made TV series was likely to have a child.

A policeman earning £570 p.a. attacked by youths with knives outside a cinema where a nineteen-year-old rock-an'-roll singer was making a personal appearance for £600.

'Would Jim Walker play for Surrey?' There was a picture of Jim Walker, and 600 words. It didn't say whether he would or not.

'Warm sunny weather expected to continue. Cologne and Athens record temperature for time of year.'

'British heavy electrical gear still world's best,' some Briton in the electrical trade had said. I held a quiet requiem for so many trees that had died in vain.

I sat there for half an hour or so. I smoked my Gauloises and thought about Keightley and Ross, and how someone smarter than I would handle Chico. Murray was the only one of the whole set-up I'd want as a personal friend, and he was only in on the deal by accident. He had neither screening nor training as an operative. I thought about my desk where there would be the usual run of junk to read and initial before getting to anything important. The sight of that desk haunted me.

Most mornings I had a rough file of material from Washington – Defense Dept DSO SD CIC.*
Once a week I had what was called a 'digest' of the 'National Intelligence Estimate', the thing they give to the President. The 'digest' meant I got a

* Director of Special Operations: State Dept. Counter Intelligence Corps US Army.

copy of the parts of it that they decided to let me see.

Then there were six to eight foolscap sheets of translations of passages from the foreign papers – *Pravda*, *People's Daily*, the main paper of the Chinese Communist régime, and *Red Flag*, the theoretical organ of the Chinese Central Committee, and perhaps a few Yugoslav, Latvian or Hungarian accounts.

All this stuff had piled up on me the last few days. I decided to let it go another day. This was a warm London summer's day, the sooty trees were in sooty leaf, and the girls were in light cotton dresses. I felt relaxed and simple. I called for another cup of thin coffee and leaned back reflectively.

She came into Led's old broken doorway and into my life like the Royal Scot, but without all the steam and noise. She was dark, calm and dangerous-looking. Under her pinned-back hair her face was childishly wide-eyed as she stood momentarily blinded by the change of light.

Slowly and unflinchingly she looked around, meeting the insolent intensity of Led's loose-lipped Lotharios, then came to sit at my small, circular, plastic-topped table. She ordered a black coffee and croissant. Her face was taut like a cast of an Aztec god; everything that was static in her features was belied by the soft, woolly, quick eyes into which the beholder sank unprotesting. Her hair, coarse and oriental in texture, was drawn back into a vortex on the crown of her head. She drank the brown coffee slowly.

She was wearing that 'little black sleeveless dress' that every woman has in reserve for cocktail parties, funerals and first nights. Her slim white arms shone against the dull material, and her hands were long and slender, the nails cut short and varnished in a natural colour. I watched her even, very white teeth bite into the croissant. She could have been top kick in the Bolshoi, Sweden's first woman ship's captain, private secretary to Chou-en-lai, or Sammy Davis's press agent. She didn't pat her hair, produce a mirror, apply lipstick or flutter her eyelashes. She opened a conversation in a tentative English way. Her name was Jean Tonnesen. She was my new assistant.

Alice, the cunning old doll, not missing a trick, had given Miss Tonnesen a file of urgent matter including a written note from Chico saying he'd 'gone away for the day would phone in at teatime'. It was pretty infuriating, but I didn't want to start the day's business by getting mad.

'Have another coffee.'

'Black, please.'

'Which department did you come to us from?'

'I was already in Dalby's – I was holding down Macao sub-office.'

She must have seen the ego in my face take a bend. 'I suppose we'll have to stop saying Dalby's now that you're running us.'

'That won't be necessary. He's only temporarily

detached. As far as anyone has told me, anyway.'

She smiled, she had a nice smile.

'Must be terrible to be back in Europe – even on a fine summer's day. I remember going to a restaurant in Macao. It was built over a gambling casino. An illuminated sign reported the results at the tables downstairs. The waitresses take the bets, take the money; you eat, the sign shows the results – Bingo! Indigestion!'

She smiled again while shaking her head. I liked sitting here watching her smile her clear white smiles. She managed to let me play at being boss without being obsequious about it. I dimly remember her being in Macao, that is to say I remembered the odd papers and reports from her.

'I brought my transfer card,' she said.

'Let's look.' I was beginning to confirm the picture of me that Alice had sketched in roughly. Even though Led's wasn't the place, she passed me a pale-green filing card. It was about six by ten inches. It was a personnel-type card, such as any large commercial firm might employ, but in the space for name and address there was only an irregularly spaced series of rectangular holes. Under this in panels was information. Born twenty-six years ago in Cairo. Norwegian father, Scottish mother, probably not short of the stuff since she went to school in Zurich between '51 and '52, and decided to live there. Perhaps working for British Diplomatic Service in Switzerland – it wouldn't be the first time an

140

Embassy typist came into the department. Her brother holds Norwegian citizenship, works for a shipping firm in Yokohama – hence presumably HK then Macao – where she worked part-time for the tourist bureau there – a Portuguese set-up. The panel marked T was bursting with entries. She spoke Norwegian, English, Portuguese, German, French, 'FSW', that is 'fluent in speech and writing', and Mandarin, Japanese and Cantonese 'SS, some speaking'. Her security clearance was GH7 'non stopped' which means that nothing had been found to prevent her having a higher clearance if the department wanted to classify her higher.

'It doesn't say whether you can sew,' I said.

'No,' she said.

'Can you?' I said.

'Yes,' she said.

'Trousers?' I said.

'Yes,' she said.

'You're in.'

I thanked her and handed the card back. It was fine; she was fine, my very first beautiful spy, always presuming of course that this was Jean Tonnesen's card, and presuming that this was Jean Tonnesen. Even if she wasn't, she was still my very first beautiful spy.

She put the card back into her small, for a handbag, handbag.

'What do you have there?' I asked. 'A small snub-nosed, pearl-handled .22 automatic?'

'No, I've got that tucked in my garter. In here I have the flare pistol.'

'OK,' I said. 'What do you like for lunch?'

In London with a beautiful hungry girl one must show her to Mario at the Terrazza. We sat in the ground floor front under the plastic grapes and Mario brought us Campari-sodas and told Jean how much he hated me. To do this he had to practically gnaw her ear off. Jean liked it.

We ordered the Zuppa di Lenticchie and Jean told how this lentil soup reminded her of visits with her father to Sicily many years ago. They had friends there, and each year would coincide their visits with the Feast of San Giuseppe on 19th March.

On that day the wealthier families provide gigantic amounts of food and open house to the whole village. Always the feast begins with lentil soup and spaghetti, but on St Joseph's day no cheese must be eaten, so, instead, a mixture of toasted bread-crumbs, sardines and fennel is sprinkled over the dish.

'Those days in the hot sun were as perfect as anytime I remember,' Jean mused.

We ate the Calamari and the chicken deep in which the butter and garlic had been artfully hidden to be struck like a vein of aromatic gold. Jean had pancakes and a thimbleful of black coffee without mentioning calories, and went through the whole meal without lighting a cigarette. This showed virtue enough, she must have some vices.

Mario, deciding that I was on the brink of a great and important seduction, brought us a bottle of cold sparkling Asti 'on the house'. He filled and refilled Jean's glass then turned with the bottle still in his hand. He pointed the neck at me. 'Is good?'

It certainly was. The wine and Jean had conspired to produce in me a gentle euphoria. The sunlight fell in dusty bars across the table-cloth and lit her face as she grinned. I watched her image inverted in the clear coolness of the wine in her glass. Outside, the driver of a wet fish van was arguing violently with a sad traffic warden. The traffic had welded itself into a river of metal, and from a taxi a few yards up the road two men paid off their cab and continued their journey on foot. The glass of the cab permitted only a momentary glimpse, then the traffic moved together; closing like the shutter of a camera.

One of the two men had the build of Jay, the other Dalby's style in shoes. I was suddenly very wide awake.

17

*[Aquarius (Jan 20–Feb 19) This can be a week
of scrambled emotions. Seize any opportunities
that come your way and be prepared to change
your plans.]*

On the filing cabinet was a vast jugful of yellow
daisies, my new carpet had been tacked into the
dry rot, and the window was open for the first
time in months. Below in the street a couple of
young men, collegiate in a Cecil Gee way, were
hammering the neighbourhood eardrums with their
motor scooters. There was a colliery brass band
in the dispatch office with a xylophone that made
my daisies quiver. Alice sent Jean out on some
errand or other, then brought me the real file on
Jean Tonnesen. A thick foolscap loose-leaf book
held together by a brown lace bearing a small metal
seal with a number on it.

It followed the transfer card roughly, although
this wasn't always the case with all our people.

144

There was the Zurich business – an affair with a man named Maydew, who had some connection with the US State Department. Her brother in Yokohama worried the author of this file – some anti-nuclear warfare activity, declarations, letters to Japanese papers, etc, but that was all pretty standard stuff nowadays. A brother missing 1943 in German-occupied Norway. On the last summary page there was the word Norway followed by a mathematical plus sign. This meant that she should not be involved in work that would call into question her loyalty to the Norwegian Government, but was recommended for anything involving Norwegian co-operation. It was all straightforward.

'I say – like a look see at the latest? New set of figures you might just . . .'

I groaned, 'No time now, I'm afraid.' I just didn't want any more of Carswell for a long time, but I just couldn't raise the energy to transfer him. In any case, lose him, we'd lose Murray, and I wanted to hang on to the only muscular intelligent adult male we had.

Carswell came nearer and dusted off the old velvet cushion. 'How's things?' I asked. I capitulated.

He lowered his creaking bones into my wicker chair.

'Very fit, very fit indeed. Plenty of exercise and fresh air, that's the secret – if you don't mind me saying so, you could do with a little of the same.

Overdoing it a bit, old chap. Can see it; dark here!'
He ran a finger under his large red staring eyes.

The door opened noiselessly and Alice came in to collect Jean's file. I was getting used to having my own department. My history books, notes and unpaid bills were scattered through our only light clean office in such profusion that I had almost forgotten the rigorous tidiness it had enjoyed when it was Dalby's domain. Alice hadn't, however, and was constantly straightening files and hiding things in places where 'Mr Dalby keeps them'. I found the crossword puzzle I had been working on. Alice had completed it. I had got ten down correct. It was EAT. 'Not so funny, rheumatism,' Carswell was saying. DITHYRAMBE had been quite wrong. I don't know why I'd ever thought it otherwise . . . 'With white horse oils,' Carswell was saying, 'and go straight to bed.'

I wished Carswell would stop talking and go home. He smoked his cigarette with a nervous concentration taking it compulsively out of his mouth, but never more than three inches away. Alice watched Carswell as he scratched his shoulder blades upon the carved uprights of the guest chair. She knew, as I did, that he was settling in. She gave me the rolling eyes and screwed face of sympathy. I pretended I hadn't seen the completed puzzle.

At that moment Chico was pressing button A.

My outside phone rang. And everyone began talking.

'Where are you speaking from? Yes, where are you now? What the hell are you doing in Grantham?'

'Let me talk to him, sir. There are the film requisitions, he hasn't done anything about them and they must go off today.'

'Well, you've no business in Grantham. Who signed your travel form? Oh, did you? Well, you needn't think you're charging it on expenses.'

'Murray,' Carswell was going on relentlessly. 'A dashed good trooper, mind you, without your confidence, nothing. I appreciate it. Working very closely, restraining the impulse to guess hastily. Thoroughness is the essence of a statistical operation.'

'Just what do you think my role is in this drama of your life?'

'Yes, sir, I know, sir, the commanding officer, sir, but when I saw . . .'

'Right, Chico, that's right, you've got it right for once. That's what I am, the, and more immediately, your commanding officer. But that doesn't worry you, does it? Would you have just minced off into the blue if Dalby had still been in charge here – would you?'

'I've seen Dalby, sir, spoken with him. I'm seeing him again this evening.'

Carswell spread some sheets of paper across my desk. He said, 'These figures I've brought along here are only the briefest possible extract, I don't want to worry you with the nuts and bolts. What you want is results, not excuses, as you are always saying. There's a lot more work if they are to be made convincing. I mean really convincing. At this stage it's more of an analytical hunch.'

'You have no business seeing Dalby.'

'It's wrong to say commanding officer on a clear line, sir.'

'You stay out of this, Alice.'

'An analytical hunch, but nevertheless, a hunch.'

'You have no business going above my head. It's a most despicable thing and it's damned unmilitary.'

'You shouldn't say unmilitary – that's a clear line. He's on just an ordinary GPO line.'

Carswell was still talking. 'Reading the results, old boy, is where the skill comes in, I always say. Just needs a trained mind. I know you thought some of our whims a little odd at times. Oh, I know. No, no, no, you see, you are a man of action. Pater just the same, the same exactly.'

'I recognized this fellow, sir. In the film at the War House, sir. A friend, sir, of my cousin, and frightfully good at chemistry. It really is, sir. I'll see Dalby again tonight. He thinks I should have a few days here, sir. Dalby said to tell no one but I knew you'd wonder where I was, and there is the film requisition too, sir. I haven't done them for a few days.'

Carswell was folding his sheet of statistics and replacing it in the large laced file. 'Murray will do all the action stuff, phoning and carrying on. But

I want your OK to say he's from the Special Branch Metropolitan Police. I wanted to see you last week, but Murray said without a few figures to start on we had just no case at all. We'll have to check hospitals, nursing homes, convalescent homes – nut-houses too, old boy, I said, if they are scientists. Ha ha. But it is convincing, I want to stress that.'

Nut-houses, I thought, whatever would Carswell be on about next. Meanwhile Chico was saying, 'Shall I phone you back tomorrow after I've spoken to Dalby, sir?'

'Jean is here, sir,' said Alice, trying to hide Jean's confidential file under her mauve cardigan with the blue buttons.

'Hello, my dear young lady.'

'No, don't ring off, I haven't finished with you yet!'

'I had a lot of trouble, Alice. They said it wouldn't be ready till morning.'

'Have my seat, it's not awfully comfortable.'

'They distinctly said four-thirty. It's always the same. The more time one gives them the more unreliable they are.'

'This friend of my cousin, sir, top ranker with the Chemical Warfare people. I knew if I spoke to him.'

'No, I've been sitting down all day.'

'How did you come to see Dalby?'

'Dalby came in after the ad in the *Stage*.'

'Well, why didn't you tell me, Alice?'

'I'd rather stand really.'

'No, I was talking to Alice. How did *you* see Dalby?'

'Can't I tell Murray to go ahead then, sir, acting most discreetly, of course. Mustn't upset the guardians of the law.'

'Did they say what time in the morning, Jean?'

'Just by accident. Horrid little place. It's where he usually meets you.'

'I've never been to Grantham in my life, not to get out of the train, anyway.'

'It cheers me up, my dear. When you get old, the sun warms your bones.'

'Remind him about the reqs, sir. He's the only one that understands them.'

'No, there's a chair there if I want one, really, umm.'

'Distinctly: where he usually meets you. That's what he said.'

'I'll go through all the results with you, if you like. You'll be impressed, I know. Cracked it wide open.'

'No, sober as a judge.'

'Shall I hang on, sir? It's almost five-thirty.'

'Me, sir. No, sir. You know I almost never tipple, sir.'

'OK,' I said. 'I like you, Chico. Phone in this time tomorrow. I'll be finished doing your damned requisition by then if I start now.'

The reputation of the department needed another crack-pot scheme from Carswell like it needed more film requisitions. But my little phone conversation with Chico left me too weak to argue. I gave him the OK in the hope that Murray was intelligent enough to keep him out of harm's way. He shuffled out with his big brown file of statistics. That was Wednesday. I finished the reqs by ten-thirty, had a drink at the Fitzroy and then went back to the office to phone for a car. We had a lot of taxis in the car pool. They were the least noticeable car and the blue glass was great for observation. As I crossed the road there was one of our cabs there already. It seemed unbelievable that Jean or Alice had predicted to a few minutes how long the reqs would take. I looked in the cab but it was empty. As I got to the top floor I saw the light was on under the door of my office. I hadn't left it on. I moved near. Inside there was someone moving the paper work about on my desk. I could hear two voices having a row in the street below. Near to my head the office clock was ticking gently. I reached for the big metal ruler from Alice's desk and found myself rubbing the scar tissue from my descent into the gaming room. I turned the brass door handle as silently and as slowly as I could. Then I kicked the door and dropped in the doorway on my knees, the steel ruler poised behind my head.

Dalby said, 'Hello,' and poured me a drink.

Dalby's clothes were tweedy and shabby. Silhouetted grey in the red neon-lit sky were Jean's big armful of daisies. Dalby sat heavily at the desk on which the Anglepoise light splashed across the large piles of non-secret office work that I never seemed to complete. The low place light emphasized his dark deep-set eyes, and his quick nervous movements belied his slow reactions. I realized that he hadn't out-thought me when I rocketed in the door. He just hadn't begun to react.

There seemed so much I wanted to ask him. I wondered whether I'd have to go right back to Ross with my cap in my hand and tell him that we'd be very happy to have the *Gumhuria* stuff. He poured me a large Teacher's whisky and by now I needed it – I had the shivers. I held the glass in both hands and sipped it gratefully. Dalby's eyes came slowly back into focus on his surroundings as from a long, long journey. We looked at each other for perhaps two minutes, then he spoke in that careful deep voice of his, 'Did you ever see a bomb explode?' he asked. I wanted him to explain things to me and here he was adding to the confusion by asking me questions. I shook my head.

'You're going to now,' he said. 'The Minister has particularly asked for us to be at the next American test. The American Defense Department say they've got a way to jam seismographs; they are going to try to double the Russian readings. I told him that we had a file on some of the British scientists who are there.'

'Some of them,' I said. 'If we are prepared to think that Carswell has got anything on the ball at all, then we've got a file of eighteen out of a

British total of fifty, that total including eleven lab assistants.'

'Yes,' Dalby came alive for a moment. 'Alice told me about what you and Carswell have been up to. You can drop it and get Carswell and his sergeant out of this department; we are overcrowded now.'

A load of help Dalby was being; he stays away a couple of months, then when he does come back it's unannounced in the middle of the night and all he does is criticize.

'This bomb test, it's Tuesday. I'll be going along. You can bring an assistant if you want to.'

I wondered if he knew about Jean and if I'd still be entitled to an assistant if Dalby was back to take over.

'Will you want Chico to go with us?'

'Yes, get him on the phone. He can arrange the tickets and passes.'

'It's eleven-fifteen,' I said. 'Do you know where I can get him?'

'Do I know? Who's been in charge here the last few weeks? You've got his number, haven't you? I haven't seen him for weeks.'

'He's in Grantham,' I said weakly.

'Who sent him there and what for?'

I didn't know why Dalby was playing close like this, but I decided to cover up. 'We had a file to be moved and there was no courier with high enough clearance. He'll be back in a day or so.'

'Oh, leave him be. Alice can arrange things.'

I nodded but for the first time I began to suspect that something odd was going on; from now on I was keeping my head down.

The next morning I completed a little private task that took an hour of my time once every two months. I collected a heavy manilla envelope from an address near Leciester Square, inspected the contents and mailed it back to the address from which I'd got it.

18

[*Aquarius (Jan 20–Feb 19) You will have a chance to follow new interests, but old friend-ships should not be forgotten. For those in love a thrilling development lies ahead.*]

Tokwe Atoll was a handful of breakfast crumbs on a blue coverlet. Each island had its little green bays that resisted the blueness of the vast Pacific which struck the reefs in hammers of fury and shattered into a swirl of enveloping whiteness around wrecked craft sunk along the shore line since 1944. The open mouths of the tank landing craft gaped toothless at the barbed-wire-strewn beach. Here and there were bright red rusting tanks and tracked vehicles, broken, split and open to the timeless sky. As we came lower we could pick out painted ammunition boxes and broken crates. The huge Vertol helicopter that had lifted us from the aircraft carrier in which only an hour ago we had been enjoying icy orange-juice, cornflakes and waffles with maple syrup, swooped across the water on to the concrete of 'Laboratory Field', an air strip that didn't exist ten weeks ago. As we dismounted, a jeep, painted white, sped towards us. The four air police inside wore shorts (shorts always look wrong on Americans), khaki shirts open at the neck, with white side-arms and cross-belt. On the right chest of the shirt they carried their names on leather strips.

'Laboratory Field', or 'Lay Field' as the Americans had rather perversely shortened it, comprised the whole of this island, which was one of the hundred that made up the whole atoll. In ninety days they had equipped the islands with an airfield, suitable for dealing with both piloted and non-piloted aircraft; two athletic fields, two movie theatres, a chapel, a clothing store, beach clubs for officers and enlisted men, a library, hobby shops, vast quarters for the Commanding General, a maintenance hangar, personnel landing pier, mess hall, dispensary, a PX, post office, a wonderful modern laundry and a power plant. At one time during the test we were told there were ninety baseball teams in ten organized leagues. The telephone exchange could handle more than 6,000 calls per day; one mess alone served 9,000 meals per day, and a radio station operated around the clock, and buses across the island did likewise. I wish that London could match it. Dalby, Jean and I wore plastic badges showing our photos and description. Across the badge a large letter 'Q' was printed. It granted us entry to even the secret laboratory areas.

We spent the first few hours looking around the project. An army major with an amazing memory for facts and figures went around with us. The bomb to be exploded was a 'fractional crit bomb', the major explained to us. 'Uranium, when enough (that is a critical mass) of it comes together, explodes. But if the density is squeezed, the same explosion can come from a smaller quantity. So high explosive is placed round a small sphere of U-235, or plutonium. This means that only a fraction of the critical mass is needed, hence "fractional crit bomb".'

The major looked at his audience like he expected applause and went on to explain about ways in which it had become possible to dispense with tritium and with refrigeration, so making the bomb cheaper and easier to produce. He left me back there with the 'fractional crit' stuff, but we let him go on.

We flew out to the island where the detonation was to take place. The whole island was a mass of instruments, and it coruscated in the bright tropical sunshine. The major pointed them out to us. He was a short thickset man with rimless glasses and a blue chin who looked like Humpty Dumpty in his white helmet liner with 'Q' painted on it, but then perhaps we all did. There were the photo-cells, photo-multipliers, ion chambers, mass and beta ray spectographs. Standing in the middle of this sandy arena, surrounded by machines, with dozens of human attendants, in godlike splendour, was the shot tower. A great red-painted metal tower 200 feet high. Round the base of the tower were huge notices reading 'DANGER' and under that, with not so typical American understatement, the words 'High Explosives'.

The sun sets and goes out like a flash-light in the tropics and it was low in the sky as we clattered along the hardboard corridors of Main Block Three. It was the third conference of the day and the ice-water was slopping around inside me like the documents in an untidy brief-case – my brief-case for instance. We got there before the meeting had begun and everyone was standing around giving each other the old stuff about retreads, PTA meetings, and where to go for a good divorce. I could see many people I knew. From ONI; from State Dept Intelligence, and the many separate US Army Intelligence departments. Standing alone in the corner were three young crew-cut collegiate men from the FBI – pariahs of the US Intelligence Organization – and not without reason.

Against the shuttered light of the window I saw a couple of colonels I remembered from a stint with the CIA Bankrolls – thicker, hair thinner and belts longer. 'Skip' Henderson had made major, I noticed – one of the brightest Intelligence men I knew. His assistant, Lieutenant Barney Barnes, wasn't with him today. I hoped he was around somewhere. Barney and Skip were people who listen a lot, tell you that you are a sensation, and at the end of a couple of hours you begin to think it's true. Skip gave me the high sign. Dalby was well into a finger-stabbing duel with Colonel Donahue. Jean was sifting through her shorthand notes, and pencils to separate them from skin food, wych-hazel, eyebrow pencils and lipstick. Before I could edge round to Skip, the chairman, Battersby, the US Intelligence Department's logistic king, made coughing noises. He felt he'd left enough time between the late arrivals – us – and starting the motors, to save us embarrassment. We sat down, all fourteen of us round the long mess-hall table; in front of each of us stood some white paper, a Zippi Speedball pen, a book of matches that said, 'Pestpruf roofing' followed by an address in Cincinnati, and a clean drinking-glass. In the centre of the table four plastic jugs held cold American water in vacuum-stoppered frigidity. We all waited for Battersby to kick off.

'Well, we've all had a tough day, so we won't . . . say – get one of those guys outside to fix these darn fans, will you?'

Someone slid across to the door and held a whispered conversation with the Air Policeman outside. We all tried to listen to both conversations at once. A white plastic helmet liner looked round the door. He wanted to make sure that a roomful of people without fans really existed. Battersby saw the movement.

159

'Just get some fans on in here, son, will you?' he boomed, then turned back to us. 'Try to get a little agreement round here. Guess all you people know each other.' This was a cue for all those healthy well-laundered Americans to politely display thirty-two teeth at Jean. I shifted uncomfortably in my drip-dry shirt that had become a bundle under my arm-pits.

The little information officer who had been showing us the set-up went to the blackboard and drew a circle; inside it he wrote 'Uranium 235 (or Plutonium)'. He tapped the circle with his chalk. 'Hit this with a Uranium 235 bullet and you get fission – a self-sustaining reaction.' Over on the right-hand side of the board he wrote 'July 16, 1945.'

'Exactly the same principle gave us the "thin man" bomb. Hiroshima.' The major wrote 'August 6, 1945' under the first date. 'Now for the "fat boy". That took out Nagasaki.' He added August 9 to the list and drew another circle. 'This,' he made the circle very thick with the side of his chalk, 'is made of plutonium with a hollow centre; you implode it. That is to say let it collapse on to itself like a burst balloon by having it surrounded with something that gives you a big bang forming,' he wrote 'crit mass' in the centre of the thick circle. 'A critical mass. OK?' He wrote 'August 28/29? 1949' and turned to face us again. 'We are not sure of the exact date.' I'll bet Ross could tell you, I thought, and I felt a little glow of vicarious pride.* The major went on, 'We think that is the sort of bomb the reds exploded in 1949. Now then we get to the Eniwetok blast.' He wrote 'November 1, 1952' under the other dates.

He drew another circle on the board and wrote 'deuterium' inside it. 'Also called heavy hydrogen,' he said, tapping the word deuterium. Alongside the first circle he drew two more. Missing the centre circle he wrote the word tritium into the third circle. 'Tritium is also called super-heavy hydrogen,' he said, tapping it. 'Now what happens in a hydrogen blast? These two fuse. It is a fusion bomb which creates a chain reaction between these two: heavy hydrogen and super-heavy hydrogen. It heats them by a trigger of what?' He turned to write the answer into the centre circle. A colonel said, 'Super-duper heavy hydrogen.' Humpty Dumpty turned round and then laughed, but I wouldn't have cared to be a captain that said it.

The major drew a chalkline connecting the earlier diagram with the centre circle. 'The trigger is an atomic bomb. Making it a fission-fusion device. Now in the larger bomb we use a different substance. Uranium 235 is expensive, but Uranium 238 is cheaper but needs a lot more get-up-and-go to be triggered. You surround the trigger with a layer of 238,' he drew a diagram. 'But this tends to give a lot of fallout as well as a big energy

* See Appendix: Joe One, p. 329.

161

release. Now you can see that all these bombs, including the red H-blast . . .' he wrote 'August 12, 1953' on to the list . . . 'These bombs all have a standard primitive A-bomb centre and are called fission-fusion-fission bombs. OK?'

The major was stabbing the air with his chalk like a medical student with his first thermometer. 'Now we come to our little blast-off here at Tokwe. We have a standard 238 bomb, but here,' he tapped the centre of the inevitable circle, 'here we have a trigger of an entirely new pattern. The only purpose of the trigger is to get extreme temperatures. OK? Suppose in here we put a king-size shot of TNT and get enough temperature to flash the bomb. Right?' He wrote 'TNT' into the centre of the chalk circle. 'Then that would be what we call a "high explosive to fusion reaction".' He wrote 'H.E.-fusion' under that drawing. 'We haven't done that and nor has anyone else – in fact it's probably impossible. Practically all the little countries have got their labs working on this because if they ever do it bombs will be a dime a dozen.' He rubbed out 'TNT' and tapped the blank space. 'So what do we have here? I'll tell you. Not a thing.' He paused while we were all registering appropriate types of surprise. 'No, we have nothing inside the bomb, but we do have something here.' He drew a small rectangle at the extreme edge of the board (he could draw any shape, this boy). Inside the rectangle he wrote 'SVMF'. 'Here there is the Super Volt Micro Flash mechanism, the

SUVOM which for a millionth of a microsecond builds up enough voltage to trip the mechanism. Now as you see, this power is taken into the bomb,' he drew a long squeaky chalkline joining the bomb to the mechanism, 'by the umbilical cord. Without the A-bomb trigger there will be no fallout. This will be the first entirely clean bomb. OK?'

The major carefully picked himself a fresh piece of chalk and I sneaked a look at my watch. It was 6.10 P.M. 'Size,' he said. 'What size bomb is this one we have here? This is a fifty-megaton bomb.* In terms of the destructive area, this is a bomb that would take out a whole city and make the "thin man" look like a dud. We expect Type 2 destruction – that is to say everything flammable gone and severe damage to metal and brick across a thirty-five-mile radius.' Someone at the other end of the table said, 'Diameter,' and Humpty Dumpty said, 'No; radius!' There was a low whistle. I guessed that the officer who said diameter had been asked to do so, but it was quite a statement just the same. The major pressed on. 'In terms of territory it means that a bomb in Bernalillo brings Type 2 as far as Santa Fé and Los Lunas (these were towns in New Mexico near Los Alamos which almost everyone knew in terms of flesh, food, and furlough). There were more exclamations. 'Or to take another example, from Sacramento right the way down to Redwood City,

* Approximately 2,500 times the destructive power of the Hiroshima explosion.

and that includes the Sheraton Palace.' It was a private joke and someone laughed at it. The little major was quite enjoying his lecture now, what with everyone being awake and all. 'For the sake of our guests, I'll give you another demonstration that may help. Think of Type 2 from Southend to Reading.' He pronounced it Reeding. He looked at me and I said, 'If it's all the same to you I'll think of it from Santa Fé to Los Lunas.'

The little major gave me a millionth of a microsecond smile and said, 'Yes – sir, we had to select a jumbo size atoll for this baby. We're not commuting between here and the shot island every day for the ride. OK?' I said it was OK, by me.

Next, Battersby stood up and the little major collected his notes together, lit up a two-bit cigar and sat down while a provost lieutenant came in with a little compressed air machine and sprayed water over the blackboard before giving it a thorough cleaning. Other officers told of detection methods used to judge the size and positions of explosions, and how they intended to jam the Russian detection devices like the radar that detects changes in the electric charges in the ionosphere, and the recording barometers that record air and sound waves and produce microbarographs, and the radio signals that are picked up from the release of radio energy at the time of the explosion. The standard and most reliable detection system of analysing fallout residue to find the substances from which the bomb had been constructed was ruled out in this case because it was to be a 'clean' bomb.

Battersby told us the structure of the security arrangements, the echelon of command, the dates the firing was likely to take place, and showed us some beautiful diagrams. Then the meeting broke up into sub-meetings. I was to go off with Skip Henderson and a Lt Dolobowski and Jean, while Dalby went into secret session with Battersby's assistant. Skip said that we may as well go across to his quarters where the fans worked properly and there was a bottle of Scotch. A few of the eager beavers down the other end of the table were destroying notes they had made, by burning them with Messrs Pestpruf's matches.

Skip had a comfortable little den in the section of camp that came nearest to the sea. A tin cupboard held his uniforms, and an old air-conditioning unit sat astride the window-sill beating the air cold. On the army table were a few books; German grammar; *Trial by Ordeal*, by Caryl Chessman; two paperback westerns, *Furnace Installation – a Guide*, and *A Century of Ribald Stories*. On the window-sill was a bottle of Scotch, gin, some assorted mixes, a glass containing a dozen sharpened pencils, and an electric razor.

From the window I could see a mile or so up the beach one way, and nearly half a mile the other. In both directions the beach was still encrusted with debris, and a flimsy jetty limped painfully into the water. The sun was a dark red fireball, just like the one we were trying to create on tower island a few miles north.

Skip poured us all a generous shot of Black Label, and even remembered to leave the ice out of mine.

'So that's the way it is,' he said. 'You and this young lady here decide to catch a little sunshine at John Government's expense?' He waited for me to speak.

I spoke. 'It's just that I have so many unsolved crimes on my hands that I have become the unsolved crime expert – anyone with an unsolved crime on their hands, they send for me.'

'And you solve it?'

'No, only file it.'

Skip poured me another drink, looked at the dark-eyed little lieutenant, and said, 'I hope you've got a large family economy size file with you this trip.' He sat down on the bed and unlocked his brief-case. I noticed the steel liner inside it. 'No one can tell you the whole picture because we haven't put it together yet. But we are in a spot; the stuff we are getting back from EW 192 is verbatim stuff we are putting in our files. Verbatim. No sooner is a discovery made in our labs than it is broadcast to the other side of the world.'

The CIA numbers its rooms with a prefix telling which wing it's situated in. Room 192 in the East Wing is really a large suite of rooms and its job is relaying information from the heart of foreign governments. It deals only with agents getting stuff from sacrosanct crevices available to highest-level foreign officials. It would certainly be the best possible way of checking the US's loss of its own information.

'It's from labs? It's strictly scientific information then?'

Skip pinched his nostrils. 'Seems to be at present.'

Jean had/made herself comfortable in the non-army-style wicker chair. She had that quiet, composed, rather stupid look that I had noticed before. It meant she was committing the bulk of the conversation to memory. She came back slowly to life now.

'You said "at present". I take it the volume of this stuff is increasing. How fast?'

'It's increasing, and fast enough for the whole department to be very worried – can I leave it at that?' It was a rhetorical question.

Jean asked, 'When did you first suspect there was a multiple leak? It is a multiple?'

'A multiple? I'll say it is – it's a multiple multiple. It's from a range of subjects so vast there isn't one college, let alone one lab, that could have access to it.'

The dark-eyed Dolobowski went for some more ice from the fridge. Skip produced one of those vast cartons of cigarettes and talked Jean into trying a Lucky. He lit his own and Jean's, and the dark-eyed one gave us more ice and Scotch all round.

'The first leaks,' Skip mused. 'Yes.'

Dolobowski sat himself back in the chair and it was suddenly clear to me that he had some sort of authority over Skip. That was why he'd said nothing while the dark-eyed one was out of the room. He was here to make sure that Jean and I came away with just the amount of information we were allowed. I didn't blame anyone for this, after all we hadn't told the Americans that we were having the same problem. In fact, goodness knows what cock-and-bull story Dalby had cooked up to get along here. Skip was staring defensively into space and blowing gently on the ember of his cigarette.

'With these international conferences it's difficult,' the dark-eyed one had decided to answer. His voice, pitched low, came from far away. 'Scientists use the same sort of jargon, and anyway, discoveries tend to run parallel. We think that eight months cover the broad front leaks. Before that there may have been the odd thing here and there, but now it covers the whole scientific programme – even non-military.'

You could see that the non-military bit really hurt; that was below the belt.

I said that I wouldn't mind if it was a small one, but that then I had better go, no really – perhaps another time. We fenced off a few questions about leaks in the UK, to persuade them that we didn't know what was happening. It wasn't difficult. Skip saw us off down to the little white-painted fence by means of which a considerate army enabled him to feel he had never left New Jersey. He was going back to the States the next day – I said to give my regards to Barney, and he said he would, and did I have plenty of cigarettes. We shook hands and I remembered Skip Henderson as he used to be; with hair to spare for barbers, and a fund of stories upon which every barman in town would refuel. I remember him carrying his old camera, and stopping every pretty girl he saw, saying he was from *Life* magazine, and how he hoped they didn't think him rude for speaking to them without being introduced. The pictures he took with that old camera, 'And now perhaps a really sophisticated shot in case we make the cover again this week.' I don't think Skip knew how the film fitted into it even. Everyone in town knew that Skip was always good for a laugh and a couple of dollars.

'I'm sorry,' Skip said, 'for not having sherry. I mean I know you hate whisky before dinner really.' Skip kicked the toe of his elegant, hand-tooled Italian pointed non-army brogues in the sand. I knew that Skip knew that I knew who dark-eyes was.

I gave him the two-handed pump-handle grip that in the old days we used as a joke. 'That's OK, Skip. You'll find yourself in London anytime, and our liquor supply isn't all it should be. You know?' He brightened up a bit and as he said good-bye to Jean I saw a flash of the old technique for an instant. It was almost dusk now. Here and there in the dingy sun-charred palm trees a bird fidgeted, and the waves hit, dragged at and sank into the shingle beach and wore the pebbles smoother. We walked across the sandy compound in silence, Jean and I, and the sun was leaving us to go to India, and the sand was red and the sky was mauve and Jean was beautiful and the wind was in her hair and her hand was in mine.

From half a mile away the juke-box in the officers' club rubbed the smooth night sky with sandpaper sounds. Inside, the tension bubble of the hard day had burst into the inconsequent chatter of martini-lubricated relaxation. From the far corner a barbecue fire sent up spluttering spitting sounds like a thousand captive kittens to accompany the bright flashes of flame. A white-clad Mephistopheles poked, prodded and mothered the thick slabs of prime American beef, and dabbed at them with the contents of a can of 'CHARKOL Barbecue flavor dressing'.

A pink-faced boy in a white jacket found us a little check table-cloth in the corner. There was some very old Ellington that some very old fan like me had selected from the juke-box murmuring low. A candle in a chianti bottle flickered across Jean's pale flat face, and I wondered how many US Officers' Clubs in France had a Pacific-style décor. Outside, the night was clear and warm.

'I like your friend Skip.' Men's friendships are something that women wonder at and fear slightly. 'He seemed a little withdrawn, as though . . .'

'Go on,' I said. 'Say it.'

'I don't know what I was going to say really.'

'You know, so say it. We can use a few extra opinions as things are.' The candlelight swerved across Jean's face as the candle was lifted away. We both turned to see Dalby lighting a cheroot from it. He drew deeply on the small black leaf. Dalby had changed into a red Hawaiian shirt with large blue and yellow flowers across it; put on a pair of lightweight trousers, and gone to the barber's shop. Dalby had this knack, or art, or charm for sinking into such a combination without looking different from all the Americans wearing it.

'You're making with the native costume.'

He dragged on the cheroot before replying, then carefully put it to rest in an ashtray. It was his claim to a seat at the table. He was just crazy about symbolism, Dalby. He finished looking casually round the room and directed his attention back to us.

'Are you sure I'm not intruding?' he said, sliding into the seat beside Jean.

'Jean was going to give me her opinion of Skip Henderson.'

'I would be most interested to hear it,' said Dalby, his small bright eyes looking over the menu carefully. He gave me the creeps when he did this. It was almost Yogi the way he diverted his eyes to an object or a piece of paper to enable him to concentrate. Jean had a similar habit. I wondered if I did the same thing and I wondered if Ross had managed to get hold of him about the file.

'Well, he looked frightened almost,' I was watching Dalby; his eyes were fixed on one place on the menu. He was listening.

At the next table I could hear a loud American voice. 'Soldier, I said, that's my wife's personal baggage and you'll move your tail back into that baggage-room . . .'

'Frightened? Of me, you mean?' I always seemed to get embroiled in nutty conversations when Dalby was with me. I wished Jean would drop it. She just didn't know a thing about Skip Henderson. Skippie Henderson who went to Korea and let himself be captured just so he could find out about collaborating in the prison camps; who came back to Washington with three bayonet wounds, a lungful of TB and a dossier that put a lot of ex-prisoner brass into the hot-seat. In a court-martial hot-seat. Skip stayed a captain for a long time after that. Prisoners' friends had friends. But frightened? Skip? who had the only Negro officer in the CIA as his assistant – Barney Barnes, and kept him against every sort of opposition that could be mustered. She just didn't know what Skip was like. Smooth smiling Skip. Twenty years and they'd finally made him a major, and detailed a major to listen to his nightmares.

'No,' said Jean. 'And I don't mean frightened of his tame policeman either. I don't mean frightened of anything. Sort of frightened for. He kept looking at you like he wanted to save you up, remember you very thoroughly for some reason. A last look almost.'

'So you thought that he was ... Skip had a strong-arm man with him,' I said to Dalby. 'Did your boyo have one, too, or did he have enough rank to be trusted?'

Dalby spoke without looking up from the menu. 'I don't think you should get too paranoiac on Henderson's behalf. He's done a lot of silly things in his time. They are pretty worried about this situation and my personal opinion is that Skip Henderson's policeman is at least there with his "OK", and may even be his idea. They don't want to spread the word too wide, and this way they stopper up the information without offence to old buddy buddies.'

'Yes,' I said, 'I can hear McCone laying awake all night worrying whether Skip and I have lost a beautiful friendship.'

'Oh, I can understand that,' said Jean. 'It's well worth a little trouble to see that valuable contacts are not lost when a little trouble could preserve them.'

'I'm still not convinced. Skip would have no difficulty in closing the questioning. He's never had any trouble with a "no" in his life.'

'That's true,' said Dalby. 'If he'd been just a little more parsimonious with his "no's" he'd be a lieutenant-general by now.'

I wondered if this meant that Dalby had said a

clear unequivocal 'yes' to Ross's offer of the *Gumhuria* file. I tried to catch Dalby's eye, but if it was intended as a hint he was doing nothing to confirm it. Dalby was giving all his attention to landing a waiter, and in so doing succeeded.

'Well, folks, what's it gonna be?' The young muscular army steward rested his hands gently on the table top. 'We have a really nice porter-house on the menu tonight; there's a fresh lobster salad all frozen and flown out from the mainland. OK then, three porter-house steaks it is, one rare, two medium. How you folks gonna start? A Collins, Rob Roy or Mint Julep, or how about one of the Bar Specialities – a "Manhattan Project" or a "Tokwe Twist"?'

'You wouldn't kid me would you?' I asked.

'No, sir,' said the young waiter. 'They are two really fine drinks, and we have another called "Greenback"* and another . . .'

'Enough of these complexities of modern living,' said Dalby. 'We will have a simple gin and vermouth combination called, if my memory serves me well, a martini.'

The waiter clawed his way back into the crowd and smoke. The vibration of a plane coming over the main runway told me the wind had swung round to SSE. One or two of the women army officers had been persuaded to dance, and after a decent interval, some of the civilian girl

* For details see Appendix, p. 333.

secretaries would condescend a slow gyrating movement.

The laughs were louder now, and our waiter used his elbows skilfully in protection of our martinis. Dalby had half-turned in his seat and was watching the room in a casual way of business. The waiter put down the large glasses heavily; the huge green olives rolled like eyes. 'Like t'pay for the drinks, folks?'

I had the wallet open and reached my fingers for the fresh dollar bills. 'One twenty-five.' My fingers touched the hard plastic edge of my security card as I paid him.

I sipped the icy drink. In spite of the air-conditioning the club was getting quite warm. More couples were dancing now and I was idly watching a dark girl in a translucent chiffon gown. She was teaching me things of which Arthur Murray never dreamed. Her partner was several inches shorter than she was. As she leaned forward to listen to something he said I caught sight of Barney Barnes through the crowd.

Skip had let me infer that Barney was still Stateside, and Barney wasn't the sort of man it was possible to miss on a small island. The music had stopped now and the couples were dissolving away. Barney was holding a handbag, while the girl he was with slipped out of a red and gold Thai-silk evening coat. The pink-faced boy took the coat over his arm and showed them both to a table under the vast map mural with the rotund cherubims blowing winds upon golden galleons.

175

'Barney Barnes – Skip Henderson's friend – him I must see.' Jean lifted a beautifully manicured eyebrow at me round the edge of an enamel compact with Tutankhamen's tomb pictured on it in gilt.

Dalby said, although I hadn't once seen him look in that direction, 'The lieutenant in uniform sitting under Australia.'

'I didn't know he was a Negro,' Jean said. 'You do mean the tall Negro with a crew-cut. The one sitting with the Statistics captain?'

Statistics, I thought. There are an awful lot of Stats people on this atoll. I began to wonder if Carswell hadn't had something after all, and whether it didn't all connect up. 'You know her?' I asked Jean.

'She was attached to the Tokyo Embassy last year and went to just about every party there ever was. She was on the verge of marrying somebody mostly.'

'Can I get you a saucer of milk?'

'But it's true and you should tell your friend Barney Barnes if you really are a friend of his,' said Jean.

'Listen Jeannie, Barney has done all right for a number of years and has never needed any help of the sort that I would be able to give, so take your elbow out of his friend's eye.'

'If I wait any longer for this steak,' Dalby joined the conversation.

'Hey there, welcome back to the human race,'

I said. 'I thought we'd left you way back there taking orders from Lt-General Skip Henderson.'

'The next table but one has emptied and filled up twice while we've been sitting here drinking this terrible gin that's probably distilled by some avaricious procurement corporal in one of the battery huts.'

'Stop getting excited,' Jean said. When off duty, she had a knack of reverting to a domineering feminine role in life without being noticeably insubordinate. 'You know there's just nothing you would be doing if we'd finished dining except arguing with the waiter that the brandy isn't what you're used to back at the castle.'

'I'll be dashed if I've ever encountered a more mordant pair.'

'You can't say "dashed" in an Hawaiian shirt,' I said to Dalby.

'Most especially not out of the side of a mouth ninety per cent occupied by a twenty-five-cent black cheroot,' said Jean.

'But since the waiter is having trouble getting the cows to stand still I'll dive across for a word with Barney – about stats.'

'You just sit still where you are. Social life can come to a standstill till I've eaten.' I knew Dalby by now, and I could recognize moods in his voice. He wasn't kidding and he hadn't enjoyed us fooling with him. To make Dalby happy you had to listen to and commiserate with him, just every little thing that marred his day and then make with the feet to rectify things. By Dalby's understanding of life I should be standing in the kitchen now making sure that only the finest fermented wine vinegar went into his salad-dressing. It doesn't take much to make the daily round with one's employer work smoothly. A couple of 'yessirs' when you know that 'not on your life' is the thing to say. A few expressions of doubt about things you've spent your life perfecting. Forgetting to make use of the information that negates his hastily formed but deliciously convenient theories. It doesn't take much but it takes about 98.5 per cent more than I've ever considered giving.

'Be back in a minute,' I said, and edged past a red-faced colonel who was saying to a waiter, 'You just tell your officer that this young lady here says that none of these Camembert cheeses are ripe, she knows what she's talking about. Yes, sir, and just as long as I'm paying the bill around here I just don't intend to have any more arguments . . .'

I didn't look back at Dalby but I imagined that Jean was trying to placate him in some way.

A long bar filled one end of the restaurant. The lighting was low and arranged to shimmer translucently through the bottles of drink that stood back to back with their reflections across the mirror wall. At the far end, the 'Parisian décor' was completed with the largest size in Espresso machines, which stood silent with the message 'No Steam' glowing blue from its navel. Behind the bar, spaces between the bottles were found for wooden slats

with decorative serrated edges that held prefabricated jokes in Saxon lettering. Under one: 'Spit on
the ceiling. Any fool can spit on the floor' stood
a little knot of flyers in uniform. I moved slowly
through them. A young sun-bronzed pilot was
doing a trick on the counter that involved a glass
of water and fifty matches. My guess was that the
pay-off was likely to be the distribution of the
water and matches among his not altogether unsus-
pecting colleagues. I moved a little faster. Barney
was lighting a cigarette for the blonde now. I
walked across the handkerchief-sized dance floor.
The enormous juke-box glowed like a monkey's
bottom, and the opening bars of a cha cha cha
rent the smoke. A fat man in bright Hawaiian shirt
lumbered laughingly towards me, his fists shadow
boxing in time to the music, the perspiration sitting heavily across his face. I negotiated the floor
ducking and weaving. At closer quarters one could
see how much older Barney had got since I last
saw him. His crew-cut was a little frayed on top.

Barney saw me across the floor and gave me
the big-smile treatment. He spoke suddenly and
quickly to the blonde who nodded. I smiled inside
as I thought I detected another little Barney 'If-
anybody-asks-you're-my-assistant-and-we've-been
working-till-late-and-we-are-finishing-the-last-
details-now' sort of conversation.

I was sufficiently English to find it difficult to
say nice things to people I really liked, and I really
liked Barney.

Barney's blonde leaned forward, face close against the table-cloth as she ran a forefinger round the heel of her shoe to ease it on. She was losing a hair grip from the ocean of hair drawn tight against her neck. Barney looked anxiously into my face.

'Pale-face I love,' Barney said.

'Red man, him speak with forked tongue.'

'So what's the good word, kid?' His rich bluey-brown face was lit by a smile. His crisp uniform shirt carried the insignia of a lieutenant of Engineers, and a plastic-faced white card showing two photographs of him and a large pink letter 'Q' hung from the button on the pocket of his shirt. According to this card he was Lieutenant Lee Montgomery, and I could make out the word 'Power' against unit. Barney had come to his feet now and I felt dwarfed by his bulk.

'Just through eating, man.' He fed a dollar bill under the ashtray. 'Must be stepping, just about shot with these early morning, late night routines.'

The waiter was helping the blonde back into her silk coat. Barney fidgeted his way around the table tightening his tie, and rubbing the palms of his hands against his hips.

'I saw an old friend of yours the other day from Canada. We were talking about how much dough we spent in that bar in King Street, Toronto. He was reminding me about that song you always sang when you were plastered.'

'Nat?' I said.

'That's him,' agreed Barney. 'Nat Goodrich. What's that old song you were always singing, how'd the words go now? Shoot, I know. "Be first to climb the mountain and climb it alone".'

I said, 'I sure do, I sure do,' a couple of times, and Barney was rattling on in a cheerful sort of way, 'Maybe we'll do a night out sometime real soon. What were those things you were drinking in that bar next door to the Embassy that time? Remember those vodka benedictine concoctions that you christened E-mc2? Oooh man, but lethal. But can't do the night out, pal, for a little while. I'm shipping out in a day or so. Must go.'

His blonde had been standing listening in a bored sort of way, but now she was getting impatient eyes. I put it down to a hunger. A sudden belt of laughter fanned from the bar. I guessed that one of those transport pilots had collected the glassful of water. It was the only correct guess I made that puzzling day, for about the only thing less likely than me drinking a mixture of benedictine and vodka was me singing. And I'd never been in Toronto with Barney, I knew no one named Nat, and I don't suppose Barney knew anyone named Goodrich.

19

The heat rocketed back from the burning sand underfoot. The red painted framework of girders that made the shot tower blistered the careless hand. Wriggling away from the legs of the tower, black smooth cables and corrugated pipelines rested along each other like a Chinese apothecary's box of snakes. Fifty yards away a twenty-foot-high electric fence, circumscribing the tower, was manned by white-helmeted police with panting Alsatian dogs on short leashes. A white amphibious jeep was parked near the only gate, its awning modified to permit the traverse of a half-inch-calibre machine-gun. The driver sat with hands clasped high on the steering-column, his chin resting on the back of his thumb. His helmet liner was painted in lateral black and yellow two-inch stripes to show he had a 'Q' permit. He looked like Danny Kaye.

Half a mile away across the flat sand I could see small shimmering black figures adjusting the automatic cameras which at this range could only be preserved by a freak of failure. With a well-oiled sound a three-man lift dropped down the tower with the accuracy of a guillotine blade and bobbed gently on its spring cushion. My guide was a small lizard-like civilian with hard, horny hands and face, and the lightest blue eyes I ever saw. His white shirt had small darns such as only a loving wife can do, and only a tight salary bracket make necessary. Across the back of one hand was a faded tattoo, an anchor design from which a name had been erased. The plain gold signet-ring caught the sun through his copious white hair.

'I've got a meter here with mercury in it.' I tapped the old leather brief-case. 'It had better not go near the cold box.' I looked up to where the pipes got thicker and more numerous two or three platforms up. I pointed vaguely. 'The refrigeration chamber might react.' I looked up again, and he looked at my badge and read the words, 'Vickers Armstrong Engineering'. He nodded without much emotion.

'Don't let anybody touch it.' He nodded again as I opened the wire gate of the lift and stepped in. I pulled the little handle and we stood motion-less, looking at each other as the motor whirled away its inertia. 'Down in a minute,' I said, rather than just stand there dumbly. He nodded his white head slowly and deliberately, as one would to a sub-intelligent child or foreigner, and the lift surged upward. The red girders cut the white hot sand into Mondrian-like shapes moving before me more quickly as the lift gained speed. The wire roof divided the dark-blue sky into a hundred rectangles as the oily steel lift cable passed me on its journey downward. No sooner did the platforms permit me to peek over them than they fell away beneath my feet. For 200 feet I rocketed into the air, the circle of fencing falling around my feet like a spent hula hoop. Through the crack in the floorboard I watched the white police jeep lazily trot round the tower, on the sand that the explosion would transform into glass.

Suddenly the motor cut out and there I hung bouncing in space like a budgerigar in a sprung cage. I slid the gate aside and stepped out on to the top platform. I could see right across the island. To the south the sharp runways of Lay Field contrasted strangely with the irregular patterns of nature all around. A B52 was taking off from the field. Its heavy fuel for the long transpacific journey challenging it to defy gravity. Other smaller, rockier islands played bob-apple in the ocean waves. Beneath my feet the complexities of machinery reached their most frenetic maze. I was standing atop the thing that all this was about, this atoll, this multi-million-dollar city, this apogee of twentieth-century achievement, this focus point of hemispherical animosity, this reason why a Leeds super-market operator can't afford a third car, and a farmer in Szechwan a third bowl of rice.

Because it was all these things the shot tower was generally called 'the mountain', and because it was called that I wasn't surprised to find Barney waiting at the summit.

Barney was dressed in white, super-lightweight coveralls. On his arm were the stripes of a master-sergeant, in his hand a .32 pistol with silencer. It just happened to be pointing at me.

'I'd just better be right about you, pale-face,' he said.

'You'd just better had, Sambo. Now ease down the drama and tell me what's on your mind.'

'You are.'

'You're nice.'

'Don't fool, because I'm sticking my neck right out, but I can rack it in, but very fast. We knew each other well once, but people change and I just need to look, to see. Have you changed?'

'Probably I have.'

There was a long silence. I didn't know what Barney was talking about, or what Barney was getting at. I was almost thinking out loud when I said, 'One morning you wake up and find *all* your life-long friends changed. They had turned into the sort of people you mutually despised not so long ago. Then you start worrying about yourself.'

'Yeah,' said Barney. 'And they've stopped being

interested in doing anything about those same jerks.'

'I'm interested.'

'That's 'cos you don't know when you're licked.'

'Maybe it is. But I don't lure people into the barrel of a police special to prove it.' He didn't smile. Maybe I hadn't made a joke.

He said, 'So *I've* changed, so I'm a nut. Listen, white man, do you know the hottest piece of merchandise on this island . . .'

'Aren't I standing on it?' I said.

'Not unless you're standing on your own neck; the hottest thing on this island is you. You're bugged, you're strapped down, you're pickled. "The friends"* have the word that you've walked away. Have you walked away, just a little way? Did you put a down payment on a dacha with some old stuff you knew they had anyway? Just tell me.'

'Just tell you?' I said. 'Just tell you? So the friends fling me half-way around the world for you to finger me on a bomb platform. But before that happens I just tell you? Are you crazy?'

'Am I crazy? Are you crazy? One of us probably is but there's a wild little chance that we are both smarter than anyone else around here.' Barney's hot glistening face was three inches from mine. And time stopped in a frozen minute of suspended silence. My mind photographed a wave in

* MI5.

186

mid splash; Danny Kaye far below me, helmet off, wiping his brow on a white handkerchief. 'I'll be DED if anyone knows I've even spoken to you. Why do you think that they have that creep fixed on Skip as firmly as a scar, and that blonde cow welded to me? I'm greasing the skids to the morgue just coming within loudhailer distance of you.'

'So why aren't you buying a subscription for my funeral?' I asked.

'I don't know why. I suppose because after a little while in this business you start getting egoistic about judging character.'

'Thanks.' It seemed a pretty lame thing to say. We stood looking at each other and Barney went across to the lift and jammed a glove into the handle so that it couldn't be controlled from the ground. Barney spoke quietly – 'I'm the only character around here who'd give you half a whirl, the only one.' He paused. 'Even that girl is half-way convinced.' He flapped a hand. 'Never mind how I know; I know. But on the other hand I've seen a few coloured guys given the heave-ho. I'm difficult to convince when it comes to concerted action against a guy who maybe doesn't know what it is tiptoeing up behind him. Afterwards it tends to be too late to find out if anyone made a mistake.'

I started to speak. I don't know whether I was going to argue, thank him or apologize, but he waved his heavy pink palm across his chest.

'Don't thank me. Skip didn't have the opportunity I had. It's my sergeant you should be

187

thanking. He's out there on one of those generator trucks making like he's me. We're just relying
on the fact that most tall niggers look alike to
pale-faces.' Barney opened his mouth in a symbol
of a grin; there was no mirth in it whatsoever.
'Anything he gets will *really* be for nothing.'

'Wait a minute – let me fasten on to all this,' I
said.

'You haven't got the time, fella. Just forget you
ever saw me and light out, especially both those
things.'

My mind was dizzy trying to think. Maybe, I
kept thinking, Barney had slid off his trolley. But
I knew Barney was right. It made sense from too
many puzzling things to be anything but true.

'We daren't be seen here, man. I must bend the
shoes!'

'Will you let me have the gun, Barney?'

'The heater, man. You ain't going to shoot your
way out of this installation. If you want to do
yourself a favour, start talking, and talk your way
on to a fast plane OUT.'

'The gun.'

'Okay. Be a nut.' Barney threw me the gun and
a small metal reel all prepared for me. I raised the
leg of my trousers and using the reel of sticking-
plaster, stuck the gun to the outside of my right
leg. When I covered it again, Barney passed me a
dark-blue thin canvas belt. It was about five inches
deep and similar to the ones used by gold smug-
glers. I undid my trousers and strapped the heavy,

188

sweaty belt, full of automatic clips, under my shirt. Barney having retrieved his glove, climbed out over the rim of the platform. He swung down the narrow ladder and paused as his neck came level with my feet. I guess he was wondering whether I might not kick him into oblivion. He looked at the toe of my shoe reflectively, and hammered his fist softly against it in a gesture of farewell. As he looked up, I once more found my mind committing the details to memory. I remember his wide handsome face like we all remember the rivets on our dentist's spectacles.

'And don't go sobbing to your new boss, pale-face.'

'Dalby's convinced, too, huh?' I paraded all Dalby's words and attitudes over the last few days through my mind.

'Him speak with *knife*-and-forked tongue, man.'

I put the sole of my shoe on Barney's knitted hair. 'Get out of here, you bum,' I said.

'You could do yourself just that favour,' Barney said. 'Try for vertically.'

The journey down seemed faster than the journey up. The white-haired little guy had put my case out of the sun. I picked it up and we walked back towards the gate. A truck had stopped at the gate and the driver was getting out so that a policeman could drive it up to the tower. In the jeep Danny Kaye was talking to the gunner earnestly. I suppose they were discussing whether to make anti-clockwise the next time round the

189

tower. The white-haired one and me flipped them our security cards but they didn't seem to know that the hottest piece of merchandise on the island was padding out of their vicinity. We had a new Chev parked outside the gate. We got in to drive back to the mess.

'Meters don't have mercury in,' said the old man; he had a hoarse voice like Fred Allen.

I didn't want to argue, I was too hungry. Anyway, a hydrogen bomb tower doesn't have a refrigeration chamber, so who cared.

So Jean was 'half-way convinced'. I remembered her the night previous. Her hair shining and her eyes full of consolation for Barney's obvious snub. I remembered the way she'd said, 'He wanted you to know he was doing it under orders, that's why he said he'd eaten. He knew you wouldn't believe it. If he's anything like the cool character you've been talking about he'd certainly be able to think up an excuse for leaving a restaurant.' I wanted to believe that. I remember Jean damping Dalby down when she could have made a better score by agreeing with him. On the other hand perhaps they had a deal about me already, and she cooled him off when I was around to soften me up. I remembered the smell of her hair when we danced, and the soft warmth of her body as we danced. And pretending to whisper things as we danced to annoy Dalby. I remembered her concern about Skip and about Barney. I remembered her red finger-nails on the back of my hand

190

as she asked if I couldn't understand their position and what had they said. And I could remember not telling her a damned thing.

The Officers' Mess was a large prefabricated building near the Administration Compound. The front was decorated with small stunted flowers in the shape of a badge of the unit that built it. 'You are now getting indigestion through the courtesy of the Army Catering Corps.' A blast of barbecue-chicken-hot-air hit me as I went in.

Then all was cool and calm. The long white crispy tables, the jugs of ice-water making noises like the treble end of a xylophone. The stainless steel, the low murmur of serious masculine conversation, the purr of air-conditioning units. This was reality, this was the world – not the scene through the window; that was a fable.

The vichyssoise was rich with fresh cream, through which the fugitive flavour of leek came mellow and earthy; it was cold and not too thick. The steak was tender and sanguine, dark with the charred carbon of crusted juices, and served with asparagus tips and *pommes allumettes*. The coffee came along with strawberry short-cake. I ate it all, drank the weak coffee, then settled back with a Gauloise Blue. Poisoning seemed an unlikely method of dealing with my defection.

20

[*Aquarius (Jan 20–Feb 19) Actions by friends may seem strange but remember that your moodiness may influence them.*]

The Officers' Mess was a low building, prefabricated as everything on Tokwe was, and single-storeyed. I walked out through the restaurant, through the simple starched shirts, the uniformly short haircuts. Snatches of German and small bite-sized pieces of Hungarian ran like strands of a web across the clipped Harvard speech and the drawn-out vowels of men who had been at Oak Ridge for so long that it had become their permanent home. I moved slowly listening with my finger-tips. No eye followed me as I entered the lounge where gaunt tubular frames had large floral-patterned plastic padding impaled upon them in relentless discomfort. Near the window I saw Jean; the group of aircrew I had noticed at the bar the previous evening were flying close formation on her. I knew they were SAC lead crews. The lead crews were the ones with the higher scores at bombing and navigation. They are raised a rank when they become lead crews, and so these boys were majors and lieutenant-colonels. One of the biannual exams they had, involved the committing to memory of one complete enemy target briefing. If they fail the exam they revert to their old rank. This had been a complicated session in 1944, but now, flying these eight-engine B52s at 600 mph after a thirty-minute check over the intercom before take-off, it was cosmic! Finding the tanker aircraft whose crew, one hoped, was similarly skilled in navigation; refuelling in flight while moving at stalling speed behind a tanker only three feet away, and then moving on a town they had never seen except in photographs; to drop a thermo-nuclear bomb, was a test of mathematical skill, dexterity, memory, and of confidence in the judgement of their leaders unparalleled since Constantine's Edict saw the last Christian share a double bill with the lions. Soviet air space was often penetrated at a time when an explosion or a launching was expected. These SAC people were going to observe this one from the air as a comparison. To know which Soviet ground targets these three-man crews had committed to memory would be a very valuable 'intelligence sequence'. The chances of Jean unloading such an item from them was remote, but I sat down a few chairs away and busied myself with some old unchecked expense accounts and indents that Alice had slipped into my case at the last moment without my noticing. Jean was doing a thing that men agents have to learn, but most women do naturally. She stood back and let the conversation move between the others, listening or guiding as needed. I hope she didn't do that funny stare she tended to do when concentrating, because these charácters wouldn't miss it. They were tumbling over just to talk in front of her.

'Yes, sir,' a balding man of about thirty-eight was saying; his eyes were too small but his jaw strong and tanned.

'But for me, New York is a city. I like to travel, I really do, but you just can't beat little ole New York, boy!'

'New York, I like, but it's a little like Chi, I'd say. New Orleans – there is a city, there is a city!'

'Then you've never been to Paris, France.'

'Parley Fransays. I lived six months in Paris. Now there's the last country on earth where women are subordinated to men.'

'And that goes for India. Do you know, in Afghanistan a camel costs more than a wife? This old guy was sitting riding on his camel. I'd seen him around, I knew he spoke a little English. I pulled up by him. I had a little red English MGA at the time, went like a bird. "Why aren't you giving your wife a lift, Chas?" I said. (We all called him Chas.) "No, there are minefields here near the aerodrome," he said. "You let her walk then?" So he said, "Yes, it's a very valuable camel." Can you beat that? He said, "It's a very valuable camel."'

A tall fair-haired major diluted his drink with a splash of ice-water. 'Bel Ami who was French, and knew all about women . . .'

'You know he's using the worst mix in the world?' Jean opened her eyes an eighth of an inch.

'Alaska, that's the biggest state. Ask any Texan,' said the balding one, and laughed.

'And I'll tell you the Texan answer – "Oil".'

The tall major who knew Bel Ami, lifted his glass and contradicted, 'You see this drink? If you were gonna measure the volume of this drink do you take account of the ice?' He paused. 'You don't. And that's how it is with Alaska. It's all ice.'

The chuckling was interrupted by the lounge door opening; a plump major looked quizzically around the room, dark glasses bisecting his large globe-like face. Beside him a neatly assembled girl army secretary in khaki shirt and slacks, both a carefully chosen size or so too small, shifted uneasily before the clear, unequivocally carnal gaze from so many efficient male eyes. Hoping to break an atmosphere as thick as cooling fudge, the newcomer asked if anyone had seen his navigator. No one answered, and here and there an unkind grin clearly stated the alienation that his social success had wrought. He turned awkwardly in the doorway and someone said affably, 'Give my love to your wife and children.'

The balding one took advantage of the time pause. He went on going on. 'My pappy used to say, "Drink Scotch by itself; with rye mix a little water, bourbon, mix it with something strong, something really strong."' He laughed loudly. 'Something really strong,' he said again.

'I like Germany. I like to eat there. I like to drink there. I like German girls.'

'I was living in Scandinavia.'

'It's not the same. It's different in Scandinavia.'

'I was at school in a big town in northern Scandinavia,' said Jean, jumping in agilely as an agent must, and speaking the truth as an agent should.

'Narvik,' said the balding one. 'I know it very well. I knew every bar in Narvik this time last year. Right?' he asked Jean.

She nodded.

'How many's that? Three?' said the man who knew Bel Ami.

I had completed most of the indents for the typewriter ribbons, recording tape and assorted junk of every day by the time the airmen had 'holycowed' and 'go-go-goed', 'see you latered', 'izz at the timed' out of the lounge. She came up behind me and touched the top of my head. I found the unexpected intimacy of her physical contact as shocking as if she'd undressed in public. As she moved into view and sat down opposite me I reappraised her attitude. She was anxious to let me know, to reassure.

The sheer effectiveness of her reassurance precluded my trusting it. Perhaps she was my Dolobowski. She offered me one of those menthol cigarettes that taste like paint remover. I declined.

She said, 'SAC lead crews flying B52s working out of Bodo, Norway and the new field near Herat.' She took her time to light it with a small silver cigarette lighter. 'I'd say committed targets; those launching sites West South West of Lake Balkach and the underwater nuclear submarine harbours in eastern Novaya Zemlya that Bobby did the work on. You probably already saw the modified bombbays on two of the planes.'

I nodded.

'Two of the crews have ex-Navy bombardiers; probably a delay device operating by water pressure.' She tilted her chin as high as possible and exhaled a stream of smoke vertically at the ceiling in an unusually theatrical way. From somewhere she had obtained a WAC officer's summer dress, and like Dalby she had this quality of looking right in whatever she wore. She waited for praise as a small child does; posturing and preparing declaimers of skill or virtue. The days of Pacific sunshine had made her face a deep shade of gold, and her lips were light against the dark skin. She sat there studying the evenness of her finger-nail polish for a long time, and then without looking up said, 'You went to Guildford?'

I nodded without moving my head.

'In the first week when it's all physical exercises

and IQ tests and you mostly sit around waiting to be interviewed and talked out of staying on for a second week, there's one lecture about cell construction and cut outs?'

I knew that she knew that this isn't the sort of thing anyone ever talks about. I hoped that the lounge wasn't bugged. I didn't stop her.

'Well, Alice is my only official contact, through her you were my permanent contact. As far as I'm concerned . . .' she paused. 'Since then I have used no other as the man in the Pears soap advertisement said.'

I sat saying nothing.

'The complexities of my job are greater than they were in Macao. Greater than I suspected they could be,' Jean said very quietly. 'I didn't see myself doing that.' She moved her head towards where she'd been sitting. 'But I'll go along with it OK. But there has to be a limit as far as personalities are concerned. I am a woman. I can't switch allegiances easily, and I am biologically incapable of answering to a group.'

'You may be making a big mistake,' I said, more in order to gain time than because it meant anything.

'I don't think so, and I'll show you why,' she said, 'if you've an hour or so to spare.'

I had. I followed her out and across to the car park. She climbed behind the wheel of a Ford convertible, the metal and leather hot enough to produce a sickly smell. Attached to the sunshield on

198

the driver's side was a grey painted metal box. One face of it was perforated; it was a little larger than an English packet of twenty. This was a monitoring radio sending conversation to a receiver up to three miles away, and by means of a compass device sending a signal to show the direction and travel of the vehicle. It was a compulsory fitting to all cars on Tokwe. It was attached by means of two magnets, and I pulled it off the metal of the sunshield and buried it deep in a big box of Kleenex in the rear seat of a pink Chevrolet parked alongside. I hoped no one would bother to tune us in. If they did without a visual check we'd be just another silent vehicle in a car park outside the Mess.

The tyres made an ugly noise on the gravel as Jean let in the clutch and swung the power steering into a fierce lock. Neither of us spoke until a mile down the road we stopped to fold back the hood. I took a close look around the windscreen and door tops.

'I think we are probably clean now but let's be careful just the same – you were smart to take the convertible,' I told her.

'It cost me a four-ounce bottle of Arpège perfume to find out not to pet in any other sort of vehicle.'

'Put it on expenses,' I said.

For a mile or so the road was first-rate, and except for a couple of police jeeps, quite clear. Jean moved the accelerator firmly down and I heard the faint snickering noises from the gear-box as the ratios automatically changed until the road wavered under us like a heat haze, and the roar of the wind dragging across the spotlight and aerial produced an unbearable battering on the eardrums. Small flying creatures hit the wind-screen and burst in ugly blotches. Jean, her head tilted back, held the wheel in a confident, loose hold, unusual in women drivers. I watched the coast flash by until we began to lose speed. I felt her foot lift from the accelerator. She'd judged the distance nicely and scarcely used the brakes. Instead of following the road where it curved left inland, to the Administration Centre, we turned off the road to the right. The wide over-sprung car lurched into the soft edges of the road and its big blue nose lifted as the tyres engaged the soil of a rough pathway. Now the going was much slower and it took nearly an hour to reach the cluster of undergrowth to which we had seen the track leading from the hard road. Jean pulled us well in under the low vegetation, and cut the motor. We had left the desiccated sectors upon which both the Administration Centre, the Mess and Living Quarters were built. This lee side of the island, shielded from the prevailing wind, was cloaked in luxuriant vegetation and punctuated by razor-sharp layers of volcanic rock. Here and there large cone-shaped mustard-yellow flowers were beginning to close their fleshy petals.

The sun was low towards the west by now, and

the spiky leaves of the palms sliced the heavy blue sky. Jean took a rubber-covered torch out of the glove compartment and we continued along the same pathway on foot. Through the undergrowth we passed the cheap-wristwatch sounds of a thousand insects kicking the heavy air.

'I don't want to pry or appear paranoiac,' I said, 'but what's the deal?' She took her time about answering and I supposed that she had as many doubts and puzzlements as any of us at that time.

'Last night I was up here with Dalby. He took me along so that if anyone found us off the road it would just look like a petting party. I'm returning on my own account. You're along for the ride. OK?'

I said 'OK.' What else could I say? We went on in silence.

Then she said, 'Last night I was left in the car. Now I want to see the part I missed.'

I helped her over a rusting coil of barbed wire. We went out of sight of the road, and unless anyone looked very closely, the car was well hidden, too. Over to the right, the shore line, away from the new road, had been left littered with World War II debris. Golden-brown rust patterns grew over the broken landing craft. One on the far side gaped with rectangular holes, as though someone had attempted to salvage the metal with a cutter, but had found the market price out of proportion to the work. The one nearest me, a Tank Landing Craft, was charred at the front. The heat had bent the steel doors like a tin toy under a child's foot. Below the water-line rich wet greenery busied itself in the lapping, clear movement of the water. The land was at its most uneven here and had clearly provided opportunities for a tenacious defensive. So well had the Japanese engineers merged their defence works into the terrain that I wasn't aware of the enormous Japanese blockhouse until I saw Jean standing in its doorway. It was nearly twenty-five feet high and built of tree trunks with steel rail supports here and there. The weather had eaten at the poor-quality cement, and the vegetation had run riot. The entrance was low even for a Japanese, and waist-high scarlet flowers followed the great burnt scars along the timbers as though the plant gained a special nutriment from the carbonized wood.

Jean's rubber-soled shoes left waffles in the sand, and where the ground was damper I noticed Dalby's. His were deeper, especially at the heel.

'Was it heavy –' I said.

'The box he carried? Yes, it looked heavy. How did you know?'

'I guessed he didn't drop by for the view, and something kept him too busy to notice you behind him.'

She stood aside as I climbed up the partly blocked entrance. 'He told me to wait by the car, but I was curious. I came after him as far as the entanglement.' Her voice changed and echoed mid sentence as we moved into the fort. It was a well-made one. The island had been one of the well-prepared outer-perimeter island bases bypassed until the latter days of the war. Through the entrance a narrow passage led down a gentle slope into a pitch-dark little room about twelve feet square. The air was cold and moist. We stood there in silence hearing the steady crunch and whoosh of breakers on the shore, and the constant rasping of insects. I'd taken off my dark glasses and slowly my range of vision increased.

The greater part of the room was taken up by olive-coloured metal boxes, upon which the faint English words like 'Factory' and some numbers could be read. In the far corner bars of sunlight revealed broken wooden boxes, large metal cartridge clips and some rotting leather straps. On a level with the top of my head a platform extended the width of the blockhouse, and provided slots for the machine-gunners and riflemen. Jean's torch made yellow ovals as it splashed over the emplacement walls, and held in one spot almost over the entrance door. She'd seen Dalby's torch shine through that particular port. I moved the green metal boxes to make a step. The paint on the underside where they had been packed together was fresh with stencilled lettering: '.5 Machine-Gun. US Army. 80770/GH/CIN/1942'. I moved a second box to put on the first, and fifteen inches of brightly coloured lizard flashed away under my feet. I climbed up on the platform and edged slowly along the crumbling earth ledge. Close to, the sand was almost black, and stank of death and the things that lived on it.

There was not room to stand upright, and I went slowly on my hands and knees. The bright daylight burned my eyes through the narrow slot, and I could see a small traverse of beach. The largest of the grey landing craft was directly in line with me, and from this angle I was able to see a burnt and battered tank jammed into the open doors like a squashed orange in the mouth of a barbecued sucking-pig. A red and yellow butterfly entered the white chalky bars of light from the aperture. Slowly I moved towards the corner position. It was darker and damper there. Jean threw the torch to me without switching it off. Its beam described a curious parabola. I used it to probe the thick roof timbering above me. Part of the ceiling had given way when the flame-thrower had poured its jet of flaming petrol into the firing position. The timber supports were charred, and under my hands, only the metal parts of a heavy bolted-down machine-gun remained. I could see nothing that looked recently disturbed. I moved the light a little to the left. There was a wooden crate with writing on it. It said, 'Harry Jacobson, 1944, 24 DEC. OAKLAND. CALIF. USA.' and was empty. Jean said why didn't I try the box underneath. I'm glad I did. It was a new cardboard box and carried the words 'General foods. One gross 1 lb packets Frozen Cranberries'. Under that was printed a small certificate of purity, and a long serial number. Inside was a brand new short pattern seven-inch cathode ray tube, about a dozen transistors, a white envelope and a yellow duster containing a long-barrelled machine-pistol shiny with fresh oil. There were no cranberries. I opened the envelope, and inside was a small slip of paper about 2 in by 6 in. On it were written about fifty words. There was a VLF (very low frequency) radio wave-length, and a compass bearing and some mathematical symbols that were a bit too post-graduate for me. I held it up for Jean to read. She looked up and said, 'Can you read Russian?'

I shook my head.

'It's something about . . .'

I interrupted her. 'That's OK,' I said. 'Even I know the Russian script for "Neutron Bomb".'

'What are you going to do with it?' she asked.

I took the paper, still carefully holding it by the edge and dropped it back into the cranberry box. The envelope I burned, and ground up the ash under my heel. 'Let's go,' I said.

We scrambled down the steep approach to the beach. The sun was a two-dimensional magenta disc, and the sunset lay in horizontal stripes like finger-nails and torn golden lacerations across the ashen face of the evening. I wanted to be away from something – I don't know from what. So we walked along the water-line, stepping around crates full of death, Coca-Cola and Band-Aids.

'Why would anyone,' Jean didn't like to say Dalby, 'take a cathode ray tube up there?'

205

'He didn't want anyone to know that he can't bear to miss "Wagon Train".'

Jean didn't even contract her lip muscles.

'I don't want to pry,' I said, 'but I'd find this whole thing more simple if you'd tell me what he said about me.'

'That's easy – he said that one of the departments of the "friends" is sure you are working for the KGB.* They told the CIA direct and everyone is pretty steamed up. Dalby said he wasn't sure one way or the other but that the CIA are keen to believe it since you killed a couple of their Navy people a long while ago.'

'Dalby said it's not him that laid the complaint?' I asked.

'No – he said that one department gives you a higher clearance than he has at present – him working away from the office caused that of course – he didn't seem very happy about that, by the way.'

She paused, and said apologetically, 'Did you kill those men?'

'Yes,' I said a little viciously, 'I killed them. That brought my total up to three, unless you count the war. If you count the war . . .'

'You don't have to explain,' Jean said.

'Look, it was a mistake. There's nothing anyone could do. Just a mistake. What do they want me to do? Write to Jackie Kennedy and say I didn't mean it?'

---

* The Soviet spy apparatus: 'Committee on State Security'.

Jean said, 'He seemed to think they'd wait to see if you made a contact before doing anything. He wondered if Carswell was working with you, and radioed a code message to have Carswell and Murray isolated.'

'He's too late,' I said. 'They bludgeoned me into giving them a leave of absence just before we left.'

'That will probably convince Dalby,' Jean said. She looked great with the sun behind her and I wished I had more of my frontal lobes to spare to think about it.

'That Carswell's my contact?' I mused. 'Maybe. But I'd say he's more likely to suspect you.'

'*I'm* not your contact.' She almost seemed not sure.

'I know that, dope. If I was really working for the KGB I'd be smarter than to be suspected, and I'd know who my contact was before I reached an island like this one, or there'd be no way for me to cross-check on you. But since I'm not working for that six-storey building in Dzerzhinsky Street, there isn't a contact, so you're not one.' Jean splashed a foot deliberately into the water and smiled a childlike smile. The sun was behind her head like the open door of a Scunthorpe steel furnace. A light breeze coming off the ocean had her dress clinging like cheap perfume. I dragged my mind back to earth. She said, 'It seems I didn't listen as closely as you did at Guildford.'

A tank track lay half out of the water like a

giant caterpillar, and the waves spurted and splashed through the intricacies of the interwoven castings. Beyond us, B61, the tank with one track missing, lay head down in the glistening foam. The sea, to which it had returned in a great involuntary semicircle, drummed and slapped at the great metal hull in restless derision. Jean stopped and turned back to me; across her gold face a strand of black hair hung like a crack in a Sung vase. I must concentrate.

'Suppose you don't work for the KGB but whoever thinks you do, wants to do something to stop it, what will they do?'

'It's something no one in our position ever dares think about,' I said.

'But suppose it happens. Then they have to think about it.'

'OK,' I said, 'then they think about it.'

Jean's voice was husky, a bit edgy and rasplike. I realized she'd spent a lot of night time wondering what to do about me, and at least I owed her enough not to kid her around.

I said, 'They don't give them free legal aid at the Old Bailey, and let them sell their memoirs to the Sundays if that's what you mean.'

'No, that's what I thought,' she said. 'It's only multiple murderers who are allowed to do that.' She paused. 'So what does happen?'

'I don't know,' I said. 'It's never happened to me before. I suppose it's "Slip your feet into this bag of wet cement, the boat's just leaving."'

The breakers bombarded the reef in thundering crashes that shook the sand beneath our feet.

'It's getting chilly,' she said. 'Let's go back to the car.'

21

[Aquarius (Jan 20–Feb 19) You may meet delays in private plans, but be circumspect. Your well-meaning efforts may well be misunderstood.]

The next two days were nerve racking. Life on the atoll busied itself into a frenetic but organized scramble as the day for the explosion neared. As far as I could tell, my role as observer was uninterrupted, and my entrée to the dreariest possible conferences unfortunately unimpeded. Jean and I had few opportunities for more than a word or so without the risk of being overheard or recorded. Our decision to appear rather distant meant a chance of remaining unimplicated for her – but a feeling of sharpened desire in me that no man should feel for his secretary if he wants to stay in a position to fire her. I saw her waiting for signatures or documents in the long grey fibreboard corridors. While standing still, her smooth body would move – slowly and imperceptibly – under

210

the thin summer uniform fabric, and I would think of the small circular gold ear-ring of hers that I had found in my bed-clothes on Wednesday morning.

More times than I care to provide excuses for, I edged past her in narrow corridors and doorways. Electricity passing between us assuaged the deep aloneness I felt. My desire wasn't a burgeoning pent-up explosive fullness, but a gentle vacant need. Fear brings an edge to physical desire sharper than a Toledo blade, and a pitch more plaintive than a Dolmetsch flute.

I'd spent most of the two days working closely with Dalby. It was a pleasure. The difference between Dalby and the other people from the Intelligence units with his background was his readiness to use information from his inferiors – both socially and militarily speaking. He was prepared to let the technicians conclude opinions from their data, where others would try to understand the techniques in order to jealously guard the privilege of deciding anything at all.

Jean and I had discovered the box in the blockhouse on Tuesday. On Thursday the General Commanding – General Y. O. Guerite, had invited all commissioned men and available girls to a party in his house.

The General's house backed on to one of the coves on the rocky side of the island. The sun made the tree trunks a pink that stampeded the gastric juices. Once more the sunset was a layer cake of mauve and gold. The insects had come out to do their daily battle with the resources of the American chemical industries, and through the trees an obliging Engineers Corps had remembered to provide lines of winking fairy lights. Large martinis clinked with ice and glowed with lemon and cherries. Small pasty-faced waiters walked heavily on their flat, perpetually aching feet, and looked ill at ease out of doors. Here and there well-built clean-cut figures, tanned and alert, moved briskly to distribute trays of drinks, and tried to look like the pasty-faced aching waiters whose white jackets they shared.

Three army musicians moved coolly and mathematically within the modal range of 'There's a small Hotel' and linking modulated inversions walked around the middle eight with creditable synchronization. Here and there a laugh walked up the foothills of noise.

Beyond the lights at the far end of the General's little garden, Dalby was sitting perched uncomfortably on a rock edge. Two or three feet below him the water moved quietly. Out at sea a grey destroyer sat at anchor, a trace of smoke demonstrating its ever-ready head of steam. On its sides, a huge white 'R' told me it was one of the ships used to measure force and radiation underwater by means of vast wire nets to which measuring equipment was attached. Upon a launch alongside, shiny black rubber-garbed frogmen climbed, explained, ordered, carried and descended, as they checked the net fittings on the hull.

Dalby made circular motions with his glass of martini, swirling it into a thin layer of clear centrifugal controlled violence. He sipped a little of the undulating alcoholic surface and rubbed the glass edge on his lower lip.

'There's no way of contracting out,' he was saying.

I couldn't help connecting his remark with myself, but he went on, 'To do any sort of bargain with them is quite out of the question, merely because there is no guarantee that their word will be kept. The minute war becomes the better way to expound Communism, war will be begun by Communists. And make no mistake, they won't be using kids' stuff like this bomb. It will be area saturation with suitable nerve gases.'

He looked across the imported and carefully laid out grass turf now crowded with summer-uniformed men and women. Between me and the big long tables of food a plump girl in white held the arms of two Marine Corps lieutenants, and all three heads bowed as her white pointed shoes nimbly followed the triple rhythms and superimposed discords of a cha cha cha.

'Don't make any mistake, Jimmy,' Dalby was speaking directly to a staff-brigadier. 'Where your military system has the direct support of commerce and industry, you are absolute world beaters. This whole atoll is an unrivalled feat: but it's a feat of logistics and organization that you've had a lot of practice in. There is not much difference between creating, at a speed fast approaching the Biblical record, a Coca-Cola plant with a shooting gallery for employee recreation, and creating a shooting plant with a Coca-Cola gallery for recreation.'

'So does it matter, Dalby?' The Brigadier, a big-boned athlete of sixty or more, hair grey and one eighth of an inch long, spectacles with their fine gold frames glinting as the reflections of a hundred fairy lights ran across his eyes. 'Who cares where the credit lies. If we can make the biggest damndest greatest bang no one is going to give a damn about details. They're just going to stay well clear of Uncle Sam.' Finding something lacking in the audience reaction, he hastily added, 'And well clear of NATO too. The whole free world in fact.'

'I don't think that's what Dalby means,' I said. I was always explaining to people what other people meant. 'He grants you the ability but is unsure if you will use it correctly.'

'You're going to give me the old "Europe: home of diplomacy" stuff, eh boy?' The Brigadier turned his huge grey head to face me. 'I thought Khrushchev tactics had brought you guys up to date on that stuff.'

'No, merely that Europeans have a firm and fearful knowledge of what happens when diplomats fail,' I told him.

'Diplomats and surgeons never fail,' said Dalby.

'They have too strong a union ever to have to admit it.'

I went on, 'Americans are not noted for assuming failure to be possible before starting something.'

'Oh heck, relationships between any rival business outfits are the same as between nations.'

'I think that was true at one time, but now the destructive capabilities are such that, to extend your analogy, we must think in terms of cartels. Rivals must unite to live and let live.'

'You Europeans always think in terms of cartels. That's one of your worst failings. An American guy figures out how to make a ballpoint pen, he figures on selling them at a nickel a throw. In Europe when you first had speed-balls I saw them on sale nudging two English pounds! The difference is: the English guy makes three and a half *thousand* per cent profit, and his competitors steal his ideas, but the American with a two per cent profit sells so many no one can catch up – he winds up a millionaire.'

A tall, very thin girl with large teeth and a streak of silver hair across the crown of her head came up behind the Brigadier and touched her elegantly manicured and varnished nails to his mouth. In front of the musicians, a wooden dance floor as big as a gramophone record was as crowded as a magnet dipped in iron filings and only half as comfortable. The Brigadier was led off in that direction. Dalby and I stood submerged in the sea sounds, the wind in the trees sound, the chatter and ice and 'Lady Be Good' and hand-hitting-shoulder sounds, passing police jeep and 'Why don't we drive out there while it's a lovely moon,' and pebble in the sea sounds, glassful down uniform, and 'if he's a very close friend of yours' and flattened sevenths and 'you do that up this very minute' sounds, and Dalby said, 'Americans are funny.' Getting no response from me he went on, 'Americans are much too brutal while they are trying to make money, and much too sloppily sentimental and even gullible after they make it. Before: they think the world is crooked. After: they think it quaint.'

'Which category does your Brigadier friend come into?' I asked.

'Oh neither,' said Dalby, and little decisions about saying more filtered through his eyes. 'He had one of the best brains I have ever come across. He owned a small publishers in Munich between the wars and then after the war, was in and out of all kinds of things. Three times, so the stories go, he's had a million dollars, and twice he's had only the battered old Riley car he runs around in, and a suit. A couple of months ago he was heading into the ground very quickly, when the army conscripted him into this project! An extraordinary fellow isn't he?'

I could see the Brigadier now: his dark-green tie, tucked neatly into the opening of his light-buff shirt, a slab of ribbons as large as a half-pound of chocolate, and his big beat-up face with pockets of light and shadow running across it as he performed the slow motion 'running on the spot' movements of the dance.

'Wanted to borrow you for a year,' Dalby said. We both continued to look at the dance floor.

'Did he get me?'

'Not unless you particularly want to go. I said you'd prefer to stay with Charlotte.'

'Let me know if I change my mind,' I said, and Dalby gave me the slanted focus.

'Don't let the last few days put a scare into you,' Dalby said. The plump little girl in white was still demonstrating dance steps. 'I shouldn't tell you this, really. It was planned to keep you on the hook for a day or so,' Dalby went on, since I hadn't replied, 'but they were anxious to take the heat off a high-ranking suspect, so they did a phase two on you so he'd stick his neck out helping to clobber you. Just grin and bear it for a little while longer, and look like you're suffering.'

I said, 'Just as long as the executioner is in on our cosy little secret,' and I headed across to the girl in white for a cha-cha lesson.

By twelve-thirty I was loaded with anchovy, cheese dip, hard egg and salmon, and about 300 geometrically shaped pieces of cold toast. I cut out by the side entrance of the garden, across the service road at the side of the post office. Blue light glowed from within the sorting office, and a radio played soft big band music which jarred against the music and laughter from the General's garden. Beyond the post office a white quonset hut stood alone. Inside, behind the counter, a young blond PFC with an almost invisible moustache handed me two cablegrams that had arrived since I last saw him at 6.30.

'A spy has no friends' people say; but it's more complex than that. A spy has to have friends, in fact many sets of friends. Friends he's made by doing things and by not doing other things. Every agent has his own 'old boy network' and like every other 'old boy network' it cuts across frontiers, jobs and every other loyalty – it's a sort of spy's insurance policy. One has no specific arrangement with anyone, no code other than a mutual sensitivity to euphemisms.

I opened the first cable. It was from a man named Grenade.* He was a political man now, and of high enough rank never to have it used as a prefix to his name. The cable said, 'YOUR NOMINEE REDUNDANT STOP 13BT1818 WILL PAY BERT.' It had come from the main post office in Lyons and there was no way of associating it with Grenade except that I had monitored some stuff when he was working for French Intelligence, and Bert had been his cover name.

The PFC lit a cigarette for me and coughed his way into the harsh French tobacco of one of mine. I looked at the other cable. It was an ordinary

* See Appendix: Grenade, p. 333.

civilian cable handed over a post office counter, and paid for in cash. It had originated at Gerrard Street post office, London. It said: 'READING A PAPER IN JC ON 3rd OF SECOND.' It was signed: 'ARTEMIDORUS.'

I looked at the two sheets of paper. Each sender had implied his message in different ways. Grenade was clearly telling me that I was for the high jump, but that I could use the funds he'd stacked at that number bank account in Switzerland. To find which bank would be easy enough, since they had different codes, and anyone quoting the number can draw without too much trouble. I smiled as I wondered whether this account was the result of the American Express forgeries he had once been involved with. It would be ironic if I was clamped for being an accessory when I tried to draw on it. The second cable was from Charlie Cavendish, who was an undercover man for C-SICH.* He liked me because I'd been in the Army with his son. When his son was killed, I'd told him, and had got on so well with the old man that I saw him often. He had a great and devastating sense of humour that illuminated dark corners and prevented him getting a senior position. He lived in a poky Bloomsbury flat, 'to be near the British Museum,' he said, and probably had trouble finding the few bob to pay for the cable. It was the most sobering of all my messages.

* Combined Services Information Clearing House.

Back at the party, globules of people were clinging together. I smiled at a very young soldier sitting on a frame chair outside the room the General used as a second office.

'The General is definitely not to be disturbed, eh, soldier?' I leered. He smiled back in an embarrassed way, but made no attempt to stop me going into the library. I moved with a studied lack of hurry and lit another cigarette.

The General's set of Shakespeare were pigskin, hand-tooled, a pleasure to handle. I didn't need to look up Artemidorus in the third scene of Act 2 *Julius Caesar*. The old man knew that I knew the play well enough. But I looked it up.*

The library was lit by a signal rocket and a hundred 'Ahs!' lay lethargic on the air. In the anticipatory silence a voice outside the window said, 'They just don't make corks the way they used to.' Then followed a giggle-giggle of laughter and the sound of pouring wine.

The dim light of the small desk lamp enabled me to see a slim figure standing at the door. The tearing sound of another rocket made me jump. The figure was a tall young PFC with a Band-Aid on his neck and ginger eyebrows that he jammed together to simulate concentration. He marched towards me. He carefully read my identity brooch then compared the photo with me. He gave me a strange perfunctory salute.

* See Appendix: Julius Caesar, p. 336.

'Compliments of Brigadier Dalby, sir,' he said.

Brigadier, I thought. What the hell is coming next? He waited.

'Yes?' I said inquiringly, and put *Julius* back on the shelf.

'There's been an accident, sir. A generator truck has gone off the road at "Bloody Angle".' I knew the place that bore the name of one of Lee's Civil War emplacements. A low brick wall painted in black and yellow checks separated a roadway blasted out of solid rock from a perpendicular drop into empty space. It was a tricky place for cornering in a jeep; with thirty foot of generator truck it was like drinking from a square glass. He didn't have to say the next bit. 'Lieutenant Montgomery was the officer on it, sir.' It was Barney. The young soldier looked awkward in the face of death. 'I'm sorry, sir,' he said. He was being nice. I appreciated it. 'The Brigadier was heading for his car. He said that if you didn't have transport I was to . . .'

'It's OK,' I told him, 'and thanks.' Outside the clouds had put dark glasses on the moon.

It was a black night, of the sort one only encounters in the tropics. Dalby had on a lambswool US Army windcheater, and stood near a big new shiny Ford. I shouted, 'Let's go,' but his reply was lost in the crackle crackle of a big chrysanthemum rocket. I couldn't get used to the idea of a dead Barney Barnes. I told myself that it was a mistake, the way one does with facts that the brain prefers to absorb piecemeal.

221

By the time I had pulled the big oversprung Lincoln Continental on to the road, Dalby's rear lights were way down the General Guerite highway. The big V8 engine warmed to the rich mixture. I saw Dalby pull over to the left and head along the coast road. This road was less carefully made since only certain lorries carrying supplies were normally allowed to use it. To the left only a hundred metres of sea separated us from the Shot Island. Had it been a better night the 'mountain' would have been clearly visible. Dalby was drawing even farther ahead and must have been doing sixty in spite of the road. I hoped he'd be able to talk us out of trouble if any of the road sections were closed. The forty-foot towers at about 300-yard intervals reflected back the sound of the car in roars. Most of the towers held only infra-red TV cameras, but every third tower was manned. I hoped none would phone ahead to stop us taking this obvious short cut from the General's party. Odd tangles of brush obscured Dalby's lights now and again. I was peering at the blackerty that sat upon the windscreen when I caught sight of the red 'CAUTION HALT AT 25 YDS' sign. I stopped the car. It was 2.12 A.M.

They had closed this section ahead of me with only three miles of forbidden road to traverse. Dalby was nowhere in sight, he had slipped through.

As I felt for my spare cigarettes my hand touched a coarse fabric. I switched on the dashboard light.

Someone had left a pair of heavy asbestos insulation gauntlets on the seat. I wondered if Barney had been in the car; he was doing the 'power' act. Then I found my Gauloises.

I clicked the cigarette lighter on and waited for it to glow red.

I was still waiting when the sky exploded into daylight – except that daylight and I had, neither of us, been so bright lately.

22

I opened the car door and rolled out into the white frozen day-like night. It suddenly became very quiet until from the far side of the island I heard a siren wailing pitifully.

Overhead two police helicopters chug-chugged towards Shot Island, and began dropping hand grenades into the sea. Under each, a huge spotlight waved an erratic beam.

The Air Police had located, recognized and flown towards the light of the large flare, while I was still expecting my eyeballs to melt.

One of the 'choppers' stopped, did an about turn and came back to me. The flare spluttered and faded, and now the glare of the spotlight blinded me. I sat very still. It was 2.17. Against the noise of the blades a deeper resonant sound bit into the chill black air. From a loudspeaker, mounted with the light, a voice spoke from the air. I didn't hear or make sense of the words at first, although I was trying hard. They had a strong accent.

'Just don't move a muscle, boy!' the voice said again.

The two beaters were really close to the car; the one that had spoken held its light about six feet away from my eye sockets – it inched around the car keeping well off the ground. The other 'copter ran its light over the high tension lines and the camera tower. The light looked yellow and dim after the intensity of the high-pitched, almost green, light of the flare. The beam sliced the darkness, it moved up the steel ladder of the tower. Way before the top was reached I saw the dead soldier in the penumbra of the searchlight: he was hanging half out of the smashed glass window. That he was dead came as no surprise. No one could stay alive in a metal tower connected to the high tension power line, connected by angle irons and bolts in the most professional way.

It was about 2.36 A.M. when a Provost-Colonel arrived to arrest me. At 2.36½ I remembered the big insulating gauntlets. But even had I remembered before, what could I have done?

23

I opened my eyes. A 200-watt light bulb hung from the centre of the ceiling. Its light scaled my brain. I closed my eyes. Time passed.

I opened my eyes again; slowly. The ceiling almost ceased to flutter up and down. I could probably have got to my feet but decided not to try for a month. I was very very old. The soldier I'd seen outside the General's office was now sitting across the room, still reading the same copy of *Confidential*. On the front cover large print asked, 'Is he a broad-chasing booze-hound?'

I'd tell you whose face the cover featured, but I can't afford a million-dollar law suit the way they can. The soldier turned over the page and gave me a glance.

I remembered arriving in this room at 2.59 one night. I remembered the Sergeant who called me names: mostly Anglo-Saxon monosyllabic four-letter ones with the odd 'Commie' thrown in for syntax. I remembered that it had been 3.40 when he said, 'You needn't keep looking at your watch, Colonel. Your pals are well away by now.' It was 3.49 when he hit me because of the 200 times I had said 'I don't know.' He hit me a lot after that. He hurt me to the point where I wanted to tell him something. My watch said 4.22 now. It had stopped. It was smashed.

I hoped they would follow standard interrogation techniques so that the good one would appear soon. I lay on a US Army stretcher. Above me the window shutters were locked with a padlock. The room was a big one. The cream paint looked faintly green in the light of the fluorescent tubes. I guessed we were in one of the single-storey buildings of the Administration block on the north end of the island. The room was empty except for a phone, over which was a chair, upon which was my guard. He was unarmed. A sure sign that they weren't kidding.

That hard metal stretcher felt wonderful. I flexed my torn bruised muscles and tried to reopen my swollen eyes. My companion wrenched himself away from *Confidential* magazine – he walked across to me. I feigned death – perhaps I have a natural talent for it: I found it very easy. He gave me a kick in the leg. It wasn't a hard blow but it sent molten pain through every nerve-end from knee to navel. I bottled up my groaning and somehow wasn't sick, but it was very difficult. The very young soldier reached into his shirt pocket. I heard the sound of a match striking. He gently eased a cigarette into my mouth.

'If this is Ellis Island I've changed my mind,' I said.

The soldier smiled gently then kicked my leg again. He had a great sense of humour that kid; fine repartee.

I was very hungry. The kid had finished *Confidential*, *Screen Romances*, *Gals and Gags*, and *Reader's Digest* before they took me out. I read 'WAITING-ROOM No. 3' on the outside of my door. We went a short distance down the hall.

Behind a door marked 'Medical Officer Security Division' was a dark, cosy womb-warm room; well-furnished, the handsome brass lamp marshalled light into a bright circle on the mahogany desk.

In the circle of light stood a stainless-steel percolator of hot aromatic coffee, a blue jug of hot milk, toast, butter, crispy grilled streaky bacon, egg *en cocotte*, marmalade, some waffles and a little jug of hot resinous corn syrup. Behind the desk was an elderly man in a brigadier's uniform; I recognized the crown of his short-cropped head. It was the Brigadier that Dalby and I had been talking with. He was well enough involved in eating not to look up as I was brought in. He passed bacon into his mouth and pointed to a soft leather armchair with a fork.

'Cup of coffee, son?' he said.

'No thanks,' I said. My voice was strange and distorted as it left my swollen mouth. 'I've eaten just about all the rich chow I can hold for one day.'

The Brigadier didn't look up. 'You're a real tough kid, eh sonny?' He poured a coffee into a black Wedgwood cup and put four sugars in. 'Raise the sugar count,' he said.

I drank the sweet black coffee; it washed the dried blood out of my mouth. 'Good china, I mean really good, is essential in a home, a really nice home, I always say,' I told him.

The Brigadier picked up the phone. 'Let's have some hot soup and a bacon sandwich along here right away.'

'On toasted brown,' I said.

'Sounds good,' he said to me, then into the phone, 'Make that two bacon sandwiches on brown and toasted.'

This boyo knew the system. He was going to stay kind and understanding whatever I did. I ate the sandwich and drank soup. He gave no sign of recognition, but as I finished drinking he offered me a cigar. When I declined, he produced a packet of Gauloises and insisted I keep the packet. It was very quiet here. In the gloom beyond his desk I could see a large grandfather clock; it ticked very softly, and as I watched it, it discreetly struck 10.30. Here and there antique furniture and heavy curtains announced a man important enough to have shipping space devoted to his gracious living, even here on Tokwe Atoll. The Brigadier went on writing. He was very quiet, and without looking at me said, 'Every time some stinking detail comes up I find myself doing it.' I thought he was referring to me, but he passed some photographs across his desk. One was a sepia-toned vignette such as any small town photo studio would take for a dollar. The other two were official identity photos, full face and side view. Each was a photograph of a corporal about twenty-two–twenty-four years old, fair-haired, open face. I'd guess a mid-west farmer's son. There was a fourth photo, a poor blurred snapshot. This time with a young girl, pretty in a conventional way – they were standing alongside a new Buick. On the back it said, 'Schultz Drug Store. 24-Hour Foto Service.' I handed the pictures back.

'So?' I said, 'a soldier.'

'A very nice soldier,' the Brigadier said. 'He has been in the Army six months. You know something? The first time he saw the ocean he was passing through Frisco last month.' The Brigadier got slowly to his feet. 'If you've finished your coffee I'll show you something.' He waited as I finished.

'It could easily be a long time before my next,' I said.

'It certainly could,' he agreed, and smiled like the man who's pleased with himself in the last photo of the Canadian Club ads. 'We'll go back to your room,' he said.

The corridor was lit by blue strip-lights and I found Waiting Room No. 3 unlocked. I opened the door and suddenly it wasn't 10.40 P.M. any more. It was morning.

The light was blinding: the big shutters had

been drawn back letting in midday tropical sunshine. The chair and phone were still there, so were *Confidential*, *Screen Romances*, *Gals and Gags* and two *Reader's Digests*. Against the wall was the olive-coloured metal Army stretcher that I had so recently vacated. The blue blanket on the stretcher was still specked with my blood. There would have been no detectable change in the room at all if a horribly scarred, naked corpse had not been occupying the blanket and stretcher.

The Brigadier walked across to the body. 'This is Corporal Steve Harmon,' he said. 'I'm writing to his folks; he's the boy you killed last night.'

24

[*Aquarius (Jan 20–Feb 19) Irksome regulations seem to impede your progress, but do not be impulsive. Chances to meet lots of new exciting friends.*]

Of the next twenty-four hours I probably spent about fourteen with the Brigadier, although doctors and psychiatrists gave me the usual working over. That same evening we were back in his office. There was plenty of hot coffee and plenty of toasted bacon sandwiches. The Brigadier poured himself his sixth cup in half an hour and broke the long silence.

'You're marked down on my dossier, Colonel, with three stars – like Michelin it's the highest rating we use. It doesn't necessarily mean that you're good at your job, it means that you are a three-star potential danger to us. As far as I'm concerned though, it's a rough guide to the fact that you are a skilled investigator. Now I don't claim to be that. I'm just the feller they send to places like this to check the barbed wire for moth holes. You tell me you didn't signal to that Russian submarine on Thursday night. I want to believe you. OK. Thread up my information and show me your movie, mister.'

I appreciated that the old man was being even nicer than his role demanded, especially considering that he was sure I had connected his nice new tower to his nice new electric line, and made a cinder out of one of his policemen.

'Well,' I said, 'I'm not convinced that the submarine didn't fire its *own* flare,' I said.

'Don't get really smart with me, sonny, it's obvious that it did.'

'OK. So why does there have to be an agent working here at all?'

'Look at it this way, sonny, we monitored the signal for one thing . . .'

'I keep asking you what sort of signal but you won't tell me!'

'The one you sent, sonny, the one you sent . . . because you're . . .' he searched for a word, 'just dirty, just dirty.' He flushed in embarrassment at his outburst and began cleaning his spectacles. 'I'm too old for your sort of war, I suppose . . .'

A good agent follows up any debating advantage, especially when it's a continuation of his life that's the subject of discussion. I said, 'I thought we were pretending that I'm innocent for the purposes of this short interrogation.'

He nodded and said, 'The signal was high-speed electrical impulses. Just as Morse can be sent in such high-speed bursts that long messages can be transmitted in seconds, recorded, then read slowly later, so the scanning of a TV picture can be sent. Last night a camera-transmitter, small enough for one man to carry, was directed towards the mountain, and no matter how much the camera was joggled about, the speed of the impulses transmitted clear pictures.'

'Just as a slow-motion movie would be less subject to camera shake,' I said, just to sound intelligent.

'Exactly,' said the Brigadier, who had no doubt that I had used this equipment the night before and was just sending him up.

'But last night was really dark. Could it have got pictures in that light?'

'I shouldn't really tell you but since we've started this comedy . . .' He lit a cigar from the ivory box. He lit it with a match as a connoisseur does a good cigar, he rolled it in his mouth, then removing it he exhaled and studied the bright red ash '. . . our boys are not really sure: perhaps the high-speed impulse gives an unprecedented aperture enough to photograph in the dark. If not, perhaps the submarine put an infra-red searchlight on to the cloudbase for reflected light. It would be invisible to human eyes of course.'

'Then . . .'

'Then why the flare? Yes, it's a contradiction,

the flare, but with a zoom lens, one that would change its focal length, at an extreme length, the sort of thing they use at ball games, the light transmitted would be very little. But with the flare and the high-speed transmission, it would be possible to get very close-up pictures of the mountain. Probably the flare was triggered automatically by the reception apparatus as soon as the "picture", so to speak, was too dark. The camera was held on to the mountain by an electro gyroscope controlled by a compass set to the correct bearing.'

'They don't leave anything to chance, do they?' I said. He gave me a sour look. I went on, 'It's a wonder they couldn't do without the flare, then no one would have known about any of it.'

'Not at all, we monitored the whole thing as I keep telling you. I'll demonstrate if you like. You won't do anything silly, will you?' the old man asked. 'Because . . .'

'I'm not under-rating you, sir,' I said.

'Swell,' he smiled. 'Nor I you,' and carried on. 'Obviously the party last night was because of what we were doing on the mountain. I don't have to tell you that.' I tried to look like a man who knew, but in reality kicked myself for being fooled so easily. A party: I should have suspected that it wasn't that social here. I wondered if Dalby knew that secret experiments were planned for that night of the garden-party. The Brigadier had been there perhaps to make sure we were. It all made sense now. I guessed that it was the neutron bomb that they were about to explode.* The information we had been given about it being a Uranium 238 bomb with a SUVOM trigger had been true but on the night of the party a team of people had been 'crash programmed' into the explosion area to modify the bomb. Without a break in the conversation I said, 'You mean the insertion of the neutron device?'

He nodded.

'What did you do, a 'copter shuttle from the flat top?'

'Something like that,' the Brigadier said, with a smile like a scythe.

He wheeled a metal trolley to the centre of his office. He began to talk as he threaded up the 16mm projector that stood on it.

'We have infra-red cameras on towers monitoring the road and the shipping channel. Some towers are manned, most are remotely-controlled. Each camera transmits on the same frequency and the receiving apparatus shows . . .' He threaded the last loop of the big crackle-finish grey machine, and closed the metal gate. The desk lamp went out and a grey scratched rectangle of light fell across the wall as a screen rose into position with a soft purring sound. 15. 14. 13. The large leader numbers gave place to the hastily processed film.

The Brigadier continued '. . . shows the pattern as a distorted map of the side of the island.' The

* See Appendix: Neutron Bomb, p. 336.

236

screen was dark except for a white worm-shape that came into the frame from the bottom centre, moving upwards. 'That's your car,' the Brigadier said. I guessed that it was a composite of Dalby's car and my car but said nothing. As the short white worm-shape got to the top of the screen there was a horizontal flip across the screen.

The Brigadier said, 'That was when the manned tower was connected to the electric cables. That camera went out of action then, of course, but luckily we have overlap on the camera fields. Now you see.' The white worm had shrunk to a dot as my car halted, and suddenly the screen became a confusion of very intense horizontal bands of varying widths and intensity. 'That's the high-speed TV transmission; so fast that we are getting hundreds of TV pictures per frame.' The bands became darker now. 'Somewhere here the flare went off.'

Apart from the small white dot made by my Lincoln the screen was quite black.

'Egg beaters.' The two helicopters came in from the side of the frame; they were quivering little blotches. I watched them return to my car and circle round it. So far the film had shown me nothing of which I was not already aware. But the film lab had been very thorough, they had spliced on the end of the film the incident of my arrest: Two cars coming down the road from the top of the screen, one up into the frame from the bottom. Now I had learnt something. This equipment showed a distinct difference between one car and two. I knew that Dalby had made that journey a few yards ahead of me along the highway. It meant that Dalby had found a way of making his car entirely invisible to the radar defences of the island.

It was easy to understand the small slip of paper I'd found in the cranberry box now. The VLF radio wavelength was a standard method of speaking to submerged submarines. The compass bearing was to set the electro gyroscope on the camera. My only luck in the whole deal was in not putting that slip in my pocket.

Furthermore the TV transmission was required because a neutron bomb is not one big flash like an H-bomb, it is designed to hang over a city, bombarding it with neutrons. Only pictures of its progress would be any use. A still picture would reveal little or nothing.

The next day they showed me the black metal twisted parts of the HSTV unit. The big heavy-weight handles were less twisted than the thin metal casing. They showed me photos and stuff. It seemed they'd got a pretty fair set of finger-prints off the unit. They were mine, of course. I'd never touched the damn thing, but I didn't doubt that everyone was being sincere.

25

[Aquarius (Jan 20–Feb 19) Handle the people around you with tact. New acquaintances could provide prospects of travel and excitement.]

The days following were clotted together in an inseparable mess. It stayed 4.22 all the time – one long fluorescent day punctuated by interrogations like TV commercials in a peak-hour play.

For an hour each day I was medically examined. I had IQ tests, interviews, and was told to write my autobiography. I matched triangles and circles and put wooden rods into racks. I was tested for reaction, speed, co-ordination and muscular efficiency. My blood was measured, and identified, its pressure checked and recorded. Birth marks, I never knew I had, were photographed and tape measured. Cold showers and hot lights blurred into a month, like blades of grass blur into a field. I ceased to remember that Jean or Dalby existed, and sometimes I doubted if *I* did.

Sometimes the guards would tell me the time, but mostly they'd say it had just turned 4.20. One day or perhaps night, it was the first guard change after cornflakes, anyway, a US Army Captain came into Waiting Room No. 3. I didn't get up off the stretcher, I had begun to feel at home there. He was about forty-two and walked like a European, that is, like a man who wears braces to hold his trousers up. His hands were wrinkled and looked like no amount of soap would ever remove the farm soil that lay dark and rich in his pores. The lobe of one ear was missing, and it was easy to imagine the village midwife, tired and clumsy in the small hours of a Balkan morning.

'Jo napot kivavok,' he said.

I'd met this greeting in the Café Budapest a couple of times and had always found that 'kezet csokolom' (kiss your hand) had given good mileage with the younger waitresses.

With this boy it went over like a lead balloon.

'Make on the feet, mack,' he said, changing his approach.

He spoke with a heavy accent liberally sprinkled with idiom. The idiom was to convince you he was the all-American boy, and gave him respite during which to translate the next sentence.

'No spik Inglese,' I said, giving a characteristic shrug and presenting the palms of both hands upwards.

'Op, or I kick you some!'

'Just as long as you don't damage my watch,' I said.

He opened the breast pocket of his uniform jacket and unfolded a white paper about 10 in by 8 in.

'This is your deportation order, signed by the Secretary of State.' He said it like he was going to paste it into the back of his vest pocket edition of Thomas Paine. 'You can think yourself stinking lucky that we are exchanging you for two fly boys that know senators, or you'd be for a slow tcheeeek.' He made a revolting noise as he ran his finger across his windpipe.

'I don't dig you, Uncle Tom,' I said. 'Why is England exchanging me for two fliers?'

'England ho ho ho!' he said; it was a merriment symbol. 'England! You're not going to stinking England, you pig, you going back to stinking Hungary. They'll like you there for fouling up the detail. Ho ho! They'll tcheeeek ho ho!'

'Ho ho to you,' I said. 'I'll save you some black pudding.' I didn't take the idea of being sent to Hungary very seriously at first.

There was little I could do. Neither Dalby nor Jean had had a chance to speak to me. I could reckon on little or no help from any other source. Now there was this Hungarian stuff.

I worried about it for two hours then a medic came with a long trolley and an enamel tray containing ether, cotton wool and a hypodermic. He fluffed up the clean white pillow on the trolley and smoothed out the red medical department blanket. He took my pulse, pulled up my eyelids and listened to my chest with a stethoscope. 'Would you lie on the table, please. Relax completely.'

'What's the time?' I asked.

'Two-twenty, roll up your sleeve.' He rubbed a little ether on the skin and eased the sharp shiny needle into the unfeeling flesh with a professional flourish.

'What time?' my voice boomed out.

'Two-twenty,' he said, again.

'What, what, what. Time, time, time.' It wasn't me talking; it was a curiously metallic echo, 'Time, time, time.' I looked up at the white-coated boy and he grew smaller and smaller and smaller. He was standing far away near the door now, but still he was gripping my arm. Was it possible? Time, time, time. Still gripping my arm, arms, I mean, both of them. Both those men, both my arms. So far away; such little men near that tiny door.

I rubbed my forehead because I was slowly going round and round on a turn-table and sinking down. But how did I get up again because I kept going around and down but I was always high enough to go sinking down and around again. I rubbed my forehead with my huge heavy hand. It was as big as a barrage balloon, my hand; you'd expect it to envelop my head, but my forehead was so wide. Wide. Wide as a barn. I was being wheeled along. Towards the door. They'll never get huge me through that little door. Not me, never. Ha ha. Never, never, never. Thud, thud, thud, thud.

Into my subconscious the drumming of engines brought me almost to the threshold of awakening. But each time there came a body bending low over me. The sharp pointed pain in the arm brought the noisy throbbing nausea breaking over me in feverish waves of heat and intense cold. I was moved on stretchers and trolleys over rough ground and polished wooden corridors, handled like a dust particle and like a dustbin, dropped into trains, helped into planes; but never far away was a blurred moon bending over me, and that sharp pain that pulled the blanket of unconsciousness over my face.

I came up to the surface very, very slowly; from the dark deeps I floated freely towards the dim-blue rippling surface of undrugged life.

I hurt, therefore I am.

I hugged close against the damp soil. By the light of a small window I was able to closely inspect the broken wristwatch upon which I was gently vomiting. It said 4.22. I shivered. From some-where nearby I heard voices. No one was talking, merely groaning.

I gradually became sentient. I became aware of the heavy hot humid air. My eyes focused only with difficulty. I closed them. I slept. Sometimes the nights seemed as long as a week. Rough bowls of porridge-like stuff were put before me, and if uneaten, removed. It was always the same man who came with the food. He had short blond hair. His features were flat with high cheek-bones. He wore a light-grey two-piece track suit. One day I was sitting in the corner on the earth floor – there was no furniture – when I heard the bolts being drawn back. Kublai Khan entered, but without food. I'd never heard his voice before. His voice was hard and unattractive. He said 'Sky is blue; earth black.' I looked at him for a minute or so. He said it again, 'Sky is blue; earth black.'

'So what?' I said.

He walked towards me and hit me with his open hand. It didn't need much to hurt me at that stage of my education. K.K. left the room and the bolts were closed and I was hungry. It took me two days to discover that I had to repeat the things K.K. said after him. It was simple enough. By the time I made that discovery I was weak from hunger and licked my food bowl avidly. The gruel was delicious and I never missed the spoon. Sometimes K.K. said, 'Fire is red; cloud is white,' or perhaps, 'Sand is yellow; silk is soft.' Sometimes his accent was so thick that it would be hours later when I had repeated the words over and over that I'd finally understand what we'd both been talking about. One day I said to him, 'Suppose I buy you a Linguaphone course; do I get out of here?' For that I not only remained unfed by day, but that night he didn't bother to bring the paper-thin dirty blanket either. I learnt what colour the sky was by the ninth day. By then K.K. merely pointed and I reeled off all the junk I could remember. But I'd done it wrong. Somehow 'Sky is red; silk is blue.' K.K. shouted and hit me softly against the face. I had no food or blanket and shivered with the intense cold of the night-time. From then on sometimes I got things right, sometimes wrong, according to the colour K.K. had decided everything was that day. Even with gruel every day I would have become weaker and weaker. I passed the 'wisecrack stage', the 'asking questions' stage, the 'do you understand English?' stage. I was weak and exhausted and on the day I got everything so correct that K.K. brought me a piece of cold cooked meat, I sobbed for an hour without feeling sad – with pleasure perhaps it was.

Every morning the door was opened and I handed out my slop pail; every night it came back again. I began to count the days. With my fingernails I incised a crude calendar in the soft wood of the door, behind it I was out of sight of the peep-hole. Some of the days were marked by means of a double stroke; those were the ones I heard the noises. They were generally loud enough to wake me, the noises, when they happened. They were human noises but difficult to describe as either groans or screams. They were somewhere between the two. Some days K.K. gave me a small slip of paper; typewritten on them there were orders such as 'The prisoner will sleep with arms above the blankets.' 'The prisoner will not sleep in the daytime.'

One day K.K. gave me a cigarette and lit it for me. As I sat back to puff at it he said, 'Why do you smoke?' I said I didn't know and he went away; but the next day Grass was Sepia, and I got beat about the head again.

After I had marked twenty-five days on my calendar K.K. brought me a slip that said, 'The prisoner will receive a visitor for six minutes only.' There was a lot of shouting in the corridor and K.K. let in a young Hungarian Army Captain. He spoke reasonably good English. We stood facing each other until he said, 'You requested a meeting with the Great Britain Ambassador.'

'I don't remember it,' I said slowly.

K.K. pushed me in the chest with force that thudded me against the wall of my cell and left me breathless.

The Captain continued, 'I don't question. I say this. You ask.' He was charming, he never once stopped smiling. 'A secretary is without. He sees you now. I go. Six minutes only.'

K.K. showed a man into my cell. He was so tall he beat his head against the door jamb. He was embarrassed and awkward. He explained reluctantly that the decision wasn't his, that he was only the third under-secretary, and that sort of thing. He explained that there was no record of my being a British citizen, although he admitted that I sounded like an Englishman to him. He was so embarrassed and awkward that I almost believed that he was the British official he purported to be.

'You wouldn't think me impertinent, sir,' I said, 'if I asked you to give proof of identity.'

He looked madly embarrassed and said, 'Not at all,' a few times.

'I don't mean papers of identity, you understand, sir. Just something to show that you are in regular contact with the old country.'

He looked at me blankly.

'Everyday things, sir, just so I can be sure.'

He was keen to be helpful; he came back with the everyday things and a load of reasons why the Embassy could do nothing. His greatest anxiety was in case I should implicate Dalby's group, and he was always fishing for news of any statement I was going to make to the Hungarian Police.

Doing this while maintaining that I wasn't a British subject was a strain even for old-school British diplomacy. 'Don't get sent to a Political Prison,' he kept saying. '*They* treat prisoners very badly.'

'*This* isn't the YMCA,' I told him on one occasion. I began to wish he'd stop coming. I almost preferred K.K. At least I knew where I was with him.

Every day seemed hotter and more humid than the previous one, while the nights became more chilly.

Although K.K. knew enough English for everyday needs, that is, to feed me or punch me on the nose, I found I could get a cup of sweet black coffee from one of the guards when I learnt enough Hungarian to ask. He was an old man looking like a bit player in a Ruritanian smaltz opera, sometimes he gave me a small piece of chewing tobacco.

Finally the tall British man came to see me for the last time. They went through the shouting and preliminaries, but this time it was only the Army Captain who spoke. He told me that, 'Her Magestyries Government' under no circumstances can regard me as a British subject. 'Therefore,' he said, 'the trial will proceed under Hungarian law.' The man from the Embassy said how sorry he was.

'Trial?' I said, and K.K. smashed me against the wall again, so I kept quiet. The British man gave me a sorry-old-chap look with a flick of the eyes, put on his rolled-brim hat and disappeared.

K.K. had a rare flash of altruism and brought me a black coffee in a real porcelain cup. Surprise followed surprise, for when I sipped it, I discovered it had a shot of plum brandy in it. It had been a long day. I curled my feet as near to my head as possible and curling my arms close, I went to sleep thinking, 'If I don't get out of here quickly you fellows are going to miss each other.'

Some nights they left the lights on all night, and on nights when I got every single K.K. colour wrong they sent the old moustachioed guard to keep me awake all night. He talked to me, and if K.K. was there, shouted at me not to lean against the wall. He talked about everything he knew, his family and his days in the Army, anything to keep me awake. I couldn't translate a word of it, but he was a simple man and easy to understand. He showed me the height of his four children, photos of all his family, and now and again made a flickering movement with his hand that meant I could lean against the wall and rest while he stood half in the corridor listening for K.K.'s return.

Once every third day the Army Captain returned, and although I may have misunderstood, I believe he told me that he was my defence counsel. On the first visit he read my indictment; it took about an hour. It was in Hungarian. He translated a few phrases like 'enemy of the State', 'high treason', 'plotting for the illegal overthrow of Peoples' Democracies' and there were a few 'imperialisms' and 'capitalisms' thrown in for good measure.

There were thirty-four marks on my door now. By resting and sleeping in snatches I had put a few of my nerve endings together but I was no Steve Reeves. The diet was keeping me pretty low physically and mentally. Each morning I got up feeling like the first frames in a Horlicks strip. It was pretty obvious that if I didn't swim against the current there would be nothing left of me I'd known and loved. There was no chance of a 'Houdini' through the boltwork and a fighting retreat out of the main gates. It was to be a cool calm slow walk or I wouldn't be there. Thus did

I reason on my thirty-fifth day of isolation and hunger.

The only person around who broke the rules was the old man. Everyone else had the door locked behind them; the old man stood half-way out of it to give me a few minutes' sleep. There was no alternative. I had no weapon but the door. I wanted to escape at night, so that meant I couldn't use the light flex. The slop pail was too heavy to be used adroitly. No, it was the door, which meant, I'm afraid, that the old man got it. That night I was all set to try. Pretending to rest I leaned against the wall lining the door up against my target. He didn't come close enough. I did nothing. When finally I went to bed I shivered until I went to sleep. It was a couple of nights later that the old man brought me a cigarette. I hit him with the door – the bolt mechanism swung against his head and he dropped unconscious to the floor. I dragged him inside the door; his breathing was irregular and his face very flushed. He was an old man. At the last minute my training almost failed. I almost couldn't hit him as he lay there, the cigarette he'd brought me still in his hand.

I took his wooden HB pencil, relocked the door, and in his guard's jacket and cap and my dark prison trousers, I softly descended the old dark wooden stairs. A light of low wattage glowed in the main hall, and from under the door to my right a slot of light and soft American music slid across to me. The main door was unguarded from inside, but I decided against touching it. Instead I took the pencil and opened the door* of an unlit room to my right. It must have been three and a half minutes at least since I had left my cell, walked the couple of yards to the stairs and negotiated them without causing a creak.

I closed the door behind me. The moonlight showed me the filing cases and books that lined the room. I ran my fingers round the window frame and encountered the electric wire alarm. Then I stood on the desk to remove the electric bulb. There was a loud cracking noise – I had cracked a pencil underfoot. The soft music from the radio in the next room ceased suddenly. I held my breath but there was only a whistle as the tuning control was turned. The exertion of stretching my hands above my head left me shaking and weak.

From my pocket I took the English sixpence that Anthony Eden's friend had given me and slipped it into the socket before replacing the bulb. Still in the moonlight I got slowly down from the desk. I groped around the floor. I was lucky. There was a big two-kilowatt electric fire plugged into a wall point. The strong rosary that snuggle tooth had brought me as my second English 'everyday thing' I wrapped tightly round and round the elements. There was no time for electrical legèrdemain. It was the work of a minute to switch on the wall

---

* This method of opening a lock with a pencil has been withdrawn from the MS.

plug and the light switch. There was no emergency lighting system and the flash and bang was pretty good. I could hear people blundering into doors and clicking switches. The main power fuse seemed to have gone, and the window opened easily without bells or buzzers. I slipped through and closed it behind me, although I couldn't lock it.

I crouched down in the wet grass and I heard the front door open and saw a torch flash in the room I had just left. No one tried the window. I remained crouching. A car started up and I could hear two people speaking loudly close by, but the sound of the engine blotted out the words.

I walked without hurrying towards the rear of the house. I probably put too much reliance on my peaked cap. I fell into some soft earth, and backing out of it grabbed some thorny bushes. A dog barked, too close for comfort. I could see the rear wall now, it was about as high as I was. I ran a tentative finger along it, but there was no barbed wire or broken glass. I had both palms on it but it required more strength than I had, to pull myself up bodily. That damn dog barked again. I looked back at the prison building. Someone was in the conservatory now, with one of those powerful portable lights. They had only to swing it round the walls. Perhaps I should lie down flat in the grass, but when the big beam shot out I managed to get the side of one foot on the wall top. I flexed my leg muscles, and as the light skimmed the wall I rolled my empty belly over and fell down the far side. I knew I mustn't stay down, although it was very pleasant, breathing long grassy lungfuls of the wet night air. I felt soaked and hungry, free and frightened, but as I started to walk, I found myself entrapped in an intricate framework of slim wooden rods and wires that enmeshed head and limbs; the more I tried to free myself, the more tangled I was. A narrow slit of light ahead of me grew fatter to become a rectangle, and a man's silhouette was centred in it.

'Here! Is someone there?' he called, then, as his eyes became accustomed to the darkness, 'Here, get out of my bloody "runners", you silly—!'

I heard a clock strike ten P.M.

26

It would be easy now, to pretend that I knew all the answers at that stage. Easy to pretend that I'd known they were holding me in a big house in London's Wood Green from the word go. But I didn't. I half guessed, but the conviction had oozed from my body day by day. As I languished underfed and miserable, it became more and more difficult to think of anything outside of my little cell and K.K. In another ten days the theory that London was just over the garden wall would have been totally beyond my comprehension. That's why I'd escaped. It was then or never.

Getting away from Mr Keating's house, 'Alf Keating's my name, spelt like the powder', was relatively easy. I told him I had had a fight with my brother-in-law who was drunk and much bigger than me, and I'd climbed over the garden walls to get away after a neighbour phoned for the police.

'Uh!' said Alf, revealing teeth like rusty railings.

To be running away from the police was terrible

enough for him not to suspect worse; to admit to being physically inferior and cowardly guaranteed the story's veracity. I must have been quite a sight. The brambles had drawn blood on my hands, and mud was spattered all over me. I saw Alf looking at the old man's uniform jacket. 'I've got to get to work,' I said. 'I'm on the door at Shell-Mex house.' Alf stared. 'Nights,' I said lamely. 'I just can't seem to sleep in the day-time somehow.' Alf nodded. 'I'll pay for the bean frames,' I said.

Alf growled, 'Yes, you ought to do that, I reckon.' Alf took a huge watch out of his greasy waistcoat in order to get at a little bent tin of snuff that had been polished by years of use. He offered me a pinch, but if I sneezed there was a good chance my head would fall off and roll under Alf's gas stove. I didn't risk it.

I promised Alf an oil stove at cost price. He let me wash. Would Alf walk down the road with me? My brother-in-law wouldn't make trouble if I was in company I said.

Alf exploded with volubility. 'I don't care if he does, mate. You won't catch me climbing garden walls to get away from him.' I was suitably admonished. It was very kind of Alf, and could he wait till Friday for the bean frame money. 'Today's Friday,' said Alf. He had me there.

'Yes, next Friday,' I said, deciding to complete the picture for him. 'I've given my wife my wage packet for this week. Nights get paid first thing Friday morning.'

'Cor blimey!' said Alf.

At the last minute Alf gave me sixpence and some coppers and a really withering look as I got on the bus. I was what things are coming to these days.

27

[Aquarius (Jan 20–Feb 19) If you are a stick-in-the-mud you'll get nowhere. Widen your social horizons. Go somewhere gay and relaxing.]

I heard the operator asking Charlie if he'd accept a reversed charge call. He said OK. 'This is a friend of Reg,' I said.

'I recognize the voice.'

'I'm in quite a bit of trouble, Mr Cavendish.'

'That's right,' said Charlie. 'You got it?' He was referring to the cable I'd had in Tokwe.

'Yes, thanks.'

''s OK. What can I do for you, my boy?'

'Could you meet me? Now?'

'Sure. Where?'

'Thanks.'

''s OK,' said Charlie. 'Where?'

I paused. I'd prepared the next bit: '"A dungeon horrible, on all sides round . . ."' I paused and Charlie completed it for me.

257

'"As one great furnace flamed; yet from those
      flames
No light, but rather darkness visible."'

That may not appeal to you, but to Milton and
Charlie it was just the thing. 'That's it,' I said.
'OK. I've got you. I'll be there in thirty min-
utes. I'll go in first and pay for you. Anything spe-
cial you want?'
'Yes, a job.'
Charlie gave a squeaky little laugh and rang off.

There are no lights inside but through the huge windows that form one wall of the little chamber two
lights that wouldn't have chagrined a medium flak
battery, stare relentlessly. The view through the glass
is impressionist; the world outside muted by the constant dribble and trickle of hot water across the
glass. The endless crash of sheets of water hitting
the red stone floor provided a banshee background
to the sudatory heat. Through the dense vapour
Charlie's pale pink and white blotchy body wrapped
in a small gingham towel could just be seen.
'Good idea,' Charlie said. He was six inches
shorter than me and he stared up with bright myopic
eyes, now more shiny than ever. 'Good idea this.' I
was flattered at Charlie's enthusiasm. 'I brought you
some clothes. A white shirt – one of Reg's. I thought
you'd take about the same size as Reg. Socks and
a pair of old canvas shoes size ten. Too big for me.'

There was a crash as someone leapt into the cold plunge.

'Turkish baths,' said Charlie, 'and sleep here too if you want.'

The pain was beginning to trickle out of my pores. I said, 'You see, Mr Cavendish . . .' the wet heat struck the back of my lungs as I opened my mouth '. . . I had no one else to go to.'

''s OK. I would have been furious if you hadn't come to your Uncle Charlie.' It was a joke we had between us, like the joke of Charlie reciting those stanzas of *Paradise Lost* here in the steam room on previous occasions. Charlie was looking at the cuts on my face and my bruised cheek. The steam had probably made them much more visible. 'You look like you got caught in a combine harvester,' Charlie said gently.

'Yes, and now they've sent me a bill for the damages.'

'Go on. What a sauce,' said Charlie seriously, then he did his squeaky laugh. Charlie wouldn't hear of me going anywhere but back to his place. Although the Turkish bath was very therapeutic I was still as weak as a half-drowned kitten. I let him put me into his 1947 Hillman that was parked right outside the door in Jermyn Street.

When I woke up on Saturday morning it was in Charlie's bed – Charlie had spent the night on the sofa. There was a smell of freshly ground coffee, a spitting of grilling bacon, and a big coal fire that had reached that state of perfection that the manufacturers of plastic fronts for electric ones seek to emulate.

I'm not good at guessing numbers, so it would be the roughest possible estimate if I said that Charlie's little apartment contained three thousand books. Enough to say perhaps that in no room was there much wall to be glimpsed. And I wouldn't like you to think that they were paperbacks of the *Bushwacker of Deadman's Gulch* genre either. No, these wonderful books were the reason Charlie Cavendish hadn't got past 1947 with his motor-cars.

'You're up,' said Charlie, coming into the living-room with a big white coffee-pot. 'Continental roast. OK?' I hoped I wasn't becoming that sort of fanatic that people had to check blends with before they could offer me a cup of coffee. 'Great,' I said.

'Would music bother you?'

'No, it would do me good,' I answered. Charlie went across to the hi-fi. It was a mass of valves and assorted components strung together with loops of wire, sticking-plaster and slivers of matchstick. He laid a huge shiny LP on the heavy turntable and delicately applied the diamond head. Strange that he should have chosen Mozart's 41st; for the second movement took me directly back to that evening I sat with Adem listening to the song of the blackcap. How long ago was that?

After breakfast Charlie settled down with

Encounters and I tuned in to the Saturday morning concert and began to wish I hadn't eaten, I was feeling pretty sick. I walked into the bedroom and took the weight off my feet. I had to think. I'd told Charlie as much as he need know, and ideally I should get away from here. Implicating a personal friend was bad enough, implicating someone employed within the framework of the service was unforgivable.

I had got as far as this merely because K.K. and Co had divided their anxieties between recapturing me and packing up their confidential stuff and clearing out quickly. But that did not mean that they were a set of amateurs, nor that they were going to take the heat off me in any way. What to do now?

Dalby seemed out of the question, so did anyone who worked for him. Ross wasn't even on my list. I could go to the CIGS but I really wasn't under Army jurisdiction any longer. Anyway that was out because Dalby would hear about my application for an interview before the ink on it was dry. If I gave a false name they would look me up in the List and arrest me when they found it wasn't there. If I gave someone else's name? No, of the Military Police and secretaries at the War House there was too many that know me by sight. Anyway, the CIGS probably wouldn't believe me. Ripley is probably the only one that *will* believe it, I thought.

The PM? I toyed with this idea for thirty

seconds. What would the Prime Minister do? He'd have to ask advice from the next responsible security authority. Who was that? In this particular case it was Dalby. Even if it wasn't Dalby it would be someone closely associated with Dalby. It was a maze and Dalby stood at the only exit.

Then perhaps the only way was to go directly to Dalby and sort out this muddle with him. After all, *I* knew I wasn't working for anyone else. There must be a way of proving it. On the other hand there wasn't a government in the world who'd have any compunction about killing an operator who knew as much as I did, if there were any doubts about loyalty. In a way this cheered me up. Whatever else, I wasn't dead yet, and killing someone isn't difficult.

I suddenly remembered Barney on the generator truck. I wondered if it was true. It had a terrible ring of truth somehow, but if Barney was killed for warning me, what did I deserve? Perhaps the Americans who held me weren't genuine. After all, the Hungarians hadn't been. No, that was out of the question.

Those interrogations had been as American as shoo-fly pie and hominy grits. The 'Hungarians'; where did they fit into all this? Who was K.K.? Naturally he would be keeping out of the way. That didn't mean that he wasn't in British Government pay.

Did the *Al Gumhuria* file that I'd declined to buy from Ross have anything to do with it? Things seemed to go wrong for me soon after that.

I must have dozed off with my problem still unresolved. Charlie woke me with tea and biscuits and said I had been shouting in my sleep. 'Nothing that I could understand,' said Charlie hastily. All day Saturday and all day Sunday I did nothing. Charlie fed me bouillon and steak while I hung around and felt sorry for myself. Sunday evening found me listening to Alistair Cooke on the radio and staring at a piece of blank paper upon which I'd resolved to write my plan of action.

I was better after the food and rest. I was still no Steve Reeves but I was moving into the Sir Cedric Hardwicke class. The paper I was doodling on stared back at me. Dalby's name I'd underlined. Connected to it in one direction: Alice; in the other: Ross, because if Dalby was going to crucify me there's no one to give him a more willing hand than Ross and the military boys. Murray and Carswell I'd linked together as the two unknowns. Chances were that by now Dalby had detached them back into some long-lost dust-covered office in the War House. Then there was Chico. He had the mind of a child of four, and the last time I'd heard from him was on the phone from Grantham. Jean? That was another big query. She'd risked a lot to help me in Tokwe, but just how long do you stick your neck out in this business? I was probably in a very good position to find out. Any way I worked it out the answer seemed to be: see Dalby. I resolved to do so. But there was something that must be done first.

By 9.30 P.M. I decided that I'd have to ask Charlie yet another favour. By 10 P.M. he was out of the house. Everything depended on Charlie then, or so it seemed at the time. I looked at the sepia photo of Reg Cavendish,* Charlie's son. He looked down from the top of the writing cabinet in one of those large boat-shaped forage caps that we'd all looked so silly in. I remembered coming to tell his father of his death when, after four years of unscathed combat action, Reg was killed by a truck in Brussels four days before VE day.

I had told Charlie that his son had been killed in a traffic accident just as simply as I'd heard it on the phone. He went into the kitchen and began to make coffee. I sat with the smell of my best uniform wet with the spring rain, and looked around at the shelves of books and gramophone records. At Balzac and Byron, Ben Jonson and Proust, Beethoven, Bach, and Sidney and Beatrice Webb.

I remember that when Charlie Cavendish had come back with coffee we talked about the weather and the wartime Cup Final and the subjects people talk about when they want to think about something else.

I remember thinking the coffee rather strange, it was as black as coal and almost as solid. It was only after two or three subsequent visits that I realized that Charlie had stood in the kitchen that

* See Appendix: Reg Cavendish, page 337.

night, ladling spoonful after spoonful of coffee into his white porcelain coffee-pot while his mind refused to function.

And now here I was again, sitting alone among Charlie's books; again I was waiting for Charlie to come back.

By 11.25 P.M. I heard his footsteps on the creaking winding staircase. I brought him coffee in that same white German porcelain coffee-pot that I had remembered from 1945. I went to the FM and switched 'Music at Night' down in volume.

Charlie spoke. 'A cipher,' he said, 'nothing nowhere, no trace, not ever.'

'You're joking,' I said. 'You must have got the Indian Army stuff.'

'No,' said Charlie, 'I even did a repeat request under "Calcutta Stats Office". There's no Carswell with the initials J.F. and the only one with anything possible is P. J. Carswell, aged 26.'

'No, that's nowhere near him,' I said.

'Are you sure of the spelling? Want me to try Carwell?'

'No, no,' I said, 'I'm sure of the spelling as much as I'm sure of anything. Anyway, you've taken enough chances already.'

'A pleasure,' said Charlie simply and sincerely. He continued with his coffee. 'French drip. I used to make it vacuum. Another time I had one of those upside-down Neapolitan things. French drip is best.'

'I'll tell you the whole story if you like, Charlie,'

I offered. I always find it difficult to use his first name, having been a friend of his son before I met him.

'Rather not. I know too many secrets already,' he said. It was a magnificent understatement. 'I'm turning in now. If you get inspired, let me know. It wouldn't be unusual me popping into "tracing" in the middle of the night.'

'Good night, Charlie,' I said. 'I'll work something out.' But I was no longer sure that I would.

28

Near Leicester Square there are some grubby little newsagents who specialize in the fleshier style of art magazine. Carnal covers posture, peer and swarm like pink spiders across their shop windows. For a small fee they act as accommodation addresses for people who receive mail that they would rather didn't arrive at home.

From the inner confines came the smell of boiled socks and an old bewhiskered crone with a fat manilla envelope addressed to the person I was purporting to be.

I opened it right away for they have little curiosity left, the people who work in these shops. Inside I knew there was a new Chubb key, a United Kingdom passport, an American passport (clipped to which was a social security card in the same name), and a UN Secretariat passport. Tucked inside each was an International driving licence, and a few bills and used envelopes in the same name as that particular passport. There were also cheque books issued by the Royal Bank of Canada, Chase Manhattan, Westminster and the Dai-ichi Bank of Tokyo, a small brown pawn ticket, twenty used ten-shilling notes, a folded new manilla envelope, and a poor-quality forged Metropolitan Police warrant card.

I put the key, pawn ticket, warrant card and money into my pocket and the other things into the new manilla envelope. I walked down the road and posted the envelope back to the same address. A taxi took me to a bank in the city and the chief clerk conducted me to the vaults. I fitted the key into the safe deposit box. I removed some five-pound notes from inside it. By this time the clerk had discreetly left me alone. From under the bank-notes I slid a heavy cardboard box, and broke the wax seals on it with my thumb-nail. It was the work of a moment to slip the Colt .32 automatic into one pocket and two spare clips into the other.

'Good day, sir,' the clerk said as I left.

'Yes, it's a bit brighter,' I told him.

The pawn shop was near Gardner's corner. I paid £11 13s 9d and exchanged the pawn ticket for a canvas travelling bag. Inside was a dark green flannel suit, cotton trousers, two dark shirts and six white ones, a bright Madras jacket, ties, socks, underwear, black shoes and canvas ones. The side panels contained razor, shaving cream, blades, comb, compressed dates, plastic raincoat, folding knife, prismatic compass and a packet of Kleenex. Into the lining of the suit was sewn a 100NF note, a £5 note, and a 100DM note, and into the small amount of padding was sewn another key to another safe deposit box. This, too, is a spy's insurance policy.

I booked into a hotel near Bedford Square, then met Charlie in Tottenham Court Road Fortes. Charlie was dead on time as usual: 12.7 (to make appointments on the hour or half-hour is to ask for trouble). I took off the raincoat and gave it to him, producing my own plastic one from my pocket. 'I've left your door key in my hotel room,' I told him.

'Yerse?' said the girl behind the counter. We ordered some coffee and sandwiches, and Charlie put on the raincoat. 'It's just beginning to spot with rain,' he said.

'What a shame,' I said, 'it seemed as though it was going to be a nice day.' We munched the sandwiches.

'You can let yourself in and leave the key on the shelf, because I must be back by two o'clock,' said Charlie. I paid for the food and he thanked me. 'Look after yourself,' he said. 'I've got used to having you drop in from time to time.' Before he left me, Charlie told me three times that I must contact him if I needed any help. Naturally I was tempted to use Charlie to help me. He was too old to be foolhardy, too knowledgeable to be garrulous, and too content to be curious, but he was too willing to be exploited.

I left Charlie, and from Fortes I went to a black sooty building in Shaftesbury Avenue. 'Waterman's World-Wide Detective Agency' it said, in black raised letters on the door. Inside, a thin shiny-black-suited detective looked up like a subject of a photo in a divorce case. He was removing a piece of wax from his ear with a match stick. He thought I should have knocked; if it hadn't prejudiced his income he might have told me about it. Instead he took off his bowler hat and said, 'Can I be of any assistance?' He didn't like me sitting down without permission either. I told him that I was in a difficult domestic situation. 'Really, sir? I'm sorry,' he said, like he had never met anyone in a difficult domestic situation before.

I gave him a lot of stuff about my wife and another fellow, and he 'ho'ed' and 'oh deared' his way through it. I didn't *think* there would be a breach of the peace, I told him, but if he could be on hand. We agreed on a fee of eight guineas, which was pretty handsome. This character would lay on an SS Armoured Division for a fiver. I felt better now I had finally decided not to involve Charlie, and it was five o'clock that afternoon before I got back to Charlie's place in Bloomsbury. I wanted to speak to him before he went to his part-time job as barman at the 'Tin-Tack Club', and give him his key.

I arrived at Charlie's place at 5.10. I let myself in by the front door. The slight amount of day-light that filtered through the green glass window on the back stairs lit the moth-eaten stair-carpet with a dense emerald light. The place smelt of unlit corners, bicycles in the hall and yesterday's cat food. One ascended like a diver, slowly nearing the white daylight surface of Charlie's top flat. I reached the loose stair-rod two steps from the top of the first flight before I heard the sound. I paused and listened without breathing for a second or so. I know now that I should have turned around and left the house, and I knew it then. But I didn't go. I continued up the stairs towards the woman's sobbing.

The whole place was upside down; clothes, books, broken plates, the whole place a battle-field. On the landing was an old-fashioned fridge as big as a portable radio, a gas oven, a sink, and Charlie's body. He looked limp and relaxed in a way that only dead things do. As I bent close to him I saw the white porcelain coffee-pot smashed into a thousand pieces, and fresh dry coffee crunched under the soles of my shoes. In the living-room whole shelf-fuls of books had been heaved on the floor, and there they lay, open and upside down, strangely like Charlie.

Shiny records, letters, flowers, brass ornaments, and a small leather-cased carriage clock had been swept from the top of the writing cabinet, leaving only Reg's photo as the sole survivor. I removed Charlie's wallet as gently as I could to provide the police with a motive, and as I straightened up I looked straight into the eyes of a young, ill-looking woman of about thirty. Her face was green like the downstairs window, and her eyes were black, very wide open, and sunk deep into her face. The knuckles of her small hand were white with tension as she pushed it into her mouth. We looked at each other for perhaps a whole minute. I wanted to tell her that although I hadn't killed Charlie she mustn't . . . oh, how could I ever begin. I started down the stairs as fast as possible.

Whoever had slaughtered Charlie was there after me, and when the police had finished taking my description from the whimpering woman on the stairs, they'd be after me, too. Dalby's organization was the only contact with enough power to help me.

At Cambridge Circus I jumped on a bus as it came past. I got off at Piccadilly, hailed a cab to the Ritz, and then walked east up Piccadilly. No car could follow without causing a traffic sensation by an illegal right turn. Just to be on the safe side, I hailed another cab on the far side of the road, outside Whites, in case anyone had done that turn, and now sped in the opposite direction to anyone who could have followed me. I gave the cabbie the address of a car hire company in Knightsbridge. It was still only 5.25.

Not without difficulty, I hired a blue Austin 7, the only car they had with a radio. I used Charlie's driving licence, and some envelopes I'd found in his wallet 'proved' my identity. I cursed my foolishness in not having taken a driving licence from the safe deposit. I was taking a long chance on Charlie's name not being released to the Press before the various Intelligence departments had a look in, but I tuned in to the 6 o'clock news just the same. Algeria, and another dock strike. The dockers didn't like something again. Perhaps it was each other. No murders. An antique Austin 7 in front of me signalled a right turn. The driver had shaved under the arms. I drove on through Putney and along the side of the common. It was green and fresh and a sudden burst of sunshine made the wet trees sparkle, and turned the spray from speeding tyres into showers of pearls. Rich stockbrokers in white Jaguars and dark-green Bentleys played tag and wondered why I'd intruded into their private fun.

'Waaa Waaa Waaa Waaa – you're driving me crazy,' sang the radio as I changed down to negotiate Wimbledon Hill, and outside, the nightmare world of killers, policemen and soldiers happily brushed shoulders. I gazed out on it from the entirely imaginary security of the little car. How long was it to be before every one of the crowds on Wimbledon High Street were going to become suddenly interested in Charlie Cavendish and interested even more in finding me. The pianist at the

'Tin-Tack Club'; I suddenly remembered that I still owed him thirty shillings. Would he give my description to the police? How to get out of this mess? I looked at the grim rows of houses on either side of me and imagined them all to be full of Mr Keatings. How I wished I lived in one – a quiet, uneventful, predictable existence.

Now I was back on the Kingston by-pass at Bushey Road. At the 'Ace of Spades' the road curves directly into the setting sunlight, and the little car leapt forward in response to a slight touch of the foot.

Two trucks were driving neck and neck ahead of me. Each one was doing twenty-eight mph, each grimly intent on proving he could do twenty-nine! I passed them eventually and fell in behind a man in a rust-coloured pullover and Robin-Hood hat who had been to BRIGHTON, BOGNOR REGIS, EXETER, HARLECH, SOUTHEND, RYDE, SOUTHAMPTON, YEOVIL and ROCHESTER, and who, because of this, could not now see through his rear window.

At Esher I put on the lights, and well before Guildford the gentle smack of raindrops began to hit the windscreen. The heater purred happily, and I kept the radio tuned to the Light for the 6.30 bulletin. Godalming was pretty well closed except for a couple of tobacconists, and at Milford I slowed up to make sure I took the right route. Not the Hindhead or Haslemere road, but the 283 to Chiddingfold. A hundred yards before I reached the big low Tudor-fronted inn I flashed the head-lights and got an answering signal from the brake-actuated red rear lights of a parked vehicle there. I glimpsed the car, a black Ford Anglia with a spotlight fixed to the roof. I watched the rear-view mirror as Mr Waterman pulled his car on to the road just behind me.

I'd been to Dalby's home once before, but that was in daylight, and now it was quite dark. He lived in a small stone house lying well back from the road. I backed, just off the road, up a small driveway. Waterman parked on the far side of the road. The rain continued, but wasn't getting any worse. I left the car unlocked with the keys on the floor under the seat. Waterman stayed in his car and I didn't blame him. It was 6.59, so I listened to the 7 o'clock news bulletin. There was still no mention of Charlie, so I set off up the path to the house.

It was a small converted farm-house with a décor that writers in women's magazines think is con-temporary. Outside the mauve front door there was a wheelbarrow with flowers growing in it. Fixed to the wall was a coach lamp converted to electricity, not as yet lit. I knocked at the door with, need I say it, a brass lion's-head knocker. I looked back. Waterman had doused his lights, and gave me no sign of recognition. Perhaps he was smarter than I thought. Dalby opened the door and tried to register surprise on his bland egg-like public school face.

'Is it still raining?' he said. 'Come in.'

I sank into the big soft sofa that had *Go*, *Queen* and *Tatler* scattered across it. In the fireplace two fruit-tree logs sent an aroma of smoky perfume through the room. I watched Dalby with a certain amount of suspicion. He walked towards a huge bookcase – the aged spines of good editions of Balzac, Irving and Hugo glinted in the fire-light.

'A drink?' he said. I nodded, and Dalby opened the 'bookcase' which proved to be an artful disguise for doors of a cocktail cabinet. The huge glass and mirror box reflected a myriad of labels, everything from Charrington to Chartreuse – this was the gracious living I had read about in the newspapers.

'Tio Pepe or Teachers?' asked Dalby, and after handing me the clear glass of sherry added, 'I'll have someone fix you a sandwich. I know that having a sherry means you are hungry.' I protested, but he disappeared anyway. This wasn't going at all the way I planned. I didn't want Dalby to have time to think, nor did I intend that he should leave the room. He could phone – get a gun ... As I was thinking this, he reappeared with a plate of cold ham. I remembered how hungry I was. I began to eat the ham and drink my sherry, and I became angry as I realized how easily Dalby had put me at a disadvantage.

'I've been bloody well incarcerated,' I finally told him.

'You're telling me,' he agreed cheerfully.

'You know?' I asked.

'It was Jay. He's been trying to sell you back to us.'

'Why didn't you grab him?'

'Well, you know Jay, he's difficult to get hold of, and anyway, we didn't want to risk them "bumping you off" did we?' Dalby used expressions like 'bumping off' when he spoke to me. He thought it helped me to understand him.

I said nothing.

'He wanted £40,000 for you. We think he may have Chico, too. Someone in the USMD* works for him. That's how he got you from Tokwe. It could be serious.'

'Could be?' I said. 'They damn' nearly killed me.'

'Oh, I wasn't worried about you. They were unlikely to kill the goose and all that.'

'Oh, weren't you? Well you weren't there to get worried and all that.'

'You didn't see Chico there?'

'No,' I said. 'That was the only alleviating feature of the whole affair.'

'Another drink?' Dalby was the perfect host.

'No,' I said. 'I must be getting along. I want the keys to the office.' His face didn't flicker. Those English public schools are worth every penny.

'I insist that you join us for dinner,' said Dalby. I declined and we batted polite talk back and

* United States Medical Department.

forth. I wasn't out of the wood yet. Charlie was dead, and Dalby either didn't know or didn't want to talk about it. As I was about to tell him Dalby produced from an abstract painting that concealed a wall safe, a couple of files about payments to agents working in the South American countries.* Dalby gave me both files, and the keys, and I promised to figure out something for him by ten o'clock the next morning at Charlotte Street. I looked at my watch. It was 7.50 P.M. I was pretty anxious to leave because Waterman's instructions were to come at the run after one hour exactly. From his performance so far it seemed unwise to count on him being tardy. I took my leave, still

---

* It was a difficult problem which before the Castro régime had always been handled by a small private bank in Havana, which we more or less owned. Castro, however, had nationalized it, luckily not before the local police had tipped them off, so the documentation was at present intact at Saratoga Springs. Dalby asked me to submit a report about it. This was the sort of situation that I was always called in to help with. Not that I'm any sort of accountant, goodness knows; I can make two and two into something different every time I put those particularly unreliable digits together, but I had done a lot of work with the Swiss bank for Ross. By the time I came to Dalby's department, I had enough good solid contacts there to trace any secret account, given enough time. As well as this I had learned every legal and illegal way of moving money about the globe. Money is to espionage what petrol is to a motor-car, and it was because I had kept the wraps on my contacts there that I had been so insubordinate to so many for so long.

without the name of Charlie Cavendish being mentioned. I decided to leave it until we were in the office.

Half-way down the driveway I realized that between now and tomorrow morning was ample time to get myself arrested on a murder charge. Perhaps I should go back and say, 'Oh, there's one other thing. I'm wanted for murder.'

I started up the Austin, and moved easily down the road towards the big pub. It was about a quarter of a mile down the road before Waterman switched on his lights. He kept going up in my estimation. When we got to the car park of the 'Glowering Owl', I walked across to Waterman and gave him the money in cash.

'It went off all right then. I'm glad of that,' he said, his nicotine-stained moustache following his mouth as it smiled. I thanked him, and he put his car into gear, then said, 'I thought we were in for a right barny when the big Chink feller came out to look at you through the window.'

Big rain clouds raced across the moon, and an arty-looking couple came out of the Saloon Bar, arguing violently. They walked across the car park.

'Wait a minute,' I said, my hand on the edge of the wet car window. 'Chink? A Chinese? Are you sure?'

'Am I sure? Listen, friend. I had five years in the New Territories; I should know what a Chink looks like.'

I got into the car seat beside him, and asked

him to go through it in slow motion. He did so, but he needn't have done for all the extra information it gave me.

'We are going back up there right away,' I told him.

'Not me, friend, I did the job I was hired for.'

'OK,' I said, 'I'll pay you again.'

'Look friend, you've been there, you've had your say – let things be.'

'No, I must go back up there whether you come or not. I might only glance in through the window,' I coaxed.

'This is nothing to do with your wife, friend. You're up to some no-good. I can tell. I could tell you weren't a divorce case from the first minute I saw you.'

'All right,' I said, 'but my money's OK isn't it?' I didn't pause, as I considered his disagreement on this score very unlikely. 'I'm from Brighton – Special Branch,' I improvised, and showed him my forged warrant card. It passed in the poor light inside the car, but I'd hate to depend upon it in daylight.

'*You* a copper! You never are, friend.'

I persisted that I was, and he half-believed me. He said, 'I know that some of the new coppers you can hardly tell nowadays. Real mixture they are.'

'This is an important case,' I told him. 'And I want your assistance now.'

The squeelch and buzz of the windscreen wipers

continued steadily as he made up his mind. Why did I want him? I thought; but somewhere I had a hunch it would be a good eight guineas' worth. It wasn't one of my best hunches.

'Why didn't you bring one of your own constables?' he suddenly asked.

'It wasn't possible,' I said, hesitating. 'It's out of our area. I'm acting on special authority.'

'It's not monkey business, friend, is it? I couldn't be mixed up in anything funny.'

At last. At last I was getting it across to him that I was a policeman negotiating a high-class bribe. As he got used to it, he came to quite like the idea of a well-placed friend on the force, but he added, 'It will cost you another twelve guineas.'

We settled on the fee and set off up the road again, this time both in his car. I didn't want Dalby to see the blue Austin 7 coming back again. The files were the problem. I didn't know what to tell Waterman to do with them if anything happened, so I put them on the back seat and hoped that nothing would.

29

It all worked quite smoothly: approach without
lights, parking, and the walk to the house. It was
quite dark now, but gaps in the curtains let some
light fall across the flower beds. Perhaps those were
the chinks Waterman saw, I thought. I was getting quite skilled at negotiating growing plants on
foot at night. Without making too much noise on
the gravel I got close to the window of the room
in which I had spoken with Dalby. It was a bit
shattering to find Dalby was very close to the
window on the other side; like a picture on a 21-
inch screen. He wasn't, however, concerned with
prowlers in his garden; he was pouring a drink
from that damn' cabinet. On the sofa sat Murray
listening to Dalby as he poured and talked. They
were talking to someone else outside my range of
vision; he must have asked what they wanted to
drink because the third party walked across to the
drinks cabinet. I watched them only three feet away
from me. I could catch an occasional word of con-

versation even through the double glass. My hunch was right; there was no other face like K.K.'s, and every feature was inscribed on my retina. He was Waterman's 'Chink'. K.K. and Dalby. I had seen enough and was about to go – but Dalby and K.K. were both looking across the room speaking to another. It wasn't Murray, I'd seen him go into the kitchen. And then into my line of vision – like the bad fairy at the princess's christening – walked Jay.

I almost fell backwards into the *Convallaria*. After all those hours of screenings, there could be no mistake. The elusive Jay. Few members of the department had ever seen him, and yet I was always coming across him – in Led's, in the street, in theatre clubs, and now – finally the prince of evil is chatting with the head of the department. How can I tell you the impact this made on me? It was like seeing Mr Macmillan drop a CP* card out of his wallet; it was like discovering that Edgar Hoover was Lucky Luciano in disguise. I was watching the scene like a small boy in a lollipop factory. Goodness knows how long I stood petrified with surprise. K.K.'s presence shattered me, but Jay's made me forget K.K.! 'We are moving in from opposite ends to the same conclusion,' Dalby had once told me. How wrong can you get? I remembered the two men I had seen from the Terrazza Restaurant window. Undoubtedly they *were* Jay and Dalby.

* Communist Party.

283

Waterman had followed me up the path, and I reached out my hand to help him avoid the lily of the valley. After staring wide-eyed into the bright room, the darkness was a baffling blanket of void, out of which a hand smelling of toilet soap clamped across my mouth, and something very sharp penetrated the 'one-piece back' of my jacket. I stiffened and held very still.

'It's Murray, sir,' a voice in my ear said, and I thought, 'Sir? This is a nice time for formalities.'

I remembered Raven who we'd kidnapped near the Syrian border, and how puzzled I'd been to hear Dalby say, 'I'm sorry, sir,' when he injected him. Perhaps 'Sir' was something they always say when they – what were Dalby's words – 'bumped you off'.

'I'm taking my hand away now, sir. Don't shout or we've both had it.' I nodded my head but Murray mistook it for an attempt to escape, and he instinctively twisted my arm and held my mouth even tighter. Where the hell was Waterman? Come and earn your twelve guineas I kept thinking – but there was no sign of him. Murray eased me quietly away from the house, and finally let go of me altogether. He was the first to speak.

'You were walking all over the infra-red alarms.'

'I might have guessed it wasn't as wide open as it looks,' I said.

'I've got to get back to the house now, but . . .' he hesitated. There was plenty I wanted to know. I was in no position to extract a confession, but

I leaned towards him and said, 'Listen, Murray, whatever screwy damn' thing is going on, you know that all the people in that house are actionable under the Treason Act. You will act on my orders and mine only as of this moment, or you will become an enemy of HMG.'* Murray was silent. 'Can't you see, man? Dalby has sold out, or perhaps he's been a double agent for years. My task was to verify that information. I have five provost platoons in Haslemere – whatever happens the whole show is over. I'm giving you a chance, Murray, because I know you are not in as deeply as the others. Come with me now and help me assemble my data. The whole crowd of them are done for.' I stopped; my invention had flagged: I was on the verge of saying the game's up.

'My name's Harriman,' said Murray. 'And I'm a lieutenant-colonel in Special Field Intelligence, and it's *you* who must be temporarily subject to my orders.' His voice was different to that of the Sergeant Murray I had known. He went on. 'I'm sorry you've had such a bad time, but you must get out of here now. We are not out of the proverbial wood by any means. To get Dalby is nothing . . .' That was the moment when Waterman hit him with the spanner.

I looked down at Murray or Harriman or whoever he was and I knew quite clearly what I must do. I must get out of here. What Dalby & Co

* Her Majesty's Government.

would do when they found their unconscious friend with his head in the petunias was anyone's guess. Waterman, that soul of simplicity, was now bound to me by complicity in my actions. 'Did I do right, Super?' he said about three times. I told him that he was sensational, but it was difficult to sound enthusiastic. It was something though, that he was prepared to do as I told him. We dragged Murray's body into the taller flowers.

I was prepared to have to sit in Waterman's car for a couple of hours, but within ten minutes we saw the front door open and car headlights switched on. It was a large car, and as it came steadily down the drive the headlights skimmed across the prostrate Murray. We both held our breath, but I suppose we saw it only because we knew it was there. Dalby went inside, and the big Rolls turned on to the road and headed towards London.

'Catch that up,' I told Waterman. 'I want to see the driver.'

At Milford the street lighting gave me a chance to take a look at the car. It was a black Rolls Phantom IV, a straight-eight that Messrs Rolls-Royce will only sell to Royalty and Heads of State. How typical that Jay should have one. Waterman flipped open the glove compartment and produced a pair of prismatics. With them I could see Jay as he leaned back on fine West of England uphol-stery and sipped a drink from the cocktail cabinet. Now and again I could glimpse the chauffeur's face in the green-tinted mirrors. We had settled down to a steady forty-five now. Waterman was a driver in a million. He handled his car with a curious 'finger-tip' feeling that was alien to him, because out of the car he was a clumsy, heavy-handed clod of a fellow. It was important that the Rolls didn't know it had a tail, and Waterman hit upon the rather subtle ruse of trying to race it, but always losing out. The Rolls didn't take advantage of its superior power to race ahead as at first I feared it might. Not that it would have shaken us off. Waterman's little modified double-carburettor car was his pride and joy. It had dozens of instruments, temperature gauges, revolution counters, clocks and reading lights. But we kept going at forty-five all the way to London. Jay seemed to be in no sort of hurry.

30

[Aquarius (Jan 20–Feb 19) A good week for your hobbies and romance, but you can expect some difficulties with evening arrangements. Forthright talking may clear the air.]

Jay's Rolls purred along the Cromwell Road until it turned off near the Brompton Oratory. Those gaunt Victorian houses, built at the time of the 1851 Exhibition, stared down at us. Cars were parked densely along the pavements, sports cars and snob cars and cars wrapped in silvery sheets of material. We turned off the road when Jay rolled to a standstill outside a big conversion. We closed the doors quietly and moved quickly enough to see the portly form of Jay entering the front door. It was a 'tasteful' piece of contemporary; natural wood-finish doors, stainless-steel windows and venetian blinds everywhere. Waterman and I peered at the list of names and bell pushes.

'You may as well go in,' said a tall, bespectacled

city gent behind us, opening the door with a key. We went in, partly because it was convenient for us, partly because there were two more city gents behind us, and partly because they were all holding small 9mm Italian Mod 34 Beretta automatic pistols.

The man who had spoken pushed the top bell and spoke into the small metal microphone. 'Yes. There's two of them. One of them could be a policeman,' he said. They had been tailing us, and to add insult to injury had been discussing us over car to car radio-phones.

I then heard Jay's voice, 'Put the gentlemen on the detector and bring them in, Maurice.' I looked at Waterman – the edges of his stained moustache turned down: we'd been a couple of right ninnies. Followed all the way! I should have guessed that Jay meeting Dalby would take some 'beef' with him. I wondered if Dalby had phoned Jay about Murray: found unconscious in his flowers.

The entrance hall was all black mirrors, fresh flowers and genuine cut-glass chandeliers. We were stood up before the full-length mirror. There was a small buzzing noise and I was deprived of my gun by Maurice who stood well clear of his colleague's line of fire. Maurice was very professional. If you could afford a Phantom IV you could afford the best in hoodlums. We were taken upstairs.

The forty-foot living-room was ankle deep in cream-coloured long-tufted carpeting. The white walls were punctuated with large abstract paintings: Rothko, Motherwell and Hitchens. At the far end of the room a circular black-marble table of knee height, surrounded by low black-leather armchairs with high wing backs, made a cosy corner round the gigantic hi-fi unit, and TV that was telling us that 'Trill makes budgies bounce with health' over and over again.

At 'our' end of the room Jay's voice, a rather rich detergent-advertising voice, floated through the open doorway. 'Won't you sit down?'

The three city gents withdrew like the Beverley Sisters taking a curtain, but we all knew they were no farther than the thickness of the door away.

'This is Mr Waterman,' I said loudly to the invisible Jay, 'of Waterman's Detective Agency. I hired him this afternoon.' There was only silence so I spoke again even more loudly, clearly enunciating my words as one would speak to a rich deaf uncle. 'I don't think there is anything further from Mr Waterman. He may as well go home now.'

There was silence, then Jay's voice, 'Do you owe Mr Waterman any money?'

'Fifteen guineas,' I said, 'but I thought you would want to fix it.'

Jay must have pressed a button for I heard a soft buzzer. The door opened so quickly that Maurice must have been standing with his hand on the handle.

'What kept you, Maurice?' I said. I hated Maurice; he was so polite and restrained. He stood there without speaking. His spectacles were clean and efficient – the glass emphasized the deadly little eyes through which he dispassionately viewed his world, of which I was, for the time being, a part. Again came Jay's instruction. 'Maurice, you will let Mr Waterman here have a cheque for fifteen guineas. The number three account, Maurice. Then you will show Mr Waterman to the door.' Maurice nodded even though Jay couldn't see him.

Mr Waterman was pinching large sections of his nicotine-stained little moustache between index finger and thumb, and twisting it until it pained him. Mr Waterman also nodded. Mr Waterman must go. Mr Waterman was feeling a little out of place. Money is money but even at fifteen guineas a time he felt he must go. 'Good-bye Mr Waterman,' I said, and Mr Waterman left us.

I wanted to see what Jay was doing in the little annexe without a door. I could hear him moving around. I knew these big Kensington houses; visitors just never participate. I walked across to the doorway. I don't know what I expected to see Jay doing. Sitting in front of bubbling test tubes like a Bela Lugosi movie. Watching 'This is your Life', or perhaps cultivating hot-house orchids.

'You are interested in cooking?' Jay looked much older than I remembered him, and against the white cook's apron, strapped over one shoulder in the French manner, his complexion was rubicund as is a heavy drinker's. In his hand he held a three-pound lobster. The kitchen was illuminated by merciless daylight tubes. Copper, stainless steel and sharp knives were distributed with the careful forethought of an operating theatre. A kitchen with such a maze of scientific aids that would make Cape Canaveral look like a rectangular wheel. Jay put the fresh mottled black and verdigris lobster down on the white counter and picked a bottle of Moet & Chandon out of the ice bucket with a happy tinkle. He poured two generous glasses full.

'I could get interested,' I said.

'That's right,' said Jay, and I began to drink the cool clear bubbling drink.

I said, 'Didn't Lao-Tze say something like "Govern the Empire as you would cook a little fish"?'

Jay warmed to me. A smile peeped around his giant moustache. 'Montaigne said, "Great men pride themselves on knowing how to prepare a fish for table,"' he answered.

'But did he mean it as a compliment?' I asked.

Jay didn't answer; he was driving a long metal rod through the lobster. I sipped the cold champagne.

'It's quite dead,' said Jay. I could see it was a difficult job. 'I just can't bear killing things,' he told me. He'd finished getting the lobster on the spit. 'You know, I have to get the fish merchant to kill it for me.'

'Yes,' I said. 'Some people are like that, I know.'

'A little more champagne,' he said. 'I only need half a bottle for this recipe, and I don't like to drink too much.'

'Thanks,' I said, and I meant it. It was hot in that kitchen.

He poured the remainder of the bottle into a metal tray and threw a little salt into it. 'You're a cool young man,' he said. 'Don't you care about your friend Cavendish?' He added a large piece of butter to the champagne. I don't know why, but I didn't expect that the butter would float. I remember watching and thinking 'It only does that because Jay put it in.' I sipped my champagne again.

Jay picked up his champagne and drank some – he watched me intently through his tiny little eyes. 'I run a very big business.'

'Yes, I know,' I said, but Jay waved his big red hand.

'Bigger,' he said. 'Bigger than you know.' I said nothing. Jay had a jar down from the shelf and sprinkled a few peppercorns into the champagne. He carefully carried the tray and limping across the tiny kitchen clipped it into the radiant heat vertical grill. He picked up the lobster that he couldn't bear to kill and waved it at me.

'The fishmonger sells fish. Right?' he said, and fixed it to the grill. 'The wine merchant sells champagne. The French don't protest at the idea of their champagne leaving France. Right?'

'Right,' I said. I was beginning to recognize my cue.

'You.' I wondered what I sold. Jay switched on the grill and the lobster, lit bright red on one side

293

by the electric element, began to revolve very very slowly. 'You,' said Jay again, 'sell loyalty.' He stared at me. 'I don't do that: I wouldn't do it.' For a moment I thought even Jay thinks I have changed sides, but I realized that it was Jay's way of talking. He went on, 'I sell people.'

'Like Eichmann?' I asked.

'I don't like that sort of joke,' said Jay like a Sunday-school teacher at the *Folies Bergères*. Then his face cracked into a little grin. 'More like Eichelhauer let's say.' That was the German name for Jay. Jay, I thought. *Garrulus glandarius rufitergum*. Jay: egg thief, bully of birds and raider of crops, lurking, cautious Jay who flies in clumsy undulating hops. 'I deal in talented men exchanging employment of their own free will.'

'You're a talent scout from the Kremlin?' I said.

Jay began to baste the lobster that he didn't like to kill with the champagne that he didn't like to drink. He was thinking about what I said. I could see why Jay was such a big success. He took everything at its face value. I still don't know if Jay thought he was a talent scout from the Kremlin because the wall phone rang in the kitchen. Jay stopped basting long enough to wipe his hands. He listened on the phone. 'Put him through.' A pause. 'Then say I *am* at home.' He moved round and fixed me with that basilisk's stare that people holding phones have. He suddenly said to me, 'We don't smoke in the kitchen,' then, uncupping the phone, 'This is Maximilian speaking. My dear Henry.' His face split open in a big smile. 'I won't say a word, my dear friend, just carry on. Yes, very well.' I saw Jay push the 'scramble' button. Jay just listened, but his face was like Gielgud doing 'The Seven Ages of Man'. Finally Jay said, 'Thanks,' and he hung up the phone thoughtfully, and began to baste the lobster again.

I puffed my cigarette. Jay watched me but said nothing. I decided the initiative in this conversation had passed to me. 'Is it time to talk about the head-shrinking factory at Wood Green?' I asked.

'Head shrinking?' Jay asked.

'Brain Washing Incorporated: the place I jumped out of. Isn't that what we're leading up to?'

'You think that I'm something to do with that?' his face was 11 A.M. November 11th.

There was a knock on the door and Maurice brought a slip of paper to Jay. I tried to read it, but it was impossible. There may have been about fifty typewritten words there. Maurice left. Then I followed Jay across the big sitting-room. Near the radio and TV was a small machine like a type-writer carriage. It was a paper shredder. Jay fed the sheet in and pressed a button. It disappeared. Jay sat down.

'Did they treat you badly at Wood Green?' he said.

'I was getting to like it,' I said, 'but I just couldn't keep the payments up.'

'You think it's terrible.' It was neither a question nor a statement.

'I don't think about it. I get paid to encounter all manner of things. I suppose some of them are terrible.'

'In the Middle Ages,' Jay went on as though he hadn't heard, 'they thought the cross-bow was the most terrible thing.'

'That wasn't because of the weapon itself, but because it threatened their system.'

'That's right,' Jay said. 'So we let them use the terrible weapon, but only upon Moslems. Right?'

'That's right,' I said; now I was using his lines.

'What you might call a policy of limited war upon subversive elements,' Jay told me. 'Yes, and now we have another terrible weapon; more terrible than nuclear explosions, more terrible than nerve gas, more terrible than the anti-matter bomb. But with this terrible weapon no one gets hurt; is that so terrible?'

'Weapons aren't terrible,' I said. 'Aeroplanes full of passengers to Paris, bombs full of insecticide, cannons with a man inside at a circus – these aren't terrible. But a vase of roses in the hands of a man of evil intent is a murder weapon.'

'My boy,' said Jay, 'if brain-washing had come to the world before the trial of Joan of Arc she would have lived to a happy old age.'

I said, 'Yes, and France would still be full of mercenary soldiers.'

'I thought you'd like that,' said Jay. 'You're the English patriot.'

I was silent. Jay leaned forward from where he was sitting in the big black-leather armchair. 'You can't really believe that the Communist countries are going to collapse, and that this strange capitalist system will march proudly on.' He tapped my knee. 'We are both sensible, objective men, with, I think I might say, wide political experience. Neither of us could deny the comfort of it all,' he stroked the rich leather, 'but what has capitalism to offer? Its colonies that once were the goose that laid the golden egg, they are vanishing. The goose has found out where to *sell* the egg. The few places where a reactionary government has suppressed the socialist movement, why, in those places those governments are merely propped up by Fascist force, paid for in Western gold.'

Behind Jay's voice I could hear the radio playing very quietly. An English jazz singer was even now Gee Whizzing, Waa Waa and Boop boop booping in an unparalleled plethora of idiocy. He noticed that I was listening, and his attack veered. What of the capitalist countries themselves? What of them then, racked with strikes, with mental illness, with insular disregard for their fellow men. On the brink of anarchy, their police beset by bribes, and by roving bands of overfed cowards seeking an outlet for the sadism that is endemic to capitalism, which is in any case licensed selfishness. Who do they pay their big rewards to? Musicians, aviators, poets, mathematicians? No! Degenerate young men who gain fame by not understanding music or having talent for singing. He'd timed his speech well, or he had luck, for he switched the radio across to the Home Service. It was time for the news. He went on talking, but I didn't hear him. I could only hear the announcer saying. 'The police are anxious to interview a man seen near the scene of the crime.' There followed a fairly good description of me.

'Cut out all this,' I said to Jay. 'Who killed Charlie Cavendish?'

Jay got up from his chair and went to look out of the window. He beckoned to me and I went to look out. There were two taxis parked across the street. At the bottom of the street was a single-decker bus. Jay switched on the FM radio, and tuned it to the police wave-length. A police walkie-talkie outside the Victoria and Albert Museum was co-ordinating the movements.

'We all did,' said Jay. 'You, me and them.'

One of the three men across the street leaned into the taxi-cab and we heard his voice saying, 'I'm going across there now – pay particular attention to the back and the roofs. Street blocks! Hold everyone until further notice.' It was Ross's voice. The three men came across the road.

Jay turned to me. 'One of these days, brain-washing will be the acknowledged method of dealing with anti-social elements. Criminals can be brain-washed. I've proved it. Nearly 300 people I've processed. It's the greatest step forward of the century.' He picked up the phone. 'Maurice, we have callers.' Jay gave me a broad calm smile. 'Show them up, but tell them that I am already in custody.' And I remembered other things about *garrulus glandarius rufitergum* – alert, tireless, excitable, vociferous, pairs for life, sociable in the spring but solitary at all other times.

Maurice let Ross and the two policemen in, and everyone shook hands with everyone. I'd never been pleased to see Ross before. They were taking no chances and the street blocks were kept in position for another hour. Ross was pretty cool with Jay, and he was searched and taken off to Carshalton, which was a house that Ross's department owned for purposes unknown. When Jay came in to say good-bye, I noticed he had changed into a very fine grey-green mohair. I was mildly surprised to notice that he had a nuclear disarmament badge in his lapel. He saw me looking at it and removed it and pressed it into my hand without saying a word. Considering the place he was going, he could have given me the TV.

When all the commotion had faded, Ross said, a little patronizingly I thought, 'And now I suppose you've got something that can't wait another moment.'

I said, 'I have, if you like *homard à la broche*,' and I took him to the kitchen to show him.

Ross made a joke then. He said, 'Do you come here often?'

'I do,' I said. 'I know the chef.'

31

[Aquarius (Jan 20–Feb 19) Joyful renewal of old acquaintance. Throw yourself wholeheartedly into your work.]

It was midnight when I got to Charlotte Street. The whole place was a hive of activity. Alice wore green lisle stockings and asked my permission to use the IBM. Jean wore a new round-necked, sleeveless, button-through tailored dress in tangerine linen, one small gold ear-ring, the one she hadn't lost, and a centre parting. I gave Alice a list of names, and when she went away I smudged Jean's lipstick.

All the people arrested were being taken down to Carshalton, and at 3.30 A.M. they were bursting at the seams, so Alice told Ross, and he fixed an alternative detention centre because it was so important to keep all the detainees separate.* The

* See Appendix: Detention Centres, p. 341.

IBM went on buzzing and clattering, and at 6 A.M. there was a meeting at Scotland Yard. The police were very worried, but Ross had got one of the 4th Secretaries from the Home Office along there, and then they were even more worried. By 8 o'clock the worst part was over. At 8.9 A.M. Murray, who had arrested Dalby shortly after being hit on the head, phoned from Liphook to say he was holding a man named Swainson, and would I send a car. Swainson, it seemed, was K.K.'s real name. I sent the car and had it drop Jean and myself off for breakfast.

'A plan to brain-wash the entire framework of a nation,' said Jean, over the coffee and croissants. 'It's hardly credible.'

'It's credible all right,' I told her, 'and we haven't entirely eradicated it! I don't know which was more surprising even now; Dalby working for the other side, or Ross master-minding the whole operation that netted him.'

'Did Ross know what was happening when he transferred you to WOOC(P)?' asked Jean.

I said, 'He half guessed. That was why he put Murray in to spy out the land. When he heard the news of my near arrest in the strip club he let Dalby understand that he was suspicious of him. A very dangerous thing to do. In this case it paid off, for, to prove his loyalty, Dalby did a very efficient job in Lebanon. I remember seeing Ross at the airport when he returned from Beirut after seeing Dalby.

'To what extent Dalby's action in the Lebanon was against Jay's wishes we shall never know, for Dalby made a point of shooting all the people in the car with Raven, you remember.'

Jean said, 'So Carswell wasn't such a fool?'

'He wasn't,' I said. 'Even to the "concens" having fever and Right-wing views – both being conducive to Communist thought reform. Of course, at first, the fact that Carswell's statistics began to show up the whole plot was a pure coincidence. But as soon as possible, Ross had Carswell hidden away. That was why I could find no trace that he had ever existed through Charlie at C-SICH. Ross was frightened for Carswell's safety.'

Jean added, 'To say nothing of the fact that, as things are right now, if Jay says nothing, Carswell might provide the only guide to the extent of operation IPCRESS. By the way is IPCRESS a figure from Greek mythology, the allusion to which I should immediately catch?'

I said, 'No, it's a distorted word that one of Ross's men invented from the words "Induction of Psycho-neuroses by Conditioned Reflex with Stress", which is a clinical description of what they did in the haunted house.'

'And what they started to do to you at Wood Green,' said Jean.

'Exactly. They had three basic systems. The "haunted house" system, for want of a better word, depended on mental isolation. They used phoney ambassadors to convince the subject that he was completely alone, or phoney policemen (but they dropped the policeman idea after we got the fellow at Shoreditch by accident) – civilian clothes were safer. At Wood Green they even had radiant heating and cooling systems to alter the temperature as often as they wished. Switched lights on and off to give a one-hour-long day or a thirty-six-hour-long night. It was all to throw the mind off balance, and as Pavlov discovered, this is much easier to do to someone physically weak.'

'What would they have done to you if you hadn't escaped?' asked Jean. It was nice to know someone had been worried.

'Escaped is too strong a word,' I said. 'Luckily I had enough information about their methods to make an informed guess. Most of the previous inmates never dreamed that they were still in England. There was no point in getting out of the house only to find yourself thousands of miles behind the Iron Curtain. As to the next stages; the beginning is this severing of connections, a feeling of isolation and physical and mental fatigue and uncertainty; that's what they started with me. Tension and an uncertainty; about what will please and what won't please. Any sort of humour is dangerous to the technique. You'll notice how the American treatment after my arrest on Tokwe, had these same basic characteristics. Well, had I stayed at Wood Green the next stage would most likely have been the memorizing of long passages of dialect. Probably they would have told me to memorize that long document about my trial.'

Jean poured out some more coffee. I was very tired, and just talking about how near I had come to being converted made my throat nervously dry. 'After that?' Jean said. She lit a Gauloise and passed it across to me.

'Group therapy. We know they had five others there at the same time as me. Maybe even more. The tape recordings of moans and groans and talking in sleep in a foreign language must have worked everyone up to a fever pitch, but since it was identical to the tape that Keightley had found, it only encouraged me. Soon there would be group meetings, and we would be allowed to discover that one is an informer, to increase the tension. Then there is the confession and autobiography stage. This is detailed. Things like why you smoked, had love affairs, drank, mixed with certain people.'

'Had love affairs?' said Jean.

'I escaped before that part,' I said.

'Now I know why,' said Jean. 'It was very sweet of you.'

I drank my coffee. The sun shone brightly in the Soho street below. Large blocks of ice stood outside restaurants and melted into the gutter. A man in a straw boater arranged a large Severn salmon across a wet marble slab. Around it he carefully placed soles and turbot and scallops and flat oysters and portugaises that looked like pieces of rock, and herrings and mackerel, and a fountain of water played over it, and Jean was talking to me. I turned and gave her my full attention.

'What happened after the mutual confession stage?'

'You don't have an ulterior motive?' I asked.

'Oh, every woman understands brain-washing. It's letting a husband get furious about a new hat and then knowing when to ask him to pay for it. Just when he starts to feel guilty.'

'You don't know how right you are,' I said. 'The whole process is one of discovering weaknesses; preferably the subjects find their own. Self-criticism, etc. Then the third phase is using the information so far gained to create what is technically called "abreaction". This is caused by intense mental work, indoctrination by meetings. In fact by overwork and stress, and is the culmination of all brain-washing. Abreaction is the point of no return.'

'How do you know when you've reached it?' asked Jean.

'You know all right – it's a complete nervous collapse. Dilated pupils, rigid body, the skin goes clammy with perspiration. You feel you can't get your breath, you breathe in and out very quickly, but not deeply at all. That's just the beginning; after that, there's continuous sobbing hysterics, complete loss of control. In World War One it was called "shell shock", in World War Two, "battle fatigue". As soon as abreaction hits one of your

305

group, the others soon topple – one after the other they are hooked.'

'You said there were three basic systems,' said Jean. 'You've told me only one.'

I said, 'Oh, did I? I didn't mean that the systems were different – only the way the one system was applied. The haunted house was the first sort. Then Jay thought of using small private nursing homes – less conspicuous, you see, and no need for all the building work – or the conversion back to normal before they moved out again. It was the nursing home aspect that Carswell found with his "concens"; do you remember the description he gave us? The fever rate was high because that is the best physical debility to prepare one for brain-washing.'

'You mean that they were deliberately given fever, then whipped into one of these nursing homes?' Jean said.

'The other way round,' I told her. 'They were brought in, then given fever.'

'Injected with it?' Jean asked.

'Apparently medical science still uses mosquitoes. They strap a glass cup on the skin and the mosquitoes bite. That's when it's needed to give a patient fever; it's pretty rare nowadays.' Jean didn't wrinkle her nose or say 'how awful' when I got to the mosquito bit and I appreciated that.

'The fever speeded things up,' Jean said.

I agreed, 'It certainly did, which led to the third system. This was to create this breakdown . . .'

'Abreaction?'

'Yes, this abreaction. To create it by drugs alone; what doctors call a pharmacological shock. It's done by injecting lots of insulin into the blood stream; this lowers the sugar in the blood, and very soon you have the same twitches and convulsions that one sees in abreaction – shouting and sobbing and finally collapse into a deep coma. Later they gave intravenous sugar.'

'Why didn't they do that to you?' asked Jean. 'Why didn't you go to one of their nursing homes?'

'I do believe you still have doubts about me.' Jean laughed nervously, but it went home. 'That was my big worry, I can tell you, but it's tricky; they needed the man who had experience, but he was deeply involved at the place in Scotland. Luckily he couldn't be in two places at once. Plus the fact that the older system is more thorough, and I was considered difficult.'

'You can say difficult again,' said Jean. 'But I'm still not sure if I understand even now. You mean, after this brain-washing, these people, these "concens", went back to work but were really working as Russian agents, their convictions totally reversed?'

I said, 'No. It's far more complex than that. Everything revolves round Jay, really; to understand IPCRESS you must understand Jay. Jay has spent his life amidst changing political scenes. Here in England it's easy for us to have allegiance to a government that has stayed pretty constant since the Stuart restoration; but Jay has seen governments come and go too often to place too much reliance on them. He remembers the Tsars; government by ignorance; Paderewski, government by gentle pianist; Pilsudski, the general who won the brilliant battle of Warsaw in 1920, and smashed the new Soviet Armies under Voroshilov. He remembers the dictator who seized power by shouting "This is a whorehouse, all get out!" to Parliament. He remembers the government who followed Hitler's example in 1938 by grabbing a piece of Czechoslovakia by force. He remembers the Nazis, and then, after the war, the protégés of London and Moscow fighting each other for power. Jay has come through all these changes like a plastic duck going over Niagara – by floating along with the current. He has sold information. Information from Klaus Fuchs in Britain, Alan Nunn May in Canada, and the Rosenbergs in the US. Then he graduated to kidnapping and arranging that Otto John from West Germany, the Italian physicist, Bruno Pontecorvo, and Burgess and Maclean should travel eastward. But always for money. He would have sent them equally willingly to anyone who named the right price. Then one day, perhaps while he was shaving, an idea hit him; he would brain-wash a network of well-placed men, and all of them would clear their information through Jay. They would be loyal to Jay personally. Jay knew enough about psychiatry to know that it was possible (and let's not forget that it's been working very well for nearly a year), and he knew that it would make us all "trigger happy", suspicious of everyone once we got on to it.'

I ordered some more coffee and phoned Charlotte Street to see if there were any cables for me, but there was nothing fresh. I went back to Jean.

'What was that water tank that you mentioned in the "haunted house" report?' she asked.

'Yes, the water tank. I should have perhaps said four ways because that was for another system. You mask the subject's eyes and fit him with breathing apparatus, then suspend him face down in a tank of blood-heat water. At first he sleeps; when he awakes he is completely disorientated and subject to anxiety and hallucination. You choose the right moment and begin to feed him information . . .'

'Hence the tape recorder.'

'Exactly . . .'

'It's a quick way of brain-washing then?'

'It is, but they discontinued it, so it probably wasn't so sensational.'

'And they didn't use TAP* either,' Jean said.

'No,' I said, 'and I didn't know you'd read that report.'

'Yes, Alice gave it to me to read last night. There were some mentions in a Norwegian medical journal which I translated for her.'

* See Appendix: TAP, p. 341.

'Oh,' I said, 'that's all right then.'

'Alice said you'd say that.' Before I could say anything, Jean continued, 'This brain-washing . . .'

'Say "thought reform". No one says "brain-washing" nowadays.'

'This thought reform,' said Jean, 'is it . . . ?'

'Enough of thought reform,' I said, 'what are you doing tonight?'

Jean fingered the lone gold ear-ring, and looked at me from low down under her eyelids. 'I thought perhaps I should give you a chance of making your ear-ring into a pair,' she said. It was suddenly very quiet and Jean picked up a copy of the *Guardian*, and I fought back the goose pimples.

The newspapers were playing it down but London murders always found an audience. 'London Club Murder' it said, and there was a lot of stuff about the police going through the membership books at the 'Tin-Tack Club' where Charlie was a part-time barman.

'Murray said he was a close friend of yours,' said Jean.

I told her that he had warned me when I was in danger, but I didn't tell her that anyone else had.

'But why would anyone want to kill him? For helping you?'

'Oh no,' I said. 'It was more tragic than that. He'd lent me some clothes, including a light-blue raincoat. I gave Charlie his raincoat back at Fortes, and he wore it when he left me and returned home. It was a simple case of mistaken identity.'

'Who arranged it?' asked Jean.

'A hoodlum that worked for Jay's network. We'll pick him up,' I said.

'Not Jay himself?'

'No, certainly not. On the contrary. As soon as he got wind of Charlie's connection with C-SICH he rushed down to talk to Dalby, which is where I came in.'

'He hoped Dalby could black it out?' Jean said.

'Yes, but Dalby hadn't a chance with C-SICH. It's got too many direct government connections via industry, as well as the combined services side of it.'

'They must have had a fit when you arrived,' said Jean.

'Well, Jay hadn't arrived then, but Dalby knew he was coming. His infra-red detectors gave him a few minutes to get ready for me. I would have left it there if this private eye that I had with me hadn't mentioned a Chinese. It was a long shot, but I took it, and it paid off. Murray, passing Dalby's study, heard the detectors buzzing and switched them off before coming to find me. After Murray found me in the garden he was worried that I would spoil the whole thing by precipitate action.'

'How could he think that?' asked Jean.

'That's what I thought, but anyway, he knew I had little to lose, so he phoned Ross.'

'After he came conscious?' said Jean.

'After he came conscious.'

'Murray is exclusively Ross's man?'

'Not normally, but for the IPCRESS business he was. After talking to Ross he turned around, went back into the house and arrested Dalby. The Chinese man . . .'

'Who really is Lithuanian, dear,' said Jean.

'So I hear,' I said. 'That was what Murray just phoned in about. He picked him up near Liphook. I don't know the story.'

'Ross must have acted quickly after Murray phoned.'

'Well, he certainly did, but don't forget that he'd had the Home Secretary prepared for days. They knew it would come suddenly when it came.'

'Why did Jay give up so easily when Ross arrived?' Jean asked. 'It's not like him, somehow.'

'I'm not sure about that. Either because he thought Dalby would pull him out of the fire, in spite of the struggle for power that was obviously going on between them.'

'Or?' said Jean.

'Or it's something to do with the phone call from someone named Henry. Time will tell.'

'More questions,' said Jean.

'Very well,' I said.

'Why did Jay let you find Raven in that club the day you were nearly arrested?'

'Simple. Jay and Dalby had the "thought reform" going well by then, but they needed a neat punctuation mark to account for the series of kidnappings. If they could find a scapegoat, there the matter would end, and they could happily go forward with their new plan.'

'Until they quarrelled.'

'Perhaps, but they might not have quarrelled. Anyway, Dalby and Jay set me up to be found alongside Raven, with a hypodermic in my pocket, police raid and all.'

'But,' said Jean.

'But instead of waiting a few more minutes, when I would have been organized into the gaming room, I got impatient . . .'

'Extraordinary,' said Jean. 'So out of character. The man from US Naval Intelligence was only trying to help, then?'

'I'm afraid so,' I said.

'We must get back,' said Jean, 'or Alice will grumble.'

'The devil with Alice,' I said. 'I'm the boss, aren't I?'

'Not when Alice gives the orders,' Jean said.

'You know, there's something different about that office lately,' I said, and we both returned to it, although I was still thinking about the ear-ring.

32

*[Aquarius (Jan 20–Feb 19) By the week-end
you will be free to follow new interests.
Unexpected action brings happiness to all.]*

Back at the office the cables were beginning to
flood in from Washington and Calcutta and Hong
Kong. Alice was coping very well, and only a few
required a decision from me. Murray flew up to
a little country town near Grantham and brought
Chico back in an army helicopter. He looked very
ill when I saw him at the Millbank Military
Hospital. Ross put a couple of men on a twenty-
four-hour watch at Chico's bedside, but they got
nothing from him, except that he'd seen a friend
of his cousin in the piece of film he'd seen at the
WO. Instead of telling Ross, he went to visit the
man. Needless to say he was in the IPCRESS network, and Chico was at Millbank, and his friend
in Ross's bag.

Painter, the thin-faced tall fellow who'd been

with us on the Lebanon job, turned out to be a psychiatrist of some standing who had brought our captive Raven, who was half-way 'brainwashed', back to something approaching normalcy. I gave him a room with Carswell on the top floor at Charlotte Street. If we couldn't break Jay down everything would depend on those two.

By Thursday I was able to take a full night's sleep. Until then I'd kept going mainly on coffee and cigarettes and an aspirin sandwich, but Thursday I took some sleeping pills Painter gave me and didn't wake until midday. I swore off coffee for a couple of days and stepped into a cold shower. I put on Irish tweed with Veldtshoen, cotton shirt, and wool tie. At three o'clock I was summoned to the presence of an exalted military personage at the WO.

I was a minute or so late and Ross and Alice were both there before me. Ross was in a very stiff new uniform with crown and pip on the shoulder. His Sam Browne was as shiny as the doorman's head and he had his bright red OBE with the Military Stripe and the India General Service and the George VI Coronation, to say nothing of a '39–'43 Star and a Western Desert ribbon. I began to wish I'd worn the pullover with the Defence Medal sewn on it.

The EMP shook hands rather grandly and referred to me as 'the hero of the hour'. I celebrated by helping myself to a cigar and pretended to have no matches in order to have the EMP light it for me. He thanked me and Ross and Alice, but I knew there was more to it than that. When he began the sales talk with, 'Mr Ross is most anxious that you should hear this from me . . .' I knew what it was. Ross had finally taken over Charlotte Street. What timing! No one could challenge Ross's competence after this IPCRESS fiasco. I heard him going on about Ross going up to 'half-colonel' and 'seniority'. On the walls were photos of the EMP standing with Churchill, seated with Eisenhower, receiving a medal, sitting on a horse, and reviewing an armoured brigade while standing in a jeep. There were no photos of him as an inexperienced subaltern with his foot jammed in a drainage pipe. Perhaps people like him are born as brigadiers.

But now the conversation was taking a different turn. Ross, it seemed, wasn't taking over Charlotte Street. The purpose of my visit was an explanation to me!

As I sorted it out afterwards, it all began because Ross wanted to be quite sure that I wasn't working for the Jay and Dalby set-up. So he asked if he could offer me the *Al Gumhuria* work. They calculated that if I was channelling stuff out through Jay I'd jump at it. I hadn't. I had told Ross to keep it. From that moment 'my future was assured' as the old army saying has it. Now Ross wanted me to be quite clear about his hands being clean, so he had the top brass tell me in person.

The Exalted Military Personage was very keen to hear how I got out of the Wood Green house, and at one stage said, 'Good show!' again, and after that, something that I still consider rather foolish for a man of his experience. He said, 'And now is there anything I can tell *you*?'

I told him that I had overseas and detachment pay outstanding for nearly eighteen months. He was a little shattered, and Ross didn't know where to put his face for embarrassment. But the EMP adopted an 'all boys together' attitude, and promised to action it for me if I let his ADC have details in writing. Ross had the door open, and Alice was about to go through it when I leaned across the vast highly polished desk and said, 'When do you arrest Henry?' Ross closed the door and came back to the desk. The EMP came around it. They both looked at me as though I wasn't using Amplex.

At last the EMP spoke; his brown wrinkled face was close to mine. He said, 'I should be furious with you. You're implying a reluctance on my part to pursue the Queen's enemies.'

I said, 'I'm implying nothing, but I'm glad to hear that the suggestion would anger you.'

The EMP unlocked a tray on his desk and produced a slim green file; on the cover it said 'HENRY' in magic-marker lettering. It was about all we knew of the man who phoned Jay that night. Inside there was a note from the PM in his own handwriting, my report, and a long screed from Ross. The EMP said, 'We are as anxious to clear it up as anyone, but we'll have to have more facts than this.'

'Then, with respect, sir, I suggest that you pass it on to the appropriate authority,' I told him. 'To be quite frank,' Ross began, but I refused to be interrupted. I stared the EMP full in the eye. 'This report of mine was submitted to the Cabinet. Neither you nor Colonel Ross has any right to open a file, handle a file, or comment in any way. The sphere of activities are clearly defined by the Cabinet. I'll take this file with me, and I must ask you to treat its contents as top secret, pending the submission of my further reports to the Cabinet.' It wasn't that there were reasons for suspecting the EMP of attempting to cover up for the elusive Henry, but I didn't want this file to be mislaid. At that moment I resolved that one day I would track down Jay's highly placed friend. Something of this must have shown on my face in spite of my training.

'My dear fellow,' said the EMP. 'Nothing was further from my mind than treating you in a cav-alier fashion.' I had won. I had won so soundly that the EMP produced his XO Brandy. I allowed myself to be mollified, but not too quickly. It's great, that Hennessy XO Brandy.

Alice and I had a car waiting to take us back to Charlotte Street. We rode in silence almost all the way, but just before Goodge Street Alice said, 'Not even Dalby would have attempted that.' It was as near as Alice ever came to admiration. I gave her the green file and said airily, 'Give this one of our file numbers, Alice.' But my triumph was short-lived, for later that afternoon she brought in the two files I'd left in Waterman's car. You could never beat Alice.

That evening Ross rang and said he had to see me, about Jay. And Carswell, Painter, Ross and I had a conference. The end was inevitable, and it came on Saturday. Jay was paid £160,000 to open a department working directly between Ross and myself. On this same day a Jensen 541S sports car went off the Maidstone by-pass while going at an absurd speed. There was one occupant, a Mr Dalby; death, they said, was instantaneous.

There was still much work to do at Charlotte Street. K.K., late of Wood Green, wanted to claim diplomatic immunity, but failed. I put an advertisement into *France-Soir*, thanking Bert for his offer of help, and telling of my cancelled tour.

Alice bought an electric coffee-mill for the office, so that we could have real coffee, and I got all my back pay and allowances. I paid the pianist at the 'Tin-Tack' thirty shillings and sent Alf Keating an oil heater. The dispatch office was making a book on the Open; I put five shillings on Munn & Felton's (Footwear) Brass Band. A little note from Chico thanked me for doing his requisitions the night he went to Grantham, and Jean sewed a patch into my brown worsted trousers.

On Tuesday I had a visitor; the American brigadier from Tokwe. He brought two large cardboard boxes with him, and after lunching at the 'Ivy' we returned to the office to watch a demonstration.

From the cardboard boxes he brought a wooden contraption, its paint chipped and faded. When fitted together it was about six feet long; attached to each end was a red automobile light. It wasn't until he showed me photographs of the battered motor cycle they had dragged from the ocean floor that I realized Dalby's ingenious scheme.

This wooden plank bolted to the back of a motor cycle was what I followed across Tokwe the night I was arrested. The motor bike was too small to register on the radar screen. Dalby moved the block across the road, and connected the HT wires to kill the only witness. He used the High Speed TV, then threw it into the sea nice and near my car, knowing that it would be detected by echo sounders, and that my close proximity would implicate me. Then he drove away relying on wind, a good silencer, and con-fusion. He dumped the bike in the sea off another part of the island, having left the road and trav-elled across open country. The two men that Jay's network had working for the USMD* told the British authorities that the Americans were holding on to me, and the Americans, that the British had asked for my return. After that, Jay took over, and brought me into the UK as a hospital case.

I appreciated the work that this officer had done. He felt he owed me a debt. I told him about Dalby

* United States Medical Department.

being killed, and he didn't look surprised or cynical, so I left it at that.

He asked, 'This feller, Dalby; the Reds had brainwashed the guy, huh?'

I said we weren't sure, but perhaps we looked for motivation in the wrong places these days. We tend to forget that there are people who are simply after money and power, and they have no psychological complications at all. I said I thought Dalby and Jay were both like that, and that a feud had been not so far away when it all blew up in their faces.

'Money and power, eh?' said the Brigadier. 'Just a simple case of a couple of well-informed SOBs.'

'Perhaps that's about it,' I said.

'I asked Dalby for you at Tokwe,' he told me, and I said I knew.

'I just had a hunch, you know what I mean,' he said.

I knew what he meant.

And he said, 'Can I ask you just one more thing?'

'Yes,' I said.

'How were your people so sure that Colonel Ross and Miss Bloom (that was Alice's other name) – I mean to give no offence, you understand.'

I said I understood.

'But how were they so sure that Ross and Miss Bloom couldn't be . . . well, reached?'

I said that there were people who were very difficult to brain-wash.

'Is that so?' he said.

'Yes,' I told him. 'Obsessional neurotics; people who go back twice to make sure the door is locked, who walk down the street avoiding the joins in the paving, then become sure they've left the kettle on. They are difficult to hypnotize and difficult to brain-wash.'

'No fooling,' he said. 'It's a wonder we had so much trouble in the US then.'

'Yes,' I said. 'Don't quote me about Alice and Ross.'

'Not a chance,' he said. But from a couple of things Alice said next day, I think he must have done.

The 'Henry File'? It's still as slim as the day I brought it from the War House. Everyone in the department has theories of course, but whoever tipped off Jay is keeping his head well down. Mind you, as Jean said the other day, when we do identify him, it's sure to turn out to be some relation of Chico.

Another thing we never did finally work out was how Dalby got my prints on to the HS TV camera, but I think he must have screwed the handles on to something (perhaps a door) at Charlotte Street, then taken them with him to Tokwe, and fixed them to the camera before dumping it.

Jean had been back to the Japanese blockhouse the day after I was arrested, but the cathode tube, slip of information and pistol had all gone. She had then sat down with a map of the area and worked out Dalby's motor cycle trick by sheer brain-power. When the Brigadier heard Jean's story he had the three places she'd marked, dragged. With no result. She told me it was a terrible moment; but they hadn't allowed for the undertow. The motor cycle was finally found quite a long way out.* Luckily the wooden gimmick was still attached (Dalby couldn't risk it floating) and by now the Americans were really convinced. Skip Henderson was recalled to Tokwe (it seems the death of Barney was a bona fide accident) and Ross flew to the Pentagon. From then on the skids were under Dalby, but it wasn't doing me a lot of good.

That's about all of the IPCRESS story. There has been a lot of work go through Charlotte Street since; some interesting, but mostly boring. Painter has a whole medical research lab working with him, but so far they have found no way of 'de-brain-washing' people, and many of the original network are still under the threat of the Treason Act, while some still forward reports under the impression that they are going via Jay to some foreign power. Of course I don't let Jay handle them, just in case he gets ideas. I see Jay at the monthly conference with Ross, when we prepare the Army Intelligence Memoranda Sheet. He seems happy

---

* (It's my theory that Dalby had it going at high speed towards the water to take it as far as possible, but Jean says it's the undertow.)

enough, and he's certainly efficient. I remember another thing about Jays – they store food for winter. 'Moving in from opposite ends to the same conclusion,' Dalby said once, and every time I am with Jay I think about it. But I doubt if this was what Dalby meant.

Anytime I want Jay I know I can find him at the 'Mirabelle', and last Saturday morning I bumped into him at Led's. He wants Jean and me to go to dinner with him. He said he would cook it himself. I'd like to go but I don't think I will. It's not wise to make too many close friends in this business.

EPILOGUE

It's a dead sure way of getting into trouble putting too much information down on paper, but I suppose having got this far I had better tell you the true end of the IPCRESS fiasco.

The Minister just wanted to know how to evade questions, as all Ministers do. He asked me a few searching questions like, 'Any good fishin' in the Lebanon?' and 'Have another?' and 'D'you know young Chillcott-Oakes?' After leaving the Minister I drove down to a house near Staines. I knocked on the door in a rather strange series of rhythms, and a woman with a moustache opened it. In the back room there was an old man standing amid three partly packed suitcases. I gave him sixty crumpled five-pound notes, which were genuine, and two medium-quality forged UK passports.

The man said, 'Thank you,' and the woman said the same thing, twice more. As I turned to leave, he said, 'I'll be at number 19* if you ever need me.'

---

* 19 Stanislavskaya Street, Moscow (facing the East German Embassy). A building occupied by SMERSH – the counter-intelligence unit of the KGB (Komitet Gosudarstvennoi Bezopasnosti).

I said thanks and drove to London, and the little old man who had been my jailer at the house in Wood Green took the plane to Prague. This, too, was a spy's insurance policy.

APPENDIX

See page 44

MEDWAY II

During the dark days of the Mediterranean War when it looked like the Wehrmacht had finished what Darius began, Beirut was a submarine base called Medway II, and was the scene of a top-secret mission. U.307 had been sunk in thirty-eight fathoms of water not far away. In the water-filled U.307 the control room was equipped with a new infra-red sighting device for night viewing above water. It was deep for a diver, but not too deep. It was still wet when we got it aboard the plane, and it dripped over my knees on the way to London, where I met Ross for the first time.

See page 48

Extract from *Handling unfamiliar pistols* (Chapter 5). Document 237. HGF. 1960.

In handling Smith & Wesson revolvers the following rules should be observed. PROVIDING that (i) the cylinder has six chambers, and (ii) it revolves anti-clockwise. (Note that Colt cylinders revolve clockwise.) There are 4 categories:

1. *.445 inch*. Only British or US ammunition marked .455 inch.
2. *.45 inch*. BEWARE. Not .45 auto ammunition.
3. *.45 inch DA*. In this .45 auto ammunition can be used but will not extract without two special three-round clips. Extraction can however be effected with the aid of, e.g., a pencil. BEWARE. Not rimmed ammunition.
4. *.38*. Any pistol with chamber longer than 1.5 inches will take any British or American ammunition except auto ammunition.

These rules only provide a general guide and THERE ARE EXCEPTIONS.

See page 59

INDIAN HEMP (MARIJUANA)

Prices at time of writing:

Rangoon: 10/- per lb block.
UK (Dockside): £30 per lb.
Wholesale: £50 per lb.
Clubs, etc: £6 per oz, or 10/6 per cigarette.
(1lb makes approximately 500 cigarettes.)

See page 121

In 1939 British Military Intelligence used Wormwood Scrubs Prison as its HQ. The prisoners had all been evacuated and the cells were used as offices, each cell being locked when it was vacated as a security measure. However, after a bomb destroyed a section of the building, it was decided to move to a block of offices in St James's Street, where they remained until the end of the war.

See page 123

JOE ONE

Near the Holo Archipelago where the waters of the Sulu Sea dilute the Sea of Celebes and the fingers of the Philippine islands grope towards Northern Borneo a B29 of the United States Air Force led a fast-moving shadow through the hot afternoon sun of August, 1949.

Special attachments held photographic plates which soaked up cosmic rays. For months this unit had charted and flown carefully calculated routes across the Pacific. It was a boring detail, and the crews were happy when each long day's flight was ended and cold showers were waiting to revitalize cramped muscles and an open-air movie helped their minds into neutral. But this day was different, this crew had hardly parked their gum when an urgent call recalled them to the briefing-room.

The photo-lab technicians had got used to developing these plates by now. The image was generally of long wormlike strips of light and often needed a little extra development to get a good contrasty image that made plotting the results much easier. But these plates were absurdly different, they were fogged. Not fogged by daylight but soaked black by an intense concentration of cosmic radiation. Otherwise called a 'hot' area. As the Commanding General said at the time, 'If the atmosphere is taking that kind of cosmic ray penetration we'd better get into the lead suit business.' But the world wasn't taking it. This was an atomic explosion.

In that briefing-room in that Pacific USAF base a big truth slowly took shape in the minds of these airmen. There had been no American bomb exploded that year.

The whole base swung into action. One after another the huge B29s trundled around the perimeter track and stepped off the end of the runway into the heavy tropical night air. This time, however, these were planes of the Atomic Bomb Detection Unit which had been formed only the previous year. Special aircraft scooping dust particles from the air as they retraced the path of the afternoon flight. Two Atomic Energy Commission laboratories in the United States had been alerted to stand by for the dust samples.

It took five days before Washington had the detailed report. The explosion it said was almost certainly a bomb. (Until September 23 it was stated that there was a one-in-twenty chance that it wasn't a bomb.) Moreover the particles indicated a plutonium device. This was an explosion six times more powerful than the Hiroshima one and not to be compared with the first American explosion at Alamogordo.

At this time the organization called MAN-HATTAN DISTRICT (code-named Post Office Box 1663) which included the Los Alamos Weapons Laboratory near Santa Fé, New Mexico, the Isotope Separation Plants at Oak Ridge, Tennessee and the plutonium piles at Hanford, Washington had all been handed over to the Atomic Energy Commission. The AEC did the whole job, getting the ores of the fissionable heavy metals, uranium and thorium, converting them into concentrations of pure metal as well as supervising production of radio-active isotopes for ship and submarine propulsion and electricity generators.

When the report of the dust particles came through to Washington it had a 'Top Secret' rating, and was delivered to William Webster, Chairman of the Defense Department's atomic liaison committee who took it to the Secretary of Defense: Louis Johnson.

Together they surveyed the guesses of their intelligence departments. The basis of US expectation of a Soviet bomb was the prediction made in 1945 by the chief of MANHATTAN DISTRICT Major-General L. R. Groves, who said it would take the

Russians fifteen or twenty years. The Director of the Office of Scientific Research and Development, Dr Vannevar Bush, said 'ten years', in his book *Modern Arms and Free Men*, which was at that moment on the press (the presses were stopped and the prediction erased). US Navy Intelligence told the Defense Department to expect it in 1965, the Army Intelligence said 1960. The USAF Intelligence report was considered panic stricken when it put up 1952 as the year. And yet here it was September, 1949, and the bang had sounded.

The US Defense Department asked London for confirmation of the Siberian explosion and Ross made his name overnight. Ross had placed his contacts with pessimistic insight. Not only did he know about the explosion (Ross had had all BOAC aircraft fitted with scoops for two years before the bang), but through a couple of well-placed AEC officials he'd had access to the Washington report for nearly twenty-four hours by the time they came through on the transatlantic scrambled line. Just to rub it in, Ross sent the Americans a summary of the physicists working on the project (Peter Kapitza, Fersman, Frenkel, Joffe) and predicted with uncanny accuracy the awards the Soviet scientists were going to receive before *they* knew.

From 'Joe One' onwards, Ross just couldn't go wrong.

See page 174

The following recipes are reproduced by kind permission of Master-Sergeant J. B. Revelli, US Army.

TOKWE TWIST: Stir and strain on to rocks: 2 oz bourbon, ½ oz benedictine. Twist of lemon peel. Serve.

MANHATTAN PROJECT: To a Manhattan: (2 oz whisky, ½ oz sweet vermouth, dash Angostura and a cherry) add ½ oz cherry brandy.

GREENBACK (or Moolah, or Cabbage): Shake or stir: 1½ oz whisky, 1 oz dry vermouth, a sprinkle of green chartreuse and of green *crème de menthe*. Add green olive, decorate with a sprig of mint.

See page 218

GRENADE

I could see Grenade's small black eyeballs and long greasy hair, and a dour smileless face which lit up once per year. Before the war he was a radio ham and ran a little radio repair shop in Joigny, a Michelin-starred town a hundred kilometres south of Paris.

Grenade was a resistance worker in 1940 when to work actively against the Germans was unfashionable enough to make being turned in to them by a dazed patriot a real risk. Grenade was a de Gaullist when everyone else in France was rooting for Marshal Pétain. He was a Gaullist when even the Allied Governments were doing deals with

Darlan and Giroud helping them persecute anti-Axis agents and leaving de Gaulle to find out about the North African invasion from his newspaper. Grenade never faltered and never altered.

He organized a train-wrecking group until it was penetrated and the survivors fled. Grenade drifted north to Paris without friends, work or papers. In Paris he met a couple of unemployed printers. By lavish promises of money he got access to a printing machine, and they began printing false passes and papers.

To run counter to law and order was patriotic and their patriotism was in no way muted by the fact that they made a great deal of money. Some of it went into political and anti-German organizations, and without Grenade's profits from printing food, clothes and petrol coupons, one of the escape chains to the Pyrenees would have collapsed before it finally did. Over thirty Allied airmen passed through Grenade's flat and that was only an overflow accommodation. After the war such groups tended to hang on to each other and adapt to the new circumstances. They made papers and passports for 'displaced persons' who were rich enough to buy, and at one time even forged Camel cigarette packets.

In June, 1947 Grenade had been mixed up with the Perrier gang who worked from the Acceuil Café on the Left Bank, and had completed a lucrative line in hundred-dollar American Express travellers' cheques. Apart from the red serial numbers being a little dark, and the watermarks being printed instead of impressed, they were pretty good. They fetched about a third of their value on the black-market, and eagerly at that. Some were detected going across the border in diplomatic bags. Grenade got into the story because he had found a method of microfilming certain diplomatic mail. When under pressure from American Express the French police staked out the courier routes, they found Grenade with 50,000 dollars of forged signed travellers' cheques. French Intelligence for whom Grenade had worked off and on since the first radio contacts in September, 1940 were now unable to extricate him since there were political involvements. I'd known Grenade about two years and liked him. With little or no risk to me I decided he could be of use as a close friend. I knew that a contact of mine with access to US Army documents had a brother who'd come through the Paris escape route in 1944. I let him think it was Grenade's. Although there was no way of telling for sure, I like to think that it was, too. He wrote up a document, one showing Grenade as a US Army agent investigating forgeries of US military scrip money and inserted it into the files. I then leaked the information to one of the American Express detectives, and to the 2nd secretary of a senator. At the first opportunity after charges against Grenade were dropped, the forged papers were destroyed. Now Grenade was returning the favour.

See page 220

JULIUS CAESAR

Scene III. The Same. A street near the Capitol.
Enter ARTEMIDORUS reading a paper.

*Caesar, beware of Brutus; take heed of
Cassius; come not near Casca; have an eye
to Cinna; trust not Trebonius; mark well
Metellus Cimber; Decius Brutus loves thee
not; thou hast wronged Caius Ligarius. There
is but one mind in all these men, and it is
bent against Caesar. If thou beest not
immortal, look about you: security gives way
to conspiracy. The mighty gods defend thee!
Thy lover,* ARTEMIDORUS.

See page 236

NEUTRON BOMB

Even from a normal-style H-bomb there is a bom-
bardment of neutrons, but the fireball generally
eats them up before they get anywhere. Now a
neutron bomb uses a pure-fission type of reaction, and has no fission-trigger. It gets its 'bounce'
from a temperature of 1,000,000 degrees centi-
grade, generated externally. The explosion releases
neutrons which don't have an electrical charge
(therefore atoms don't repel them) and which
travel far and fast until the air absorbs them.

These neutrons penetrate buildings, water, etc., but destroy only living matter, leaving machinery in perfect working order. The Tokwe explosion was of a small tactical-size neutron weapon, although, for security reasons, it was isolated within the pretence of a huge H-explosion. Neutron bombs do not use expensive or rare ingredients and therefore information about them is as eagerly sought by the smaller powers as by the larger.

See page 264

REG CAVENDISH

I looked at the sepia photo of Reg Cavendish – Charlie's son – who looked down from the top of the writing cabinet in one of those boat-shaped forage caps that we had all looked so silly in. I remember the day Reg got that hat. He was a tall gangling boy with ginger hair that he held lowered in sympathy with the more stunted members of the human race. He was the brightest pupil in the sixth form but was never made a prefect because, '. . . there's such a thing as being too gentle Cavendish and it's called slackness.' Reg just smiled a small smile, he wasn't a great talker. That's why we were such inseparable friends I suppose – I was the most vociferous boy there – when Reg was with me he wasn't required to say much.

Reg was most at home in the country, he knew about cumulonimbus and isobars and could tell a Song Thrush from a Fieldfare at fifty yards, which is pretty impressive if you can't tell a Barn-Owl from a Buzzard. Reg knew about moles and foxes and Latin names of wild flowers. Reg came to terms with life in the army, he quietly did everything better than anyone else. Reg's style of leadership was to be out in front where things were hardest and most dangerous and he used firepower with the same economy that he used words. Reg didn't have to convert to the idea of airborne warfare, he'd never known any other kind. Dropping out of an aeroplane as an overture to battle was as natural as pipeclayed breeches, burnished firelocks and heel-balled cartridge boxes had been to other soldiers in other times.

He became Regimental Sergeant Major Cavendish; one of the youngest RSMs in the British Army during the Tunisian campaign when the parachute brigade was used as infantry. It was here he got the nickname 'Springer'.

In the fighting around 'Longstop' – the most costly of the whole campaign – Reg was in a 15-cwt lorry that lost its way while in convoy, went off the road and struck a mine. The German engineers had sown s-mines around the big ones. As the soldiers jumped down these leapt high in the air and exploded metal ball-bearings. The Afrika Korps put mortar fire amongst the flashes and screams as dawn came.

It's hot in Tunisia even in May and the heights of Longstop Hill housed a thousand keen German eyes. The bangs and smack of grenade and mortar rolled across the slopes and so did the sweet smell of hot dead flesh. Big black sated flies hovered and waited for Von Arnim's mortars to search them out and convert them to carrion. Men died all day. Some died very quickly, some took an infinite time and some slipped into impercipient dolour and came to a very private arrangement with death. Wince, writhe or ease a cramped foot, reach for a hard-tack biscuit, stifle blood, swat a dozen flies on your eyelid, touch the hot metal of your gun, these were things men did a finger-squeeze before they died. 'We went to ground like mouldwarps,' Reg said.

Slowly inch by inch it became night. A man moved but did not die. The shattered group dragged their desiccated bodies out of the moulds they had formed in the dirty sand and shuffled off, without saliva enough to spit. All the survivors had to do was walk back to their lines through a minefield. Only Reg and two lance-corporals made it. They got promotion and a 48-hour pass.

By the July of 1943 there was a change in Reg. His eyes watched over your shoulder and he looked at the ground too much. Reg had seen a lot of combat. Reg was part of the airborne attack against Catania in that July. They were blasted out of the sky in error by the Allied Fleet. He didn't need his parachute that night, his Dakota crashed. Before the night was over Reg had gained two superficial wounds, a DCM and a twitching muscle near his left eye. They sent him on leave in Tunisia that

Autumn. By now he looked nearer 40 than 20, seldom smiled and spent all his leave writing next-of-kin letters.

It was one A.M. on D-day that Reg dropped into the River Dives in full equipment. He got fifty men and an officer through chest-deep swamp and undergrowth by hitting the slowest. He wasn't a lot of fun by now. He was tense and irritable and spent every minute of every leave visiting the relatives of the dead. I told him it wasn't doing any good. He had developed a stammer and his co-ordination wasn't all it should be. 'Mind your own business,' he said, so we went to see the relatives. Hollow houses and gutted people were at both ends of dirty blacked-out trains.

'Springer' Cavendish still survived, soldiers were still drawing lots to go in his aircraft, his operations, his 'stick'. 'Springer'; Reg was you see. Always Springer survived and what's more he brought others back with him like the time he brought back a song-bird in a cage bent almost flat. They were both whistling.

When, some weeks after Arnhem had grown quiet, Reg and four other airborne soldiers paddled across the lower Rhine in a Wehrmacht inflatable boat the 1st Airborne knew it had lost 7,605 soldiers of the 10,000 who had gone in. It seemed as though Reg was indestructible. He wasn't. A rations lorry hit Reg as he was coming out of the Montgomery Club in Brussels. It was four days before VE day.

The Adjutant of Reg's unit phoned me. What should he tell Reg's father? Should he record it as it was? He could hardly believe it himself. He said that Reg was with him when he first jumped. He said it three times. I was going to London that night. I said I'd tell his father.

See page 300

DETENTION CENTRES

The last time we had seen anything on this sort of scale was when the Home Office pulled in all aliens during the war. At that time Olympia was used to house them before they were moved to the Isle of Man. But then there had been no need to keep them separate, and the numbers were kept down by the movement to the internment camps. This was a much more complex job.

See page 309

TAP

Work by Dr Holger Hyden, professor of Histology at Goteberg, revealed that Tricayandaminopropene, a substance made by manipulating the molecular structure of a series of chemicals, can change the brain's nerve cells and the cells of membrane that sheath the cells.

The fatty substance and protein of the nerve

cells is increased by 25 per cent.

In surrounding membranes the quantity of the molecule RNA was decreased by almost 50 per cent.

From this change the suggestibility of the subject is increased by the functional change of these important substances.

HORSE UNDER WATER

Len Deighton

'Lives brilliantly up to the promise of *The Ipcress File*'
Books and Bookmen

The Ipcress File was a debut sensation. Here in the second Secret File, *Horse Under Water*, skin-diving, drug trafficking and blackmail all feature in a curious story in which the dead hand of a long-defeated Hitler-Germany reaches out to Portugal, London and Marrakech, and to all the neo-Nazis of today's Europe.

The detail is frightening but unfaultable; the story as up to date as ever it was. The un-named hero of *The Ipcress File* the same: insolent, fallible, capricious – in other words, human. But he must draw on all his abilities, good and bad, when plunged into a story of murder, betrayal and greed every bit as murky as the waters off the coast of Portugal, where the answers lie buried.

'James Bond's most serious rival'
Queen

'I had a sneaking feeling I was breaking the Official Secrets Act every time I opened this book'
Daily Express

'This secret service thriller will be read; so will the next and the next . . . '
Sunday Telegraph

978 0 586 04431 5

FUNERAL IN BERLIN
Len Deighton

'A ferociously cool fable'   *New York Times*

In Berlin, where neither side of the wall is safe, Colonel Stok of Red Army Security is prepared to sell an important Russian scientist to the West – for a price.

British intelligence are willing to pay, providing their own top secret agent is in Berlin to act as go-between. But it soon becomes apparent that behind the facade of an elaborate mock funeral lies a game of deadly manoeuvres and ruthless tactics. A game in which the blood-stained legacy of Nazi Germany is enmeshed in the intricate moves of cold war espionage . . .

'*Funeral in Berlin* is splendid'   *Daily Telegraph*

'A most impressive book, a chronicle of one sad aspect of our times, in which the tension, more like a chronic ache than a sharp stab of pain, never lets go'   *Evening Standard*

'Deighton really is something special'
                    Julian Symons, *Sunday Times*

978 0 586 04580 0

BILLION-DOLLAR BRAIN

Len Deighton

The classic thriller of lethal computer-age intrigue and a maniac's private cold war

General Midwinter loves his country, and hates communism. In a bid to destabilise the Soviet power block he is running his own intelligence agency, whose 'brain' is the world's biggest super-computer.

With his past coming back to haunt him, the un-named agent of *The Ipcress File* is sent to Finland to penetrate Midwinter's spy cell. But then a deadly virus is stolen, and our hero must stop it falling into the hands of both the Russians and the billionaire madman.

'So far in front of other writers in the field that they are not even in sight'   *Sunday Times*

'Such credibility, such accurate line-by-line beaming of a sheer sense of the actual . . . a glittering, wintry entertainment'   *Guardian*

'Worthy of Raymond Chandler . . . intelligent, inventive, constantly entertaining'   *Sunday Telegraph*

978 0 586 04428 5

BOMBER

Len Deighton

Bomber is a novel war. There are no victors, no vanquished. There are simply those who remain alive, and those who die.

Bomber follows the progress of an Allied air raid through a period of twenty-four hours in the summer of 1943. It portrays all the participants in a terrifying drama, both in the air and on the ground, in Britain and in Germany.

In its documentary style, it is unique. In its emotional power it is overwhelming.

Len Deighton has been equally acclaimed as a novelist and as an historian. In *Bomber* he has combined both talents to produce a masterpiece.

'A massively different novel . . . the effect is – quite literally – devastating'   *Sunday Times*

'A massive and superbly mobilised tragedy of the machines which men create to destroy themselves . . . masterly and by far Mr Deighton's best'
Douglas Hurd, *The Spectator*

'A magnificent story . . . the characters lean out of the pages'   *Daily Mirror*

978 0 586 04544 2

SS-GB

Len Deighton

The war is over. And we have lost.

In February 1941 British Command surrendered to the Nazis. Churchill has been executed, the King is in the Tower and the SS are in Whitehall. For nine months Britain has been occupied – a blitzed, depressed and dingy country. However, it's 'business as usual' at Scotland Yard run by the SS when Detective Inspector Archer is assigned to a routine murder case. Life must go on.

But when SS Standartenfuhrer Huth arrives from Berlin with orders from the great Himmler himself to supervise the investigation, the resourceful Archer finds himself caught up in a high level, all action, espionage battle.

This is a spy story quite different from any other. Only Deighton, with his flair for historical research and his narrative genius, could have written it.

'A brilliant picture of Britain under German rule'
Sunday Telegraph

'One of Deighton's best. Apart from his virtues as a storyteller, his passion for researching his backgrounds gives his work a remarkable factual authority. With Bomber and Fighter he established himself as an expert on a period . . . the authority of these books seem absolute.'
Observer

'Len Deighton is the Flaubert of the contemporary thriller writers . . . there can be little doubt that this is much the way things would have turned out if the Germans had won the war.'
Michael Howard, *Times Literary Supplement*

978 0 586 05002 6

XPD

Len Deighton

A private aircraft takes off from a small town in central France, while Adolf Hitler, the would-be conqueror of Europe, prepares for a clandestine meeting near the Belgian border.

For more than forty years the events of this day have been Britain's most closely guarded secret. Anyone who learns of them must die – with their file stamped:

XPD – expedient demise

'A stunning spy story . . . Deighton remains the incomparable entertainer'   *Guardian*

'Exciting and well made'   *Daily Telegraph*

'Deighton in top form... the best kind of action entertainment'   *Publishers Weekly*

'Deliciously sharp and flawlessly accurate dialogue, breathtakingly clever plotting, confident character drawing . . . a splendidly strongly told story'
      The Times

978 0 586 05447 5

GOODBYE MICKEY MOUSE

Len Deighton

Goodbye Mickey Mouse is Deighton's fourteenth novel and a vivid evocation of wartime England, the story of a group of American fighter pilots flying escort missions over Germany in the winter of 1943–4.

At the centre of the novel are two young men: the deeply reserved Captain Jamie Farebrother, estranged son of a deskbound colonel, and the cocky Lieutenant Mickey Morse, well on his way to becoming America's Number One Flying Ace. Alike only in their courage, they forge a bond of friendship in battle with far-reaching consequences for themselves, and for the future of those they love.

'It is a novel of memory, satisfying on every imaginable level, but truly astonishing in its recreation of a time and place through minute detail. Deighton has written well of the air before, non-fictionally, and he informs us in an afterword that it took six years of research to do this novel. It shows. The only way you could know more about flying a P-51 Mustang, after reading this book, is to have flown one'

Washington Post

'He writes, as usual, with authority and a superb sense of period'   *Daily Telegraph*

'The sheer charge of the writing swept me into another world all the while I was reading, and now that piece of the past is a piece in my mind.'

HRF Keating, *The Times*

978 0 586 05448 2

ACTION COOK BOOK

Len Deighton

'Len was a great cook, a smashing cook. I learned a lot about food from playing Harry Palmer'

Michael Caine

Before becoming famous as the thriller writer of his generation, Len Deighton trained as a pastry chef. If you look carefully at Harry Palmer's kitchen in the classic film *The Ipcress File* you will notice a newspaper pinned on the wall. This is one of Deighton's classic cookstrips, the series that ran for two years when he was the *Observer* food writer.

The *Action Cook Book* was once an instructional book for the bachelor male – a guide to sophisticated cooking for the would-be Harry Palmer, collecting together 50 of his best one-page illustrated recipes and numerous demystifying tips. It now has a great following as a fabulous piece of nostalgia as well as retaining real credibility as a genuinely useful cook book.

'[Len Deighton's cookbooks] have attracted a cult following for their brilliant design as much as for their comprehensive approach to cooking . . .'

Guardian

'They showed the idiot novice male how to dice an onion without it falling apart; how to fine-cut parsley by rocking the blade rather than chopping it; how to sauté mushrooms without them yielding the water that would turn them into a gelatinous glop'

Simon Schama

978 0 00 730587 2